# OUT OF
## THE
# ATTIC

Center Point
Large Print

Also by V. C. Andrews® and available from
Center Point Large Print:

*House of Secrets*
*The Silhouette Girl*
*Beneath the Attic*

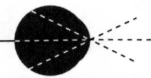

**This Large Print Book carries the
Seal of Approval of N.A.V.H.**

# V.C.
# ANDREWS®

# OUT OF
# THE
# ATTIC

CENTER POINT LARGE PRINT
THORNDIKE, MAINE

This Center Point Large Print edition
is published in the year 2020 by arrangement with
Gallery Books, a division of Simon & Schuster, Inc.

The text of this Large Print edition is unabridged.
In other aspects, this book may vary
from the original edition.
Printed in the United States of America
on permanent paper.
Set in 16-point Times New Roman type.

ISBN: 978-1-64358-555-0

The Library of Congress has cataloged this record under
Library of Congress Control Number: 2019956937

# PROLOGUE

The first time I had entered Foxworth Hall as Mrs. Garland Foxworth, I had to pause to catch my breath as if I had been racing through the entire wedding ceremony and reception. I was still a little dazed and couldn't help but imagine myself having been scooped up by a gallant, handsome, and powerful knight on a white horse who had carried me away swiftly from my carefree youthful life too soon and deposited me here at Foxworth Hall, an estate that was another world unto itself.

The grand house was surrounded by acres and acres of prime Virginia woods and fields, situated in the foothills of the Blue Ridge Mountains. There was a mile-long lake on the property, less than a quarter of a mile from the house, a stopover for Canada geese at the start of spring. It had a dock and rowboats. At night when the moon was out, it looked like a large platter of glittering liquid silver. In the valley below the estate were rows of much smaller houses. From this height they resembled toy homes. How could anyone living in Foxworth Hall not feel like an aristocrat, almost godlike, looking down on the far less wealthy inhabitants, some of whom were employed in Foxworth Enterprises and paid meager salaries?

I had been in the great mansion nearly ten days ahead of the ceremony preparing, which included having Garland's mother's wedding dress adjusted to fit me. I hated it but I wore it to please him and slip on the Foxworth name the way you might slip on a pair of too-tight shoes. Every one of Garland's parents' friends who attended told me his father especially would have been so pleased. The older men who had known him implied that he was quite aware of attractive women, maybe too aware. How many times during the reception had I heard "You are the most beautiful Foxworth ever" or "We never thought Garland would settle down, but seeing you, we understand why he has chosen to do so"?

"And so quickly! He was obviously afraid of losing you."

The leering men laughed in chorus, but I did feel like I was on a pedestal, unable to move from right to left or vice versa without all eyes turning to me as if anything and everything I did was to be noted for posterity. Foxworths made history in Virginia, and I was now part of that heritage and the future. I had every reason to be happy, ecstatic, floating on a cloud.

But suddenly that day, the Foxworth ancestors, who were frozen in portraits high up on the walls, were glaring down at me with eyes swimming in condescension and disapproval. It was as if they knew what most would consider the sordid events that had brought me here. No one would be surprised at my reaction to these paintings and the fears I had read into them.

None of the artists had captured anyone with even the wisp of a smile on his or her lips. If anything, the relatives portrayed wore fixed, piercing scowls. Those arrogant eyes followed me late in the afternoon of our wedding reception when I decided to go in to repair my hair and freshen up. As I crossed the huge entryway toward the two flights of stairs, I felt a chill at the back of my neck. In the hall above, flickering lanterns struggled to push back the thickening shadows spreading like spilled India ink. Despite the size of the mansion, the walls seemed closer, intimidating, now that they were my walls, too.

Standing at the top of the second stairway above the enormous entryway, I could hear the echo of the help's footsteps and their voices and laughter as they walked through the rear of the great house, carrying out what was needed at the wedding reception. Yet the music sounded far off, as if it had already become a distant memory. I had to pause to catch my breath and swallow back the anxiety that rose from the soles of my feet to wash over my breasts and soak my tender heart.

I was, after all, barely more than sixteen, and

I was married. I was Garland Foxworth's wife, and even though it was our main purpose for my being here these ten days, we had barely grown to know much more about each other. There was a great deal to do and Garland never stopped working at his businesses. Some days, we didn't see each other until dinner. So much of his personal past was yet to be discovered. He was handsome, charming, and wealthy, yes, but there was a great deal I didn't know about my new husband, and much I feared that I might never get to know.

It was like a chant resonating in my head: *Who really is this man you married? You have seen his loving and tender smile, you have tasted his salty, demanding lips, and you have heard him pronounce his vows with firmness in his voice that old fire-and-brimstone preachers would envy, but who is he?*

Now, after living here nearly five years and being known as the mistress of Foxworth Hall, I was often haunted by the memory of those moments passing the wall of portraits on my wedding day. I still saw myself as a stranger. It was as if the house would accept only the marriage of Foxworths. Indeed, cousins had married cousins. I could see the resemblances to each other in the paintings of the ancestors. Like some English royal family, they guarded their lineage. The house demanded it. Diluted family blood was unwelcomed in its veins. Garland's father had married his second cousin.

I never really felt the expected warmth of a new home; I never felt cozy and comfortable here. Surely most people would understand why not. None of the furniture or artifacts reflected my taste or interest even after all these years. I hadn't bought a new picture or changed a curtain or a rug, much less an ashtray or a candlestick holder. The only place I saw myself was in a mirror.

There were rooms I still had barely glimpsed and doors I couldn't recall having seen when I was in that hallway the first or even second time. It was as if the walls in that section of the mansion I rarely walked gave birth to new entrances that opened to places born out of the black, muted darkness that flooded them once the sun went down and all light, like some unwanted guest, fled.

Nearly five years ago, I had given birth at Foxworth Hall in my bedroom, a room known as the Swan Room because the headboard of the bed had a swan in ivory turned in profile, looking like it was ready to plunge its head under the ruffled underside of a lifted wing. Whatever angels I had brought to comfort me had been locked out of the house and left fluttering helplessly in the icy night. That was an evening so cold that stars couldn't twinkle. The heavens were numb, expectant, as if the universe itself was holding its breath. A new Foxworth was coming through me to enter the world. Everyone was to be told he was born premature. I quickly discovered that the richer and more powerful you are, the quicker and easier people will accept your lies or at least pretend they do.

According to my mother's descriptions, she had suffered a terribly difficult pregnancy with me, but my labor was almost a mere inconvenience compared to hers. She was unable to hide her jealousy and be joyful and grateful her daughter had less suffering. My son, Malcolm, had left my womb like a child fleeing. Anyone hearing me that day would agree that some of my final cries could have been cries of surprise and not pain, especially if they looked at my face.

It was over?

Already?

My water had broken and in less than thirty minutes, Malcolm had been born. Dr. Ross lifted him above his head, afterbirth and all, resembling some heathen warrior with bloodied hands holding up the heart of his conquered foe so that Garland, standing in the doorway like some indifferent passerby, could glance in and see his son.

"Thank God it's a boy and it's done," Garland had said, and then had gone downstairs to announce the birth of his son to three of his business associates who had been waiting in the library, smoking cigars as if they were all expectant fathers or gamblers who had bet on my baby's sex. I'm sure he had brought out his cache of limoncello to make a toast. He saved it for the most special of occasions. I had no idea whether or not he ever had shared the secret of my seduction with them in explaining why a well-known, wealthy playboy had married so soon and so young. I know he made himself seem gallant and noble any chance he had. Growing up in this house as a member of this family, he did believe and often behaved as if he was a prince who wore a crown invisible to anyone but him.

Dora Clifford, my personal maid, had assisted Dr. Ross in cutting the umbilical cord and washing Malcolm, so named for Garland's mother's father. He hadn't cried while they cared for him, not even uttering a small wail. Perhaps he had expected to be treated like a sun god who was immediately wrapped in his soft blue wool blanket and laid comfortably in the bassinet. Instantly he had known that he didn't have to depend on my heartbeat anymore.

Malcolm had not been placed on my body, close to my breast, the way babies often were placed soon after they were born. The wet nurse, Mrs. Cotter, had been waiting in his nursery, where she had her own bed. At the time I was still a bit dazzled over my being pregnant and Garland had made a wet nurse one of his promises to ease the impact on me, lustfully whispering that he didn't want to damage my perfect breasts. Dr. Ross, who was in his eighties and had delivered Garland, had thought it would be better if Malcolm was immediately attached to the woman who would feed him for months.

"We can't confuse those suckling lips, now, can we? Too many nipples spoil the kitchen," he had added, and had choked on his own laughter, coughing and sputtering like some steamboat on the Shenandoah. If he had died on the spot and fallen over me, I would have considered it divine intervention. As soon as he could, he left my birthing so he could go imbibe with Garland and his friends. Most likely Lucas, our carriage driver, would take him home passed out on the seat, snoring so loudly and hard he'd frighten the horses.

Neither Dora nor I ever liked Dr. Ross. There was nothing gentle about him, especially when he had female patients. No man felt more superior to a woman than her doctor in 1891, and none like Dr. Ross let her know it as clearly, too. There was no sense complaining about him to Garland, either. He was the Foxworth family doctor and that was that. He was something else the Foxworths owned. Sometimes I imagined the family crest stamped on the physician's wrinkled, pale-lily forehead with those dull-brown milky orbs below rimmed in faded rose. His fingers inside me felt like thorns and caused my nausea along the way as much as anything.

"That's that," he had said after washing his hands.

The moment he was gone, Dora had attended to me, her face full of *don't pay attention to him.*

I turned away and closed my eyes, trying to shut all of it out.

*I'm a mother,* I had realized, but I didn't seem to care right at that moment.

And I wondered back then and still do now if I ever would.

# 1

Something unusual was happening in the Swan Room today.

I could hear the unexpected noise resonating in the hallway, unexpected because Dora looked after my bedroom as soon as she could in the morning, so no one should be in it this late in the day. It should be deadly silent. I knew Garland wasn't yet home from his recent business venture, and he wouldn't be in the Swan Room without me anyway. Even when I was in my bedroom and he could visit me, he was rarely there. To make love I had to go to his bedroom; I had to go there even to talk privately in the later evening sometimes. Aside from one occasion when we had made love in a rowboat on our lake, his bedroom had become the only love nest for us in this grand mansion and on this large estate. We had lost the magic of spontaneity years ago. If he didn't plan it, nothing happened.

"Come to me tonight," he would say.

When I first hesitated and demanded to know why it had to be his bedroom and not mine, he said he wanted it to feel more like a discreet rendezvous because that made it more romantic and we must never lose the romance. How could I argue against that?

However, years ago I realized that the real reason wasn't the romance in him or the Foxworth arrogance showing its face; it was something else, something far worse that I would have to learn how to ignore and to live with, just like so many other dark and twisted secrets that dwelled in this mansion with its whispers and fading footsteps. Did all great families by nature have so many mysteries lingering? Should I have expected it and not been surprised?

Most girls think when they say "I do" to a man, they are saying it to him, to their new life together, but I had said it to a history captured and embedded so deeply in Foxworth Hall that opening a window didn't do much to let in new, fresher air or release the captured cries and mournful sighs one could easily imagine having been sounded over the years here. It was as if every birth in this house and certainly every death left indelible shadows on the walls, shadows sunlight couldn't push aside.

Right now I paused to listen harder on the stairway, barely breathing even though I had started up quickly, eager to bathe and change my clothes. I was nearly up to the second landing after returning from a midday shopping spree at Miller and Rhoads on High Street in Charlottesville, Virginia. I was going to send

Dora down to bring up the packages. As usual, there were quite a few.

The department store had become my opium den. Buying new things and following what the salesladies called the recent fashions lifted me out of the doldrums these days. Garland was gone so often and for longer periods of time. It wasn't like that during the first few years. Suddenly, he claimed that he no longer trusted his managers and there were all sorts of new marketing problems almost everywhere.

"I caught one manager embezzling from me," he declared before charging out one time. It was never "embezzling from us."

Whenever he left now, the house would darken even more and silence flowed in everywhere, flowed in waves, a tide of stillness. As time went by, the absence of music and laughter, almost any joviality, gave the mansion a cemetery atmosphere. Eventually, I half-expected everyone who worked here always to be dressed in black. The grandfather's clock bonged out the hours like a drummer accompanying a funeral procession.

There were some good reasons for depression and unhappiness these days, however.

Garland's factories and other investments really were struggling to stay profitable since the Panic of 1893. Whenever I complained about his leaving me so frequently and us doing so little when it came to having fun and enjoying the gay life he had promised, he went into a rant, weaving details about the overbuilt railroads and the stupid politicians who had driven the economy into shambles with the Sherman Silver Purchase Act. If I so much as groaned over these boring facts, his face would redden even more and he would pound the table after every complaint about the depleted federal gold reserves, blaming everything on stupid bankers and shortsighted investors. It wasn't lost on me that my father was a banker who often guided investors.

"We were almost better off during the Civil War," he had claimed at a recent dinner. "Not that we're not still wealthy," he quickly had added in a calmer tone. He never lost his pride. Foxworths didn't grovel; Foxworths didn't whine. "I'm not asking you to make any economies. Just understand my needs and how much harder I have to work to protect what we have."

Before that evening had ended, I was expected to demonstrate how I sympathized and understood. That was the only way to bring us back at least to a semblance of a happy marriage. Too often, especially lately, I saw myself more like a temporary wife, winding down her allotted days of matrimony and family until some other young woman captured her husband's fancy and she was sent out to pasture like a beautiful racehorse that had outlived its prime.

Perhaps some of this was my fault. I knew I

resembled a girlfriend rather than a wife, even after all this time. Right from the beginning, I was willing to accept my freedom from domestic and motherly responsibilities. But that wasn't completely my selfish doing. According to my mother, it was something I had to accept if I wanted to enjoy what she called "being part of the aristocracy." I was a woman of wealth and position now. I couldn't dirty my hands with the work and obligations ordinary married women and mothers performed. I admittedly wasn't looking forward to any of that anyway. I barely did my share of housework when I was living at home, and becoming a mother so young had been so far off in my young imagination that it was barely a thought. Back then the possibility was right up there with flying to the moon.

But what my mother didn't tell me about my "aristocratic life" was that I would have no separate identity and rarely be called Corrine instead of Mrs. Garland Foxworth. Gradually, I would lose contact with all those who knew me as anyone else. I was deposited into a world of strangers. And yet my mother insisted that love, romance, and marriage were merely baby steps taking you to a life in which you compromised; you sacrificed and your husband provided. When I complained, she nodded and with a bitter smirk said, "Of course this would happen. What did you expect? From the moment you say 'I do' until the day you take your final breath, you no longer have a different shadow. Get used to it."

How depressing, but how true that was. Sometimes I did feel like a ghost, especially here in a house that was becoming more of a museum than a home for me. Our servants looked through me, walked around me, and rarely said more than the formal greeting unless I asked a question.

At first I thought I would take care of Malcolm right after Mrs. Cotter left. I really had intended to do that, and Garland must have believed it, too. He permitted me to have a carpenter create an infant's swan bed. However, Malcolm didn't sleep through a single night after he had been brought to the Swan Room. I wasn't sure if it was because of the room or not having someone practically hovering over him constantly, which was something I wasn't going to do. His incessant crying exhausted me, and I finally gave in to Dora taking over. The bed was left in my room since it had the swan embossed on the small headboard, and a new nursery was created.

After that, with Dora caring for Malcolm, with Mrs. Steiner overseeing every little thing this mansion needed, with Mrs. Wilson ruling the kitchen like the captain of a naval vessel, and with Garland's forbidding my even changing the position of a lamp in a room, except for the Swan Room, I was beginning to see myself as unnecessary as dust. The house and the Foxworths had swallowed what little there was left of Corrine Dixon. Sometimes in dreams I saw myself swept up, bagged, and taken away. Without my portrait up on a wall, I'd be as forgotten as yesterday's yawn.

My bedroom was my only sanctuary in the great house, the one place I ruled as firmly as Garland ruled the mansion. I could breathe there and pretend to be a young girl again and think silly thoughts. I would imagine myself still unmarried, still planning how I would flirt with and tease good-looking boys. But right now, my sanctuary was being violated. I hurried to it as if I believed my fantasies could be discovered.

Near the doorway, I stopped. I was surprised to hear Malcolm's giggle, which always sounded like his father's, a mix of a laugh and a deep, guttural exclamation of self-satisfied joy. There was much about his father that he imitated, despite how little he saw of him. He often spent more time beside Olsen, our groundskeeper, than he did with his own father. However, by the time he was four years old, he had already mastered this laugh to the point where if I didn't see who it was, I wouldn't know if it was Malcolm or Garland chuckling.

What was he doing in my bedroom, and where was Dora? He was never to go into my room when I wasn't there. In fact, no one but Dora was permitted. Everyone in this house understood my strict orders about that. I especially didn't want my son to wander about in it, touching my things. Malcolm, even at this age, was too mischievous and indifferent to any rules. You could see the defiance light up when you told him something he was not to do or somewhere he was not to go. I didn't trust him to be alone with my possessions. He could strip pearls off a necklace and use them as marbles. Dora, defending him as much and as strongly as she would if he were truly her son, was quite aware of his impish behavior and did her best to contain him, but always found excuses for him, too.

Lately, however, my spoiled four-year-old too often was managing to get away from my personal assistant, who willingly had increased her responsibilities to become his nanny and tutor and, with what I saw as Garland's blessing, essentially to become his surrogate mother. Maybe Malcolm required two mothers. He was that demanding, never pausing with his questions and his complaints. Usually now, he would go to her before he would go to me. He could wind her like a clock and get her to do his bidding. Whenever he ran off, he would disappear some-where in the mansion as if it had consumed him. He wasn't afraid of any shadow, any alcove or cranny, or any room. The whole of Foxworth Hall was his playground.

Often Dora needed help to locate him after he

had snuck off. He would keep so quiet and so well hidden deeper in the mansion that it could take more than an hour to locate him or get him to come out. Punishing or threatening him with a spanking didn't get him to stop his shenanigans, either. He never cried if I spanked him; he simply turned his eyes into glass and waited as if he had left his body and was anticipating when to rejoin it. One time when my parents visited us and Malcolm was just two and a half, my father warned me I was in for it. I had no idea what that meant at the time.

I was beginning to understand and would completely, especially today.

I stepped into the doorway. He was at my vanity table, tearing pages from Garland's and my wedding album, crumpling them in his small hands, and tossing them at the wastebasket the way Garland tossed unwanted or unneeded paper at his office basket, imitating the sound of a Civil War cannonball.

My scream was shrill, frightening, even to me. Malcolm shuddered and paused, narrowed his eyes to look at me with shock at first and then defiance. Standing there in his new sailor suit with his flaxen blond hair and sky-blue eyes, he would melt the heart of any woman who saw him. Strangers, who had never been stung by his arrogant indifference or insolence, would smile at the sight of such an adorable and perfect

23

child. I had no doubt that Malcolm realized this by now and knew how to take advantage of it. Exploitation and always profiting and scheming were part of his character. He was, after all, Garland Foxworth's child, perhaps more somehow than he was mine. My mother would coldly tell me that Garland's sperm drowned my helpless egg.

"What are you doing!" I cried, my hands clenched in fists, my face surely twisted and uglier than he had ever seen it. That was my wedding album he was destroying.

But he didn't retreat. It didn't frighten him. Before he replied, he ripped out another page.

"Hate the album," he said, crumpling the page in his hands and tossing it boldly, making the same cannonball sound as if I weren't there.

Twice recently he had come into the Swan Room while I was gazing at the album. Obviously, he blamed it for my not catering to his whims, whatever they were. I was so deeply in thought both times that I didn't hear him enter and didn't realize he was standing there, waiting to be acknowledged, waiting for me to agree to do something with him or for him or maybe just to answer another one of his incessant questions, like why were there so many clouds today or why didn't worms have feet. He had screamed something mean and had run from the room.

So it didn't surprise me that he would then target

the wedding album. He knew it was something special. My spoiled son always chose a valuable item to damage or destroy whenever he wanted to express his anger or frustration. The angrier he was, the more expensive the target. Garland once joked that he had a rich man's sense of taste from the moment he could grasp something and drop it to make it shatter. "Just like a Foxworth," he had added, as if he was proud of how destructive of something valuable his son could be, and that the violence he expressed was good simply because it was what a Foxworth would do.

Our wedding album was valuable to us both, but not for Garland's reasons. He was proud of it because it had been quite unique in 1890 to hire a photographer to snap pictures of the famous people at our wedding, as well as the decoratively constructed stage and the flowery surroundings Olsen had beautifully designed and built. There were pictures of the dance floor when we were doing our waltz and portraits of me in Garland's mother's wedding dress, some only with him, some only with my parents, and some with me and Dora, who had been conscripted to serve as my maid of honor.

Garland wouldn't permit me to invite my best friend from Alexandria, Daisy Herman, to serve in that role. He wanted me to make a clean break from my earlier life, but also not have my youth emphasized at our wedding by my bringing along girls who, although not more than sixteen, too, looked it. I didn't. I overheard him clearly tell people that I was recently eighteen. How do you begin a relationship on a foundation of lies, even though in all the pictures I looked that old?

Now, five years later, having such an album was still quite rare and still quite expensive. Garland had carefully researched to choose our photographer. He wanted to impress our guests, especially his envious business associates. My mother was certainly overwhelmed after Garland had copies of her pictures made, framed, and delivered to her and my father before their new house was constructed so she would have them to hang in their entryway.

It was another attempt of Garland's to compensate and placate her because she had been left out of the great secret: I had been two months pregnant before Garland and I had married. I had confessed all to my father but not to her. Once she realized she had been kept in the dark, there was nothing Garland, my father, or I could do that would soothe her wounded ego. Even though my father and Garland had organized everything, carefully keeping her unaware, she focused her anger mostly on me.

Suddenly, now that I was mistress of one of the most impressive mansions in Virginia and married to one of the wealthiest young men in the state, our mother-daughter relationship was sacred. My not telling her the "dirty truth," as she put it, was "a deep betrayal of our trust." She was in tears.

"What trust?" I asked. "When was a strong and loving mother-daughter relationship important to you? When did you share anything personal with me to help me understand my own emotions growing up?"

She couldn't answer that. Instead, she reached into a well of popular superstitions before my pregnancy became obvious.

"A woman who hides her pregnancy will have a child who is deaf," she predicted. "Or worse."

Malcolm might be growing up spoiled, but he was as close to a perfect child physically as could be. She was forced to accept it.

"You should be grateful," I told her. "You have a beautiful grandson."

Eventually, she swallowed down her indignation, gulping down her fake tears and complaints. Nevertheless, I knew my father would probably pay the price in small stinging ways forever, and I would never be truly forgiven. Now, whenever I uttered the smallest complaint, her response always was, "You made your bed behind my back. Now sleep in it." I saw how much pleasure it gave her to say that.

And turning to my father for any sympathy wasn't going to give me much satisfaction, either, mainly because I no longer believed in him. A little more than a year after our marriage, when Garland had drunk a little too much wine and was ranting about some investment he had made that had gone sour, I stumbled into another ugly truth when I said, "Maybe you should have asked my father about it."

"Your father?" he said, and laughed as if I had said a stupid thing. Condescension and arrogance sang in harmony in this house. My self-pride rose like a cobra. Back then, I cared far more about my family pride than I did now.

"He is chairman of the bank board, Garland. That's quite an accomplishment. People in business respect him. Otherwise, how would he be where he is?"

"Really?"

He looked away and busied himself with something unimportant just as he often did when he felt so superior to me. It was like I was not worth the effort involved in saying another word, but this time I wouldn't be ignored. It was my father we were discussing.

"Yes, really," I said. "You don't know everything, especially that you don't know that." I could be as sharp as my mother when I wanted to be.

He turned and peered at me through those arrogant eyes and then smiled, but not in the sexy way I had so admired. This was what I had come to know as the Foxworth smile, cold, a precursor, a drumbeat that made you stop breathing for a moment because you knew something terrible was coming.

"The only reason your father is chairman of the bank board, Corrine, is because I voted for him. My investment gave me more votes than any other member. I agreed to that the first time he came to see me about you."

I stared at him, thinking and shaking my head. *That can't be,* I was telling myself, convincing myself. My father wouldn't have done that. He wouldn't have forgiven Garland for seducing me under the influence of his precious limoncello drink in exchange for his votes. But all that did happen at the same time. How could I deny that? Still, I wanted to hear it clearly. I wanted to be sure it wasn't simply a coincidence he was employing for his benefit.

"When did you decide to do that, Garland?"

He looked away.

"Garland? When?"

"Don't be an idiot," he said, and walked away from me, but the answer remained behind in the air, in the weight on my chest, and in the thumping of my heart. My father had convinced me that Garland was not only remorseful but fearful he would lose me. The way my father had described it helped me believe that I was the love of Garland Foxworth's life, the perfect woman to be his wife. My father said that he had never seen a man so lovesick and persuaded me that Garland wanted not only me but our child.

I was always closer to my father than I was to my mother. I practically worshipped him and assumed he would never want anything for me that wasn't wonderful and good for me. He took my side in almost every dispute I had with my mother and was eager for me to be treated like a grown woman. He was proud of me and enjoyed showing me off, having me on his arm, and introducing me to people he respected. How could I ever forget the proud look on his face when he had escorted both my mother and me up the stairs to the Wexler anniversary gala where I first had met Garland Foxworth? My father called it my coming-out party.

That Garland's vote for chairman of the banking board would be more important to him than my utmost happiness was devastating. It was truly a great betrayal. I desperately tried not to believe it for a while after I first heard it, but gradually, like the water from a heavy downpour, no matter how much and how hard I pushed it away, it eventually soaked in and drowned my childish faith.

My father was an ambitious man, as ambitious as my husband after all. Maybe all men were the same. Marriage was simply another tool to service that ambition. What they didn't realize was that love is too fragile, too easily sacrificed for selfish reasons and then the sacrifice regretted. They'd pay in the end. Surely they would suffer for this, and even though they pretended otherwise, deep down in their hearts they feared it. They knew, surely they knew. Deceit gives birth to miseries you had yet to imagine.

This was why I cherished and looked back at my wedding album from time to time. I wanted to see if there was an expression on anyone's face that revealed he or she didn't believe ours was a romantic love affair. Who besides my father and Garland knew about me, knew I was already pregnant? What was my father feeling when he stood to give me away? I studied his portrait to see if there was even the iota of regret. But I saw nothing in those smiles or in those eyes that revealed the ugly truth. Still, I turned to it as if it was a window on the past and if I looked long and hard enough, I would see and understand how and why I had been delivered so easily and quickly to my life in Foxworth Hall. That was my reason for placing so much value on these pictures.

Now much of that album was destroyed by the son whose very existence had brought Garland and me to the altar.

"How could you do such a terrible, mean thing?" I screamed at Malcolm. Some of the pages he had ripped were crumpled and balled on the floor beside the wastebasket. One had the portrait of Garland and me, Garland's face the less wrinkled.

I reached for a belt I had hanging on the door. Even his father didn't frighten him into better behavior with his threats. He often told me that it was up to a child's mother to discipline the child until he was at least ten, especially boys. After that, if a mother did a good job, a father could enforce rules of behavior with merely a stern look, because his mother could threaten that his father would do worse things to him. My stern looks certainly didn't work. Maybe they would this time. He surely could see my rage was at a new height, I thought, seizing the belt. He would cower and cry and plead. But as I turned back to him, he charged forward and ducked under my outstretched hand to run out the door.

"Come back here, Malcolm Foxworth!" I screamed, and charged after him, regardless of how foolish it made me look. I was that angry at him.

He started down the hallway, running toward the corner to follow another hallway into the darker side of Foxworth Hall, the wing that housed the rooms rarely used. They were afterthoughts long ago forgotten.

"Stop!" I screamed, and ran after him. "Malcolm Foxworth, you stop running right now. You can't hide this time. We'll find you, and it will be worse for you. Come back."

So many things were driving me to run after him. Every frustration added more angry energy. I turned down the corridor and ran into the darker hallway. I could hear his footsteps ahead. The faster and longer he ran, the angrier I got. He was running in almost total darkness. Almost any child I had seen would have been afraid to continue alone, especially in this part of the house that was rarely lit. Mrs. Steiner barely kept after it. I felt the cobwebs breaking across my forehead. I passed the area that looked down on our ballroom, now in darkness, the window curtains drawn closed. I always hated this section of the house. The whispers of the dead still hovered in the corners. He had run here almost as if he knew that. Sometimes I thought he talked to them. Perhaps he had over-heard me tell Dora how I always avoided this wing.

Moments later I heard a door ahead on the right open and close. I had been told that was the most unused bedroom in this house, never a guest room and never a room for any servant. From the way Mrs. Steiner had described it, no one had slept in it for decades even though it was fully furnished. I deeply suspected that it had been someone's personal hideaway, maybe Garland's mother's or maybe even Garland's, although he never admitted being in this wing of the house very much, either. The mansion had swelled, spawned new rooms over time along with the Foxworths' growing egos.

"Malcolm!"

*I will drag him back by the scruff of his neck,* I thought. If he wanted to be in a bedroom, he would be in his own for days and nights. That was about the only thing he feared, confinement. I caught my breath when I reached the door.

"Malcolm, you come out of there right now. Every second I wait will be another day locked in your room. Do you hear me?"

Silence was like a flame burning my heart. Any other child would be trembling and, by now, obedient. Enraged, I threw open the door. The darkness seemed even thicker, but there was enough light peeking through the heavy tapestried draperies covering the two tall windows for me to scan the two double beds. It was a large but cluttered room with a massive highboy, a large dresser, two stuffed chairs, plus a mahogany table with two chairs. He could be hiding behind anything, but I was thinking he had crawled under one of the beds. I was about to go to my knees when my eyes picked up the opened door on the left, a door I knew revealed the narrow stairway leading up to the attic.

Just how he would have the courage to go up there this time of day when the sunlight was dwindling astounded me. I had been up there only once with Garland, who obviously hadn't enjoyed showing it to me. I had nagged him into it because in those early days, I wanted to know as much as I could about this house, my new home. As its new mistress, I felt obligated to be familiar with every part of it. It wasn't a long visit in the attic. Garland wasn't afraid of anything, but it was obvious that being there resurrected some unpleasant memories, memories he didn't care to describe at the time.

He pointed out some of the very old things that had been stored. "I don't know why," he said. "I used to call this the Miser's Palace. You know what misers tell you when you want to throw something out or give it away? 'Someday this will be worth something.' It's worth something, all right, something to dust. It has a place to sleep. Now I would call it another Foxworth cemetery. You can almost hear their souls gathering up here. I used to think that was why the ceilings below creaked."

It gave me the chills to hear him say that. I didn't even like looking up the dark stairway now, but I had no doubt Malcolm wouldn't be dissuaded. For all I knew, he had been up here a number of times.

"Malcolm!" I called, and walked to the door. The waning light of the late-fall afternoon sun barely illuminated the steps.

"You'll get hurt up there, Malcolm. Come right now, this instant!" I shouted up the stairway, and then listened. The silence was broken only by the sound of the wind swirling over the roof and seeping into the cracks. It was almost a whistling. "Malcolm?"

I looked about for a candle, but this room had been unoccupied so long that no one bothered with it, especially in the evening. I was sure too much movement would stir whirling dust up from the floor. The room was more like a tomb. A rancid odor made me gag. Something might have died in it recently, I thought.

"Malcolm, you are going to be terribly sorry."

I waited, but he didn't stir.

Reluctantly, I started up the stairs.

# 2

Every muscle in my body, especially in my legs and thighs, seemed in revolt. I didn't want to go any farther. How could he run up here? Didn't anything frighten him? I was of a mind to retreat, close the door, and leave him hovering in some corner of the attic. After a while I would send Dora up after him. She should be the one going up here anyway. He snuck into the Swan Room under her watch. Garland never attached any blame to her when Malcolm did something wrong.

"You didn't let him sleep in your Swan Room when he was an infant," he would remind me, as if Malcolm as a baby was capable of resenting it. I had real doubts that he understood his own child or any child's mind. Lately, he had less to do with him than I did.

Nevertheless, I had no doubt that if a terrible thing happened to him while I went to get Dora, Garland would blame me entirely. I could just hear him. *Why did you chase him? Why didn't you just leave him be until he came back? You drove him to go up there, and I had shown you how cluttered it was, how dangerous it could be for anyone, especially in the dark.*

37

I felt the sweat break out on my forehead and my neck. It gave me a chill. Again, I heard the stiff breezes penetrating the cracks and around the dormer windows. It sounded like the attic was sucking it in. Something tinkled like chimes above. Had he bumped into it or tripped over it? I listened for his cry but heard nothing, so I went up a little farther. The steps creaked under my feet as if the wood could complain like the sleeping dead who were annoyed at being woken.

"Malcolm!" I screamed. By now he must realize I was coming up after him. "You come right down. I won't spank you. Don't make me come up there to get you."

I waited, listening hard for the sound of his small footsteps returning to the stairway, but all I heard was the wind whistling and that tinkling, perhaps of whatever was in his path. Reluctantly, I took another step and then another. The stairway was so narrow. It wasn't much wider than a ladder, and the walls felt colder than the walls anywhere else in the mansion. Every few feet or so, there were webs of dust between the steps and between them and the walls. Some ugly-looking, wormlike creature, surely comfortable in hell, crawled upward. I avoided touching it and took another step.

I was so frustrated, my rage twirling in my stomach, the muscles in my legs now aching with reluctance. I tried to swallow but couldn't without taking a deep breath, and I hated breathing this stale, rancorous, and acrid air. It was as if the great house was rotting from the top down. In years to come, we would smell it everywhere. I raked my thoughts to find words that would drive him to submission and bring him back to the stairway.

"You're going to bed without any dinner tonight, Malcolm. And Mrs. Wilson made your favorite chocolate cake for dessert, too. You'd better come out and down," I said, pausing more than halfway up.

I waited. He made no sound, but I thought I heard something scurrying across the attic floor. Visions of rats as large as alley cats ran through my imagination. Garland had told me Mrs. Steiner periodically had Olsen use arsenic. Right before winter, he would go up and pluck the dead mice, rats, and other vermin, dropping the carcasses into a sack the way a slave before the Civil War picked cotton.

What if Malcolm touched the arsenic or inhaled it?

"There's poison up there, Malcolm. You can die from it, or something bad will bite you up there and you'll get a terrible infection and die," I said. I was really warning myself. "There are evil spiders and rats and bats, too. One could bite you and give you rabies."

What else could I think of? Any other child

would be somewhat terrified of such vermin, but in my heart I knew that hearing all that could easily please him. He liked creatures and especially enjoyed tormenting them. Dora was always chastising him for it, warning him of being bitten, but her criticism came dressed in such reasonable tones he was never threatened or afraid. I thought he might care if she liked him or not, that it was important to him, but Malcolm had his father's independence and arrogance. He knew she would like him no matter what. I could almost hear him say it, even at this young age.

I waited.

Nothing, not a sound, suggested he was giving up. Maybe I should leave and not keep after him. Then he would come.

I was tempted to do just that but mainly because what I had done was frighten myself and obviously not him.

"Malcolm, I'm going back down and leaving you up here," I warned. I really didn't want to go up any farther. The autumn sun was sinking like a rock in water. The attic, the stairway, all of it, would soon be in pitch darkness. He would surely hurt himself then. The wisest thing for me to do now was simply leave and hope he would feel safe enough to follow before he couldn't see his way back.

"Maybe you belong up here, Malcolm. How would you like that? We can lock the door and keep you up here. You won't be able to go to the lake and play with your toy sailboat or go for a rowboat ride. You won't ride your pony, and I'll make sure you don't get any presents on your birthday or next Christmas."

I rattled off every threat I could imagine. There was still no sound of him, and then—

Like a rifle's discharge, I heard the door to the narrow stairway slam shut. I turned, pausing to believe it myself.

"What?" I cried. The silence was suddenly deeper. I could see the door was indeed shut.

I started down very slowly. Now that more time had passed, the steps were even darker than when I had ascended. What had he done? I imagined he had been under the bed after all, but why was the door to the attic opened? Had he thought of running up here and then lost his nerve? Or had someone else been up here and forgotten to close it?

Or . . . could he be that crafty and deceitful at almost five years old and deliberately have opened it, knowing I would think he had gone up?

I walked down to the final step and turned the door handle.

The door didn't move. I pushed it and turned the handle again, but it still didn't budge. The cold, dank air seemed to rush down the stairway and close in around me. My whole body shuddered.

"Malcolm? Are you holding this door closed?" I called.

He didn't respond. I tried again and this time put my shoulder against the door. It did not budge. Panic seeped into me, washing my neck and face in waves of heat as another frightening thought shot through my mind.

"Malcolm. Malcolm! Did you turn the key? Did you lock this door?"

It felt like it was locked. It didn't even rattle. He had turned the key. The realization stunned me for a moment. I stood there breathing fast and hard. I pounded the door and pushed on it and turned the knob, but it didn't move. I shook the handle so hard I thought it would break off, but like most doors in this mansion, this one was solid.

"Malcolm?" I screamed, and then I balled my hands and pounded on the door so intensely and fast that my hands and my wrists stung. I had to stop and then listened.

There was only silence on the other side. Above me, whatever had scurried before began to scurry again. It sounded like more than one. The thought of them charging down this stairway took my breath away. I couldn't swallow. My chest felt like it had turned to stone.

"If you're in that room and you locked this door, Malcolm Foxworth, I will punish you for a month," I said, my mouth near the jamb. I didn't want to breathe the dank, dusty air around me if I could help it.

There was no response, not a giggle, nothing.

"I will definitely have you locked up here. I swear I will. Malcolm. You're hurting Mama badly. Everyone will be angry, especially your father. Especially Dora," I added.

I waited, really in disbelief at the silence. Could he be standing there on the other side, now too frightened of what he had done to move? Something crawled over my ankle. I screamed and kicked out so hard and fast that I nearly lost my balance. I felt like I was sinking in a well of panic, sinking like someone who had stepped into quicksand. I ended up slamming my rear on the step. I was trembling badly and, despite how I had avoided it, took deep breaths of this rancid air. For a moment I simply sat there, trying to convince myself that this wasn't happening.

But it was, of course, and now there were other reasons to panic.

Who had seen me chase after him? No one knew I had come home from shopping. No one had greeted me, neither Mrs. Steiner nor Mrs. Wilson, and Lucas had gone off to finish a chore for Mrs. Wilson and then pick up a meat order. I didn't want to wait in the carriage while he had done all of that, so I had him take me home first and then sent him back.

After a good half a minute or so, I stood up and

pounded on the door again and screamed until my throat ached. There was no response. Everyone was too far away to hear. How would anyone know I was in here if Malcolm, who was surely terrified about what he had done now, didn't tell? I searched my mind for a solution and decided I had no choice but to go back up to the attic and call for help from one of the attic windows. I took the reluctant steps until I was up there, standing in the doorway looking across the vast attic that ran the length of the mansion.

It was much darker now. The shadows had merged. Every piece of old furniture was covered in a sheet. When I was up here with Garland, they looked dingy gray, but now they looked coal-black, and the shapes pressing under them appeared to be moving, changing shapes, threatening, angry at being awoken. The Confederate uniforms I had seen hanging looked like ghosts were filling them out again. A dressmaker's mannequin seemed to turn my way.

I spun around because I thought I heard the sound of a trunk opening to my right. I was stone still and listened for the sound of anything, but whatever I had heard crawling was probably just as frightened of me as I was of it and cowered in a corner or under something, its heart beating as fast as mine. I was glad of that. I'd rather not see it.

There was no time to dillydally anyway. Night

was falling very quickly; it did this time of year, as soon as summer disappeared into the beginning of autumn. That sinking sun barely scratched at the horizon. I carefully navigated between old furniture, boxes of discarded clothes and shoes, and trunks. Every movement I made seemed to stir another cloud of dust or get something to scurry into a corner. I coughed and then paused to take some deep breaths with my hand over my mouth to calm myself. I counted to ten, something my father had told me to do when I was a little girl after something had frightened me.

Gathering my strength, I continued on through the attic, moving carefully to avoid what I recalled had looked like rusted old farm equipment. I remember Garland ridiculing his father and grandfather for being so miserly as to not give it to someone who could have used it. I passed the school desks that Garland had told me the Foxworth cousins had used during the smallpox epidemic and wound around to the closest set of four deep dormer windows. Clouds were at that point between day and night when they looked more like shadows. Stars were twinkling brighter. I was never lonelier as a child than I was at evening when the world looked like it was spinning aimlessly into the vastness of space. Those memories still haunted me.

I rushed at the windows.

The first three didn't budge. I started to panic

again, but the fourth opened. I brought myself up to it and began to shout. I shouted until I was nearly hoarse, feeling embarrassed and stupid crying "Help!" but finally, I saw Olsen step around the right corner of the mansion and look up.

"Olsen. I'm locked in the attic. Hurry!" I screamed.

He rushed into the house. I hurried to the stairway, tripping on some smaller box and scratching my arm on a metal trunk before regaining my balance. It stung, but I hurried down the stairs, nearly stumbling over my own feet and falling head over heels. I pressed my palms against the door to stop my downward motion, and I waited, my eyes closed. Minutes later, I heard Olsen's and someone else's footsteps. The key was turned and the door pulled open. I nearly fell out, but Olsen stopped me with his big right palm on my shoulder. Mrs. Steiner stood behind him with a lantern.

"What in all tarnation!" she exclaimed. I was sure I looked a sight, looked like a crazy woman. I had been running my fingers through my hair, and dust probably had caked on my cheeks.

"Where is he?" I demanded.

"Who, ma'am?"

"My son," I said.

She shook her head. "I think he's in his room with Dora."

"Thank you, Olsen," I said. I started out and paused. "Take that key out of the door. I don't know why it was left in the lock."

I continued into the hallway. Mrs. Steiner hurried to move beside me with the lantern.

"What happened?" she asked. "How did you get locked in there?"

I didn't speak. When we reached the hallway to the Swan Room, Garland's room, and Malcolm's, I hesitated. Somehow I had not lost the belt. It was still wrapped around my wrist. Dora heard the commotion and stepped out of Malcolm's room.

"Where is he?" I demanded.

"He's curled up in his bed, ma'am," she said. "He's been shivering with fear."

"As well he should," I said. "Did you see what he did in my bedroom? Why did you permit him to go in there?"

She shook her head, her lips trembling.

"She was helping me, ma'am," Mrs. Steiner said. "What did he do?"

Ignoring Mrs. Steiner, I hurried past Dora and into his room. He was lying there on his bed with his face buried in the pillow. He had his left thumb in his mouth. Now he would pretend to be a baby, I thought.

"What happened, ma'am?" Dora asked, coming up behind me, Mrs. Steiner a few feet back. "He was covered in dust, too. You have a bad scratch

47

on your left arm," she said. "There's blood on your torn sleeve. I'll fetch a wet cloth, medicine, and a bandage. Did he do that?" she asked incredulously.

"He caused it. He nearly destroyed my entire wedding album and then ran away when I caught him doing it. He tricked me into going up the attic stairs and then locked the door behind me. I fell and scratched this arm on some metal trunk."

"Oh, ma'am. That's a lot to lay at the feet of one so small," Dora said.

I turned on her, my eyes probably blazing. "Are you blind, deaf, or stupid?" I asked. "One so small? You know better than I do that he's stuffed with enough mischievous behavior to choke a horse." I turned to him. "How could you do such terrible things, Malcolm, and to your own mother?"

He didn't move or say a word.

I stepped closer and raised the belt. "Maybe this will bring some answers."

"Oh, ma'am, don't," Dora said. "I'll see to him. He'll have no toys and be kept in his room for as long as you see fit."

My hand trembled. I knew I should lay at least a half dozen good whacks on his behind, but Dora was trembling almost as much as Malcolm, who I was sure was pretending, and Mrs. Steiner was staring at me, looking shocked and terrified, too. Reluctantly, I lowered my arm. I had to show some control, or they'd somehow get Garland to believe I had gone mad.

"He's to stay in here for . . . a week," I said, turning to her and speaking calmly but firmly.

She nodded, but I could clearly see she didn't believe I'd keep to a week.

"No dessert tonight, Dora. No dessert for lunch or dinner for this whole week. I mean that. He cannot go out to play with his bike or go to the lake with his sailboat toys. Nothing."

"Yes, ma'am." She looked at him. He still hadn't turned, and his eyes were tightly closed. She knelt beside him and put her hand on his back softly. Then she stroked his hair. "Why did you do such a terrible thing to your mother, Malcolm?" she asked him gingerly. "Why did you run away and hide where it is so dark and dirty? I've begged you to stay out of that part of the house. Why would you go there?"

He took his thumb out of his mouth but didn't answer.

She looked at me and then turned back to him. "Did you lock your mother in the attic?"

"She was going to beat me," he said, without looking at either of us.

"I sure was and still might," I said, "if you don't listen and sit and think about what you've done. Do you hear me, Malcolm Foxworth? You have gone too far this time. You're not a little baby. You know you've done a terrible thing."

When he didn't answer, I leaned over and whispered in a hoarse voice. I realized my throat was aching from all the screaming I had done.

"Do you hear me?"

He nodded.

"Tell your mother you're sorry, Malcolm," Dora said. "Please."

"Don't beg him to be good, Dora," I snapped at her.

She looked down quickly.

I was almost as angry at her. Why she had so willingly accepted this added responsibility caring for Malcolm puzzled me. She had enough to do caring for me and helping her aunt, Mrs. Steiner. Why didn't she want to marry and have a child of her own, a house of her own, and a life of her own? Maybe she had a hidden desire to become a nun.

I shook the belt in front of Malcolm's face.

"I'm not done with you, young man. I want you to get up right now and go to my bedroom. You take out every page you tore out of the wedding album, and you straighten it out. Get up!" I screamed.

He didn't move.

"I'll fix it, ma'am. I'll iron the pages. He can't do that," Dora said.

I looked at her and then at him. She would never see it, I thought, but there was that smug little smile forming on his lips, a smile just like his father's. He was getting away without having to repair the damage he had done. His sense of entitlement would grow bigger than his father's and his grandfather's. It was terrible, but when I looked at my own son now, I saw only the Foxworths, the arrogant and insensitive Foxworths captured in portraits forever.

"He doesn't leave the room, then," I repeated with more emphasis, turned, and paused to recapture my demeanor. "Go get my packages down in the entryway first and bring them up, Dora."

"Yes, ma'am," she said, and started out. I followed her. Mrs. Steiner stood back in the hall-way as if she really feared I would explode.

I looked back at Malcolm from the doorway. He still hadn't moved.

"Someday," I said, "you'll be very sorry you treated your mother like this, Malcolm. You'll cry for your mother's love. Nothing and no one can replace it. You grew inside me, no one else."

I stepped out and closed the door behind me. Mrs. Steiner nodded and hurried away like some-one glad to escape.

I could hear Dora descending the stairway quickly. They'd all talk about this for days. I suddenly felt terribly exhausted. My heart was still pounding as hard as it had been on the attic stairway. After glancing back at Malcolm's door,

I started for the Swan Room. A voice inside me asked why I should be at all surprised at how my son treated me. What part of being a mother had I honestly assumed? *Why would he have an ounce of love for you?* I asked myself. *Your final speech to him probably sounded like a foreign language.* How empty those threats and predictions probably had seemed.

Despite how my mother had treated me when I was younger, I never thought of her as anything but my mother, and I always longed for her love. She was there at least for my basic needs. I never thought of anyone else as a mother. But Malcolm . . . I rarely fed him or dressed him. Whenever we all sat together at dinner, he looked to Dora for instructions.

But whose fault was that? From time to time, I tinkered with letting Dora go. Maybe I was simply jealous of the affection my son showed her but not me. It wasn't her fault, but I couldn't help resenting her sometimes. I'd look for a way to find fault with her. She was too young to be someone's lifelong personal servant and a nanny. Instead of blaming myself, I constantly blamed her.

Where were her self-pride, her ambitions? Her poor self-image always annoyed me. She should be out there meeting people her own age and eventually finding herself a husband. She never asked for a vacation. Her idea of a day off was sitting in her room and reading. Malcolm would still go to her with his problems and requests even on her day off.

However, I knew that Dora had a special, mysterious place in my husband's life as well. She had whispered it to me days before I was becoming Mrs. Garland Foxworth. She had sworn that there was nothing sexual going on. I really didn't understand what it was or what it meant, but during those early days, I sensed that if I pursued it any further, everything would explode in my face, especially my wedding and therefore my future.

Who could blame me for blindly accepting the way things were back then? After all, I was just a little more than sixteen, and despite my bravado and the confidence I portrayed to my girlfriends, who had come to believe I was more sophisticated than women much older than I was, I knew in my heart that I had miles to go before I came anywhere near to knowing what was truly in the heart of a grown man, especially a man of the world like Garland Foxworth. I really had no idea even how to begin to explore it. So much of it was deeply hidden behind his smiles.

Except for my own father and some young boys I had tormented with promises of love, what experience with men did I have? What insights or visions did I really possess? I was successful in putting myself into the body of someone older, even much older, but inside I was still a little girl at heart, a teenage girl who imagined herself a femme fatale. I convinced myself that I was ready to understand and confidently twist a grown man around my thumb.

Perhaps I had never fallen in love with Garland. Perhaps I was always too in love with myself. Such a woman didn't even know how blind she really was. I had been in frightening darkness in the attic of Foxworth Hall. But the truth was, I was always in some darkness here.

The question I couldn't answer now and perhaps never would was, would I ever step out of it? To do that, I had to get better at understanding everything there was to understand about my own husband. I tried to make it seem ordinary, expected. I told myself that any woman would have to do that, wouldn't she?

Yes, Garland Foxworth was a wonderful target for my seductive smiles. He was everything I dreamed I'd find for myself. How could I not capture him and instantly know what I had to know to win his heart forever? His love for me was deep and complete. I was so sure that was what I had seen in those beautiful eyes that first night at the Wexler anniversary gala. I had convinced myself that, like any other man, he was easy to read.

I didn't know it then, but in Garland Foxworth's

case, I would never know what was looming behind those beautiful eyes.

And in the end, that would be tragic for me and perhaps for Malcolm, too.

# 3

Right after we had made love for the first time during my ten-day stay at Foxworth to prepare for our wedding, I thought I had seen a ghost going into Garland's mother's bedroom, but it was Dora in one of his mother's dresses. I confronted Dora about it, and she revealed that Garland made her wear his mother's clothes and lie in her bed. He then entered the room and spoke to her as if she were his mother.

It might have taken much longer to learn more about those strange rendezvous if we had, as Garland had promised, taken a wonderful, long honeymoon. But right before our ceremony, Garland had told me that he was too busy to take me on a formal honeymoon. He promised he would very soon, but for the time being, we would have our honeymoon at Foxworth Hall.

"How can you have a honeymoon at your home?" I asked, smiling. Surely he didn't mean it.

"You have scratched only the surface of Foxworth Hall, Corrine," he said. "For you it's as new and exciting as any place I might take you for ten days. And although I will be working daily, I will be with you most every night. We'll have wonderful dinners with champagne and wine, wines I have brought back from France, wines you wouldn't find at any honeymoon resort in America right now.

"When I have a spare afternoon, weather permitting, we'll go out on the lake, maybe picnic in the boat. I'll have musicians here playing for us often before and after dinner. I'll take you on carriage rides whenever possible. If I break down and decide to share some of my precious time with you with one or two of my closer business associates and their wives, we'll have small dinner parties. It will be good for you to begin becoming a formal dinner hostess as soon as possible, too. Mrs. Wilson and Mrs. Steiner will help you with that. You want to do everything properly and live up to expectations. In years to come, an invitation to dinner at Foxworth Hall will be as valuable as an invitation to the governor's mansion, even the White House.

"Believe me, my sweet, you'll see the first ten days as a honeymoon, and," he added with that coy, sexy smile, "I'll have you in my bed most every night."

I couldn't help being a little taken aback. All of the married women I had met and known, even my mother's boring friends, bragged about their honeymoons. Here I was marrying one of the wealthiest men in the state, apparently, and he was suggesting, no, telling me, we would have a poor man's honeymoon and stay at home. Despite the fact that this home was a mansion, except for the few times I had been driven to Charlottesville to do some shopping, I basically had been stuck here for ten days preparing for "the wedding of the century." And now I was to be stuck here again for who knew how long. Was it possible to have cabin fever in such a place? I'm sure my face reflected my disappointment at what he was saying about our honeymoon, but rather than changing his mind, he looked peeved at me.

"Surely you see no problem with any of this. There is so much more for you to learn about Foxworth Hall. The sooner the better for you. I know you want that, too."

One thing I was going to understand and understand quickly about my new husband was that he was not an easy man to contradict. It was nearly impossible to turn down any request he had made of me, not because he would pout or make my life miserable otherwise but because he always sounded right and he always made it seem as if I was just as much a part of the idea he proposed. I would look foolish opposing him, and a newly married young woman, especially one constantly on a stage, did not want to look foolish. I did feel like I was on display most of the time. Unless I locked myself in my room, and even then, because I'd have to be waited upon, I lived with an audience. The eyes of one of the servants followed me almost everywhere I went, looking for ways to please me.

One would think that in a mansion this large, there were places I could go to spend an entire day alone, especially if I wanted to pout. There were, but if I was alone too long, someone would be worried and soon appear with water or fruit or simply to ask how I was. I was piqued, but I couldn't be visibly annoyed or nasty. I understood that Garland had left an overriding commandment hovering above everyone in this house whenever he was gone after our marriage and home honeymoon. It was to watch over me very closely. They all knew I was pregnant, but keeping a Foxworth secret was expected. It was months more before anyone in the mansion would dare to mention my pregnancy, even to me.

But I could see that realization in their faces. Right from the first day after my marriage, I felt eyes on me whenever I started down the stairs or went outside. If I stumbled, caught my foot on something, no matter where I was or how alone I thought I was, I heard an audible gasp and soon saw Dora, Mrs. Wilson, Mrs. Steiner, Olsen, or Mr. Wilson rushing to see if I was all right.

Months later, during my pregnancy, I was naturally tired more often than I usually was. I'd fall asleep on the settee or chaise in the grand room and wake to find a blanket over my lap.

As if my eyelids set off a bell when they closed, Dora was at my side, and if she wasn't able to be there instantly, Mrs. Steiner would be there.

Dr. Ross left instructions about what I could and couldn't eat and drink, the amount of weight I could carry, and how much sleep I should have. I was not to go too far from the house, but he did say that I could go for a walk, should go for a walk, but he left strict orders that I should never go alone. Dora had to accompany me, and with her limp caused by one leg being shorter than the other since birth, I always felt I had to walk slower and not go too far, even though she could move as quickly as I could.

But walking with someone wasn't simply walking. You talked, told stories, and enjoyed each other's company. I missed my intimate discussions with Daisy Herman and some of the other girls. Conversation with Dora wasn't at all interesting, and almost anything I told her about myself shocked her, which after a while made me feel so uncomfortable that I stopped talking.

Dora, after all, was a young woman who had never had any romance, who had been in a servant's role her entire short life, waiting hand and foot on her parents and then her brother. She was about as naive as any of the girls who had attended my special private gatherings in Alexandria, where I would explain and tutor them about everything from flirtation to intercourse.

She had nothing to add that would interest me.

However, I couldn't avoid her. Dora was truly like another shadow for me in those early days. She would bring breakfast to my bed, and wherever I had ended up sitting after I had risen, dressed, and gone downstairs, that was where she would bring me lunch. In my seventh and eighth months, whenever Garland wasn't coming home for dinner, she brought it up to me. I never asked her to stay while I ate. It was more interesting to flip through a book or stare out the window and dream.

During those last few months, I fell into some pools of depression despite the attention and the gifts Garland sent along with flowers and candy. He made sure to have magazines and newspapers delivered so I could see any new fashions, and he arranged for me to have every new musical rendition on the Edison gramophone. By this time Dr. Ross forbade my riding in the carriage because the roads were too bumpy, and he even restricted the distance I could go for a walk.

It was during those last months of my pregnancy, when I was most depressed about myself, depressed about how my life had changed and about the world of Foxworth that twirled around me, that I most resented what went on secretly between Dora and Garland. Everything was bothering me, but this especially. He wouldn't sleep with me because he said Dr. Ross told him it was too dangerous to make love to a woman this far along in her pregnancy. He always seemed uncomfortable visiting me in the Swan Room and often stepped in no farther than inches from the doorway. I felt like I was contagious.

After a while I was convinced he avoided me as much as he could because of my big belly and my bloated face. I hated how I looked and imagined he hated it as well. But he always had a nice smile for Dora. Surely it had to do with their secret meetings in his mother's bedroom. It was then that I came the closest to confronting him and demanding to know why that was happening and, whatever the reason for it, demanding it to stop.

But Garland was still battling with all sorts of economic issues, still raging about incompetent employees and even at one point snapping at all our servants, including Dora. I was afraid to speak, much less complain about anything or pursue his secrets. He looked like walking dynamite, his eyes bloodshot, pacing in his library and office and rushing out to do this or that at all times day and night.

After Malcolm was born and I felt whole and strong again, Dr. Ross gave me a follow-up examination and then gave Garland his approval to resume sexual activity with me. Garland asked me to his room just the way he always had, in a whisper at dinner or when we were sitting together in the living room or library, each time making it seem like a forbidden tryst. Sometimes he was so convincing about how secretive we had to be that I truly wondered if he really wanted it to be kept hidden. Of course, anyone would ask, from whom? The ghosts of his ancestors, especially the ghost of his mother? What Dora had told me Garland made her do in the past never left my thoughts. I had been hoping that since our marriage, that had ended. Whatever comfort he needed he now got from me.

However, a number of times during our "Foxworth Honeymoon," after we had made love and I had returned to the Swan Room, I had heard Garland's footsteps in the hallway just as I had begun to close my eyes. By the time I rose to see where he was going, he was gone; but one time, I hadn't gone right to bed. I was fidgety and even contemplated going down to the kitchen to make myself a glass of warm milk. As I was putting on my bathrobe, I heard his footsteps and went to my door, opening it just a little to look out. He passed by, wearing his nightdress. I started to call to him until I saw he was moving like someone in a trance, his eyes almost closed and his steps methodical, with his arms at his sides.

I stepped out of the Swan Room and watched him continue down the dimly lit hallway toward what had been his mother's bedroom. He paused before it, knocked gently, and, after a moment, opened the door and went in. Why, I wondered, was he really going in there? Was Dora lying to me when she said there was nothing sexual between them?

I waited in the hallway by my room, and when he didn't come out, I approached his mother's bedroom slowly. Almost there, I heard what was distinctly sobbing. It sounded like the sobbing of a little boy, just as Dora had described.

With trembling fingers, I opened the door slowly, an inch at a time, and peered through the crack and indeed saw Dora dressed in one of his mother's nightdresses just the way she had been when I had gotten that glimpse of her before my wedding and thought I had seen a ghost.

The room was so dimly lit it was almost impossible to see anything, but gradually my eyes adjusted to the weak light and the shadows enough for me to see that Dora was sitting back against the oversized pillow. Garland was on his knees beside the bed and leaning over her legs. She had her hand on his head and gently stroked him while he uttered these sobs. He was saying something in between them, too low for me to understand it. I wanted to thrust the door open and ask what was happening, but my heart was pounding, and I was quite terrified by the scene. It was one thing to hear her vaguely describe it but another to see it, so I closed the door softly and retreated.

I lay in bed trembling until I heard his footsteps again. He was walking faster now. When I rose and peeked through the slightly opened door, I saw him slip into his own bedroom. I looked back at his mother's room when I heard that door open. Dora, now in her own clothing, walked down the hallway to the stairway and descended. I wanted to intercept her, but I hesitated too long, and she was gone.

I was still too upset about what I had witnessed to confront Garland about it the following day, and when I saw Dora, I didn't make any new reference to it. I hoped that eventually Garland would explain. Maybe Dora had told him I knew or he had realized I had seen him. However, he didn't say anything, and for a long time, it never happened again. I was always good at drowning and burying things that disturbed me. No one was more critical of that than my mother, who accused me many times of creating my own reality.

"Someday," she predicted, stating it like it was something she wanted to be true rather than something inevitable, "it will come raging back and slap you in the face."

In a way she was right, of course. Ignoring it didn't make it go away. But I feared the whole house would come down on me if I mentioned his secret night visits. Every ancestor in every portrait would come to life and scream. So I tried to talk around it and suggest some things that might get him to reveal this strange behavior himself. Wouldn't that be a better way? However, I could see the panic in his face from just a small suggestion or a question like "Shouldn't we arrange for Dora to be with people her age, maybe even find her a job where she isn't confined like this? We could find an older woman to be Malcolm's nanny and assist me with anything I needed."

I practiced saying it in front of my mirror before actually doing it so I would look and sound innocent, sound as if I was simply looking out for poor Dora.

"Dora's fine," he said. "We're all she has. Don't be selfish and cruel. A crippled woman would end up with a scoundrel."

Truthfully, even though Dora had been born with one leg shorter than the other and limped, she didn't look distorted or in any pain. She was in fact quite attractive. However, I couldn't deny that because she came from a working-class family and men of stature and wealth would not settle for anyone with any sort of deformity, much less a woman below their station, Garland was right. I stopped talking about it. I never really had any high hopes for her to have a real romantic future. To pretend so and be insistent about it would be too obvious. Garland was sure to ask what she had done to justify my passion to rid myself of her. He might even suggest I was somehow jealous of her. That would surely lead to a terrible end.

"Oh, you're probably right," I told him. "You're very good when it comes to helping those who aren't as fortunate. Look what you've done with Olsen and Lucas."

That pleased him and smothered any speck of a suspicion.

I didn't push him any further about the secret, but in the back of my mind, I was thinking of a plan. It was clearly important to him for Dora to dress in something of his mother's. What if there wasn't anything left of his mother's wardrobe, not even a handkerchief? What if one day I got rid of it all? I could empty those closets and drawers and give the clothes to the Salvation Army. Of course, they were too fancy, but they could tear up the material and have new clothes created for the poor. It was important to look charitable if you were as rich as we were. How could he blame me?

Twice during the past year, I set out to do just that and both times lost my courage.

So I left it. I left everything the way it was.

It was simply just another thing that haunted me, and in this house, being haunted seemed accepted by everyone. But it was not for me. I wished I could smother every ghost and crush every secret like a cigarette.

Maybe that was why the ancestors in the portraits scowled at me. They knew what was in my heart. I wanted to rip them all off the walls and put them up in that attic that ran nearly the length of this mansion. It was more of a proper setting for them all. Now I believed that just thinking about what it had been like locked up there for several minutes would surely give birth to new nightmares. I doubted I would ever go into that section of Foxworth Hall again. These bedrooms, Garland's, Malcolm's, and mine, the dining room and kitchen, the library and sitting room, and, if there was a gala affair, of course, the ballroom would be all I cared to frequent. The spiders and rodents were welcome to the rest of it.

These days especially, since even before the attic incident with Malcolm, I felt the mansion was closing in on me more and more, just like I had the first day of my marriage. How could I continue to walk through hallways afraid of what would come out of the shadows in my own home? However, I said nothing to any of the servants or my parents, especially not my mother.

But I was afraid. I was very afraid.

Maybe it was my wishful imagination, but when I looked closely at the faces of the servants, especially Mrs. Wilson and Mrs. Steiner, I thought I saw similar fears. They, too, seemed to remain within the boundaries of their work.

It was as if the rest of the mansion didn't exist for them. Especially during my first years here, whenever I asked Mrs. Steiner about a room or a corridor left unused and untouched, she would assure me that if and when Mr. Foxworth wanted something done with those places, she would see to it, but for now, "It's just moving dust from one wall to another, only to have it come back and no one there to see or care."

*No one but ghosts,* I thought, but never said.

My defiant and mischievous son had forced me to go to the places I had avoided so long. I hoped Garland would finally be more of a father and speak to him firmly. Apparently, his own father had been a strict disciplinarian. Why should he be so different or indifferent? He was close-lipped when it came to talking about his own upbringing, except when he wanted to describe his hunting exploits with his father. It was almost as if that was the only time they had ever seen each other.

It occurred to me that there was a way for me to learn more about my husband. Maybe today, because of all that had happened with Malcolm, I was convinced I should know more. How much of what a Foxworth was in heart and spirit determined who and what my own son would be? Why shouldn't I know my husband and his family as much as a servant did? Knowledge smothered secrets, didn't it? I dreamed of a day not a single one remained in Foxworth Hall. Why not start with this one? I had put it off too long.

Dora looked especially vulnerable to me right after the commotion with Malcolm had died down. I was resting on the velvet chaise while she was at work on repairing the wedding album. I watched her trying to restore the torn pages, ironing out as many creases as she could. She was so protective of Malcolm, so determined to lessen and hopefully eliminate whatever pain or unhappiness he experienced. Perhaps he embodied the child she believed she would never have.

"Stop that," I ordered. She looked up, surprised. "I want to talk to you. You can go back at it afterward."

"Yes, ma'am."

She put the iron down and waited. I rose from the chaise and stepped toward her. She looked absolutely terrified, which I thought was good. I knew she was surely blaming herself for what Malcolm had done both to the album and to me. She thought that was what I was going to do now, ream her out and threaten to get rid of her. I would never let her know that I had tried and failed. Maybe that was bothering me the most, that a servant commanded my husband's loyalty more than I did.

Why?

"Up to now, I have kept your secret, my

husband's secret, and not forced you to do or say anything about it. You know what I'm talking about, Dora. Don't look dumb and confused."

"Yes, ma'am." She was holding her breath.

"I'm not demanding you stop doing it, doing whatever he needs you to do, but I want you to tell me what he tells you in his mother's bedroom. Why does he cry? I've seen you together. Don't deny it," I quickly added.

"Oh," she said, and brought her hands to the base of her neck.

"Well?"

"He doesn't always cry."

I folded my arms across my bosom and pulled my shoulders back just the way my mother used to when she was cross-examining me about something I had done and didn't buy my answers. Despite my reluctance to in any way resemble her, I had to step into my mother's shoes from time to time. It was a giving-the-devil-her-due sort of thing.

"Sometimes he's just there for a while, silently, and then he gets up and leaves."

"Not saying a word?"

"No, ma'am."

"How did this start? Was it your idea?"

"Oh, no, ma'am. No." She shook her head so hard that I thought she'd break her neck. "I would never think of such a thing."

"Then how did it happen?"

She looked at the door.

"My husband is not due home until later. He never walks in without knocking anyway. Go on."

"It wasn't long after he had hired me," she began. "He wanted me to organize some of his mother's things, do some dusting in the room. He liked it to look like she was still there." She hesitated.

"Like she was still there, still alive?"

"Yes. I had to change the linen every week and wash some clothes."

I sat on the bed and thought about it. Although Garland talked about his mother from time to time, he never did so with tears in his eyes. Maybe he'd smile, remembering something she had said or done. He'd praise the way she had handled the servants and looked after the house, but he'd say nothing more informative and revealing. So much of what was here was here because she had bought it, wanted it, and designed how it should be placed, right down to candlestick holders, which was why he was so adamant about my not changing things. Was that the way he expressed his sorrow?

The most he had ever said to me about it was, "When people you love pass and you remove anything that reminds you of them, you bury them deeper and deeper until you forget them enough to feel like they never existed."

"But most people do that," I said. "Your great-grandparents' things and older ancestors' things were put up in the attic, weren't they? You called it another Foxworth cemetery."

He smiled and then looked up at one of the portraits. "And he's not too happy about it," he said, and walked off. Apparently, what his forefathers believed and did was not what he wanted to do. Perhaps that was a good thing, something for which I should not fault him. After all, wasn't there something beautiful about a son's devotion to his mother?

I looked at Dora. She was trembling a little now, wondering what I would do to her.

"People who love someone very much don't want to let go when they're gone," I said.

She looked grateful. "Yes, ma'am. That's what I believed."

"Believed?"

"Believe, I mean. Yes. It's sad."

"So if you didn't want this, how did it come to be?"

"One afternoon, when I was working on Mr. Foxworth's mother's clothes, I fancied one of the dresses. I even considered taking it to my room, and the shoes, of course."

"So?"

"I took off my dress and put it on. There I was admiring myself in the mirror when Mr. Foxworth appeared. I nearly fainted. I can tell you that. My heart surely stopped and started. I couldn't speak, couldn't swallow."

She closed her eyes as if she was reliving the fear. She clasped her hands and twisted them.

"And?" This was truly like pulling teeth.

She opened her eyes, a little more widely. "He didn't speak. He just looked at me strangely, so strangely. I became even more frightened. I thought this was it; I'm going to be sent home, and my poor brother might lose his job all because of me. But he didn't get angry. He smiled, and that took more of my breath away."

"Smiled?"

"Yes, ma'am. He said, 'You look just like her when she was about your age.'"

"You? Look like her? I've seen her portrait, Dora. You couldn't look anything like her no matter what you wore of hers."

"I thought the same, but I wasn't going to say so. No, ma'am, I wasn't. If he wanted me to look like her, that's what I'd do. I had to protect my position and my brother."

"Yes, yes. Go on."

"I told him I was sorry and that I would never do it again, but he shook his head. 'No, no,' he said. 'I want you to put that dress on again, and another dress, and another. When I want you to do so, I'll leave the dress out on the bed there. You put it on that evening.' I didn't know what to say or do. Did he want me to go about the house in his mother's dress? I knew I'd look foolish."

I nodded, waited.

"He knew what I was thinking. He said, 'After you put it on, you stay here. You lie on that bed, and you wait for me, no matter how long or how late. Understand?'

"'Yes, sir,' I said. I thought maybe he just wanted me to wear it and walk about the room to help him remember his mother. I even thought that was a very sweet thing to do. I did, ma'am. Honest."

"Of course you did. What else could you think? Did you tell your aunt about this?"

"Oh, no. I've told no one but you. He had me swear I wouldn't tell my aunt. But seeing you had seen me in his mother's clothes that night when you first came here . . ."

"Exactly. So you did what he asked? You put on whatever he left out for you to wear?"

"Yes, ma'am. And he came to the room late in the evening after I had put on the dress. That first time, I waited and waited and fell asleep. I still had some chores to do downstairs. I was afraid my aunt would wonder about me, but she had gone to sleep herself."

I nodded, waited. Maybe she was hoping that I would think that was enough. It wasn't, not nearly.

"I woke up when I felt his hand on my arm and saw he was kneeling at the side of the bed.

Before I could speak, he said, 'I'm sorry, Mama.' I was afraid to move. I was afraid to speak. He was calling me Mama. 'Please, don't let Father beat me,' he said."

"He said that? You mean, he was acting as if he was a little boy again? You didn't tell me this when I asked you the first time."

"I was afraid to, ma'am. He was like someone in a dream," she said, nodding. "I didn't know what to say or do, but he was looking at me with such hope that I said, 'No, he won't beat you.' I don't know where that came from, ma'am. To this day." She paused. "But . . ."

"But what?" I nearly shouted.

"But to this day, because I'm in her room, in her clothes, I wonder if she doesn't indeed speak through me."

"What?" Now I brought my hands to the base of my throat. "Do you hear her?"

"I don't know, ma'am. I don't know what I hear and . . . sometimes I don't remember what I said."

"That's . . . that's crazy," I said. "What did he do that first time when you told him you'd protect him from his father?"

"He smiled then, and after a moment, he lay down on the other side of the bed, curled up, and went to sleep. I didn't move a muscle. I felt so tired, exhausted from it. I fell asleep myself, and when I awoke later, he was gone. I got out of the dress immediately and hung it up in the closet."

"How often did this happen?"

"Maybe a half dozen times before you were married and three times since," she said.

"What other things has he told you in this dreamy state?"

"Nice things about his mother, not so nice about his father." She looked like that was all she wanted to say and then added, "His father locked him in the attic once."

"Yes, he told me that."

"Without food," she added, "but his mother snuck it up to him."

"Really? He didn't tell me that." I was getting more annoyed. A servant knew more about my husband's past than I did. But now I thought I had heard enough. "Okay, return to repairing the album."

"Do you want me to do anything, say anything about it now, ma'am? I mean, if you tell him or say anything, he'll know we spoke of it and . . ."

"No, I'm not going to say anything, but I do want to hear about it from time to time and immediately if there is anything sexual involved."

"Oh, that will never be, ma'am," she said, practically gasping.

"How can you be so sure? Your experience with men is, by your own admission, practically nonexistent."

She smiled. "He's as sweet and helpless as Malcolm sometimes is."

"Sweet and helpless? I have yet to see that in Malcolm," I muttered.

I left the Swan Room and walked down to Garland's mother's bedroom. Dora did keep it as immaculate as she did the Swan Room. There were even fresh flowers in the vases. I opened the closet door and looked at all the old clothes and shoes. Everything appeared clean and pressed. She hadn't exaggerated. Garland's mother could rise from the grave and continue on as if nothing had happened.

I stood there listening, wondering if I could hear his mother's voice, too. After a moment, I felt foolish. Actually, as I thought about what Dora had told me, the way she had described Garland, I felt sad for him. His manly ego perhaps kept him from sharing something so emotional with me. My hope was that as time went by and our marriage grew stronger, he would, and perhaps then Dora could be helped to do something more with her life.

I stopped in Malcolm's room on my way back and saw he had fallen asleep. Why was it that little boys, even men, when they were asleep looked so innocent and helpless? Malcolm's face looked streaked with some recent tears, but had he been crying because of what he had done or because he was being severely punished?

I wanted to sit beside him and stroke him the way Dora had described petting Garland in his dreamlike state, but I hesitated, thinking my clever little imp would see that only as weakness. He would mumble another apology and plead for me to end his punishment, even as it had just begun.

Ironically, I thought of myself and the way I used to play up to my father to get him to end some life sentence my mother had pronounced because of something defiant I had done. I loved him for loving me so much back then, but his deal with Garland right before I agreed to marry him came back up in me like sour milk.

My rage was restored. I turned and left without touching Malcolm and certainly without kissing him. After I closed his door, I stood there in the hallway a few moments and looked into the darker part of it.

*This house,* I thought, *this house makes love so difficult unless it's unusual, distorted, born out of some darkness rather than out of a heart.*

Would it always?

Why should I think otherwise?

# 4

When he came home just over an hour later, Garland made so much noise entering with Lucas that I thought he surely had woken the sleeping ghosts. He screamed for me, his voice bellowing. I had never heard him do that. In a panic I hurried to the stairway to see what was happening. Had I done something? Did he somehow hear about Malcolm and what he had done?

"My Corrine," he said in a softer voice, smiling as soon as I appeared. "My beautiful Corrine."

When I stepped off the final step in wonder, he handed a large box and a small box to Lucas and embraced me, whirling me around as if I were nothing more than a large rag doll while he peppered my cheeks and forehead with kisses, knocking off his derby. He reeked of whiskey and cigars, but I didn't care. It had been some time since I had seen him this joyful and attentive.

As soon as he put me down, he stepped back with his hands on his hips and gazed, smiling and nodding.

"What?" I asked. His stare made me instantly self-conscious. My hair was pinned up, and I was wearing an ordinary light-blue blouse with puffed upper sleeves and a dark-blue tulip of bell skirt. Did I look too common, too ordinary for him?

He continued smiling and shook his head, his expression changing to one of awe.

"You look exactly how you did that night I first saw you at the Wexlers' anniversary gala," he declared. "What do you think, Lucas? You saw her shortly after that. Am I right? She hasn't aged a day. Maybe she never will. Someday people will think she's my daughter, eh, Lucas?"

Lucas looked up quickly, obviously embarrassed. In five years, barely a word passed between us. Considering all that he did for Garland, all the places and events he had brought him to and had brought him home from quite drunk, I would have thought he would have lost his shyness long ago. However, sometimes when I caught him staring at me, he would turn red and quickly look away.

He was a slim man not much taller than I was, with dark-brown hair that was habitually unruly, perhaps because of the way the wind brushed through it during his carriage rides. Garland liked going as fast as possible. But Lucas's wild hair didn't matter. He was still somehow attractive. He would always look like a teenage boy, I thought, with those hazel eyes and almost feminine soft facial features. His facial hair was more of a cross between brown and blond. It was so light that if he wore a beard, you wouldn't see it from a dozen feet away. But Lucas's shyness aside, Garland couldn't ask for a more loyal servant. His dedication to and affection for Garland were unquestioned. It was easy for anyone to see how much he idolized him.

That made sense when you knew his history. He was another young man, like Olsen, whom Garland had rescued from somewhat dire circumstances. Olsen had been in a terrible wagon accident and still stuttered badly because of it. He was only twelve at the time, and his parents had little money. Garland had heard about his magic hands when it came to gardening. He had natural talent designing flower beds and bushes and an artistic eye for laying them out, so Garland had looked after his medical needs and brought him to Foxworth.

Lucas was an orphan working for a blacksmith in Charlottesville; "a white slave" is what Garland called him. He was barely fourteen and received no real wages. He worked for what he ate and the little he was provided in clothing. He had to sleep in the stables, in a corner where there was a coal stove at least.

"Old Dimitri Korniloff wasn't happy to lose him, but I saw how well he handled horses despite his youth, and so I gave Dimitri almost as much as he'd make in a year to let him come work for me," Garland had told me when I once asked about Lucas and how he had found him.

"Then I had Lucas trained properly to drive a carriage. Now he's the best in Charlottesville, and he works for me. Invest well in people, and you'll be rewarded," Garland added pointedly, which was something he often said. Everything in the world was a matter of profit and loss to him. Long ago I wondered if that included me.

"Yes, sir, Mr. Foxworth," Lucas said now. "She surely doesn't look a day older."

"Right," he said, taking the larger box from Lucas, who stood back holding it and the other, which I was guessing was for me because of the paper and ribbon.

"Know what this is?" Garland asked. I saw the picture of a locomotive, but I shook my head. "It's a wind-up train with tracks. You know how much Malcolm loves trains. I was thinking of setting it up in the ballroom for now."

"Not now," I said. "He doesn't get a present now."

"What? Why not?"

I described what had happened and what Malcolm had done to me. I rolled up my sleeve and showed him my bandaged scratch.

"Thank goodness Olsen heard me screaming. I fear I would still be up there."

"Our wedding album?" he asked. I was expecting him to be more concerned about me. "Why did you leave that album out where he could get to it?" he demanded, his lips twisting into an ugly grimace.

"Where he could get to it? It was in my bedroom, where he wasn't supposed to be, Garland. Dora knows that. It was on the shelf on my closet where it has always been. What did you want me to do, keep it under lock and key? That's not the point, is it? Didn't you hear all I said, what he did to me?"

He nodded but continued scowling just like his great-great-grandfather in the portrait above us.

"I paid a fortune for that album," he muttered. "That photographer is already charging three times the amount thanks to me."

I sighed. When he was fixed on something that involved money, it was difficult to get him to look elsewhere or listen. Besides, the album was first and foremost another Foxworth possession, valued only for what it cost and not what it was about.

"It was important to me, too, Garland. Dora is going to try to restore as many pages as she can."

He looked up the stairs and then at me, his eyes narrowing.

"Why would he do that? Why attack our wedding album of all things?"

"He was angry that I hadn't paid enough attention to him while I was looking at it. That's all I can think. I'm afraid your son has a vicious temper. But you should be angrier about what he did to me after I caught him doing it," I insisted.

"You shouldn't have chased after him," he said, echoing the very words I had heard him say earlier in my imagination. "He would have grown tired of hiding and come out. How did you punish him? What did you finally do?"

"I wanted to spank him, but Dora pleaded for him and promised to do what I told her."

"Which is?"

"Keep him locked in his room without any dessert for a week at least."

He nodded. And then, after another moment of thought, he smiled again and shook his head, laughing.

"What?" I asked. "What is so funny, Garland?"

"I wasn't much older than he is when my father locked me in that attic for deliberately kicking over a statue he had on a pedestal."

"Why didn't he keep you in your room? Why the attic?"

"The attic was his idea of a prison, I guess. I was kept up there three days, but I amused myself so well that he never did it again. I told him I had conversations with our Confederate ancestors, who were happy to see me. He was so frustrated and came up with other ways to punish me."

"Was he starving you?" I asked. I knew the answer, but I wanted him to say it.

"My mother wouldn't allow that. If it wasn't for my mother sometimes, I'd-a been tarred and feathered. But let's not get into all that dark stuff now."

He put the large box down.

"I'll keep it in the library until he behaves. But maybe this will help you forget and make up for your displeasure," he said, reaching for the smaller box in pink wrapping that Lucas held. "Go on, open it."

I undid the ribbon, peeled off the paper, and opened the box to gaze upon a necklace.

"Is this real?"

He laughed. "Of course it's real. That necklace comes from a famous store in New York, Tiffany and Company."

He took the necklace out and held it up with both hands.

"This is stylized fleurs-de-lis and rosettes. There are two hundred sixty-five diamonds set in the gold mounting faced with platinum, Corrine. It's worth more than most people's homes and savings."

"I'd be afraid to wear it."

"Nonsense," he said, and undid the clasp and stepped behind me to put it on me. Then he took me to the closest wall mirror. He stood behind me with his hands on my shoulders. "It belongs on you," he said. "It looks like it's come home to be around your beautiful neck and rest between those amazing breasts, which I spent good money protecting, by the way."

He leaned down to move my high collar away and kiss my neck.

"I guess you did make a lot of money," I said, touching the necklace. If anything made me feel like a queen, this did. "It's beautiful. Thank you."

He laughed. "Yes, we made a lot of money, but the bigger thing that happened is I've been invited to sell my products overseas in what anyone would call a titanic business deal. I will have to go to New York in a few days to work out the details with an exporter, inspect some factories, and then visit another exporter in Maryland. This new business will triple our net worth, and I'm including our house and land in that total. Don't even try to imagine how rich we are. My father is probably spinning in his grave with surprise. He never thought I'd outdo him."

"Why not?" I asked, leaping on the opportunity to find out more about his personal history.

He sighed and looked sadly at the big box instead of replying. "I was so hoping to celebrate all this as a family, something my father rarely did."

"If we forgive Malcolm this quickly, Garland . . ."

"I know. I know." He clapped his hands as if he could change the weather at will. "Let's not think about all that right now. I will permit no unhappiness tonight. Let's dress for dinner. I sent word to Mrs. Wilson to prepare something very special for us. We'll have champagne in the ballroom first, just the way we used to almost every night right after we were married."

"Every night you were home, you mean? And not exactly every night."

"Whatever . . ."

He laughed and turned to Lucas.

"You can go get Mr. LaRuffa," he said. "We'll be dressed by the time you return or soon after."

"Who's Mr. LaRuffa?"

"Only the most expensive and most talented musician in Charlottesville these days. I sent a telegram to him before I set out for home yesterday. He knows all the latest popular songs to play on the piano, and he'll play the violin for us at dinner, too."

It did sound festive, and he was doing all this with no other guests present. It would be a really romantic evening. For once in a long time, he was contemplating a celebration with only me and none of his business friends.

"That's wonderful. I have a new dress I bought just today. I can't wait for you to see it."

His smile faded a little. "I was thinking of that dress of my mother's I had my tailor adjust for you weeks ago, the one I told you she wore the night of my parents' fifth anniversary. The necklace is perfect for it. I was picturing you in that dress when I bought it. The governor was here that night she wore it."

"But . . . this new dress . . . I was thinking of you when I bought it," I countered.

"Were you?"

"Of course."

He nodded. "Yes, yes, it's all right. No unhappiness, not the glimmer of a frown tonight. Wear your new dress by all means. I'm looking forward to seeing you in the latest fashion. Go on. Get dressed. I have some new clothes to show you as well."

He stepped forward and kissed me, holding his lips that split second longer as if he was trying to draw something out of me, some of my energy, just the way he used to kiss me. Then he stroked my hair and looked into my eyes with that sexual intensity that could start my heart pounding.

"We'll make this a very, very special night. I promise," he said. "You'll remember nothing else about this day."

Moses on Mount Sinai probably hadn't spoken with more assurance when he had recited the Ten Commandments.

Garland turned away and took Malcolm's present into the library.

I hurried to the stairway, keeping my palm over my new, very beautiful necklace and imagining my mother's face full of envy when she saw it. Like a magician, Garland had waved his hand over my depression and sent it fleeing back into the shadows. Two years ago, he had taken me on a trip to a place called Coney Island in New York. One of his investors had put money into something called a switchback railway in an amusement park called Steeplechase. It was a ride for a nickel. We climbed a tower to board a large benchlike car and then were pushed off down to another tower and went down again. I nearly peed in my pants and remembered how other women were screaming, even some men.

That's how I felt now. Malcolm had taken me so far down into the dark of anger and panic, and now Garland had lifted me up with his happiness, his success, his beautiful gift, and his plans for our celebration dinner. My emotions were on a switchback.

However, when I hurried past Malcolm's closed door, I felt sorry for him and paused to think. Maybe he was just a lonely, frightened child after all, flailing out every which way he could. His father was absent most of the time, and I would by no means call myself a perfect mother. After all, I had never intended to be one at seventeen. How much of this should I be blaming on myself? I made a mental note to spend more time with him and to give Dora more days off, force her to go to the city or go visit her brother, maybe. Perhaps my strained relationship with my own mother had begun when she plainly looked for ways to avoid me, even as a little girl. I was treating Malcolm the way she had treated me. If there was one person I didn't want to become, it was my mother.

But there was no time for forgiveness and understanding right now. He had to serve some time for what he had done, or he would never be repentant. When I entered the Swan Room, I found Dora in the corner still with the ironing board pressing on the crumpled pages. She held another up.

"I'm nearly done getting them all back to a reasonable state, ma'am."

"My husband will be pleased," I said. "But it's time for me to dress for dinner. It's going to be a very special one tonight."

"Oh, I'll attend to the last few later. My," she said, seeing what I was wearing, "what a beautiful necklace."

"Yes, it is. Thank you. My husband just gave it to me. This is a night of celebration."

She nodded, almost as if she already had known.

"Something about profit and new contracts to sell Foxworth products internationally," I muttered. I didn't want to look totally daft when it came to business. That was my mother, not me.

"Do you want me to prepare a bath?"

"After my spending time in that attic today, I should say. Who knows how many spiderwebs broke in my hair and are still there."

I took off the necklace.

"And we should wash and redress that scratch," she said.

"I can do that after."

"Very good, ma'am."

While she prepared my bath, I took my new dress out of the box. It was a pink and cream evening dress in silk satin with uncovered arms and neck. The saleslady called it a "full dress."

I thought my new necklace would work perfectly with it. I laid it out on the bed with the necklace beside it and was thinking about the right shoes to wear just as Dora returned.

"Oh, how beautiful," she said, and looked at it through dreamy eyes.

Dora never appeared envious or jealous. There wasn't an iota of resentment in her face because I had so much and she had little. But for some reason, her purity and goodness annoyed me. She was everything I wasn't but also everything I wouldn't want to be. Women like her were like roses pressed in a book too soon. They'd never enjoy the fullness of life or their own beauty.

"You need to take some of that money you've been earning and buy some new things for yourself, Dora. I'm frankly tired of seeing you looking so matronly. You're still wearing your aunt's hand-me-downs. New, more fashionable clothes will give you a better self-image. I've never known anyone who needs it more than you."

"Oh, dear me. I don't know, ma'am," she said with her hand on the base of her throat as if I had just suggested she go dancing naked on the back patio.

"Well, I do. I'll have Lucas take you on your next day off instead of your spending it locked away with a book and Malcolm still demanding everything of you. Do not argue," I added firmly. She was probably still catching her breath from my rage at Malcolm. Even I was shocked at the heights of anger I could reach.

She nodded reluctantly.

"Good."

My secret thought was she would turn herself into an attractive woman, probably with my help, be seen by some young man who worked in the city, and get rescued from this place and this self-imposed retreat from life. Once she was gone, the strange trysts with my husband would be gone, too. I was still afraid she'd go and buy herself something unattractive, however, something more fitting for her aunt.

"Maybe we'll have Mrs. Steiner watch our little imp and I'll go along to help you," I said. Now she would have a more difficult time getting out of it, I thought, which was probably why she looked even more terrified of the idea.

"Your bath will be ready, ma'am," she said.

"Thank you."

I started out and stopped.

"Remember, he gets no dessert and is not permitted out of that room, Dora."

"He knows it, ma'am."

She started to go out with me.

"I'll do my own bath tonight, Dora. See to his dinner, and help Mrs. Steiner with dinner preparations. I imagine they'll be more elaborate tonight. Mr. Foxworth has asked for something special."

"But when you're ready to dress . . ."

"I'll do it all myself, Dora. Before I married Mr. Foxworth, I always did. I was looking after myself from the age of five. That's when I had realized my mother would stifle me and turn me into a nobody," I said.

The intimate revelation about my feelings toward my mother shocked her. I smiled at how it had left her speechless and then left to take my bath. Tormenting and teasing Dora had become my daily entertainment.

Afterward, I spent a lot of time on my hair and used a little blush on my cheeks. Garland didn't want me using any of the cosmetics some wealthy women were using these days. Most people still thought they were only for prostitutes. But my mother had given me some good advice when it came to how I should treat my face. She warned me about getting sunburnt. I didn't want to look pasty, so I got some sun, especially when I rode my bicycle, but I wasn't riding anymore. Garland wouldn't permit it. "Mrs. Foxworth should always be transported in our gilded carriage," he had declared. We literally looked down on most people. The best dash of sunshine I got was walking to the lake. Even so, afraid for my face, I was careful to wear a wide-brimmed hat.

Dora stopped in to tell me she had given Malcolm his dinner without dessert, and although he wasn't crying, he was very sad. She thought he was remorseful.

"We'll see," I said. "He can be quite the little actor—liar, I should say."

"Oh, no, ma'am. He's sincere."

"We'll see," I said.

"You look beautiful, ma'am. The necklace is the most beautiful I've seen, but it looks more beautiful on you."

"Thank you, Dora. It is quite stunning, isn't it?" I touched it and smiled at myself in the mirror. Then I looked at her. I knew what she was up to. She was trying to soften me so I'd be more lenient on Malcolm. "Don't keep him company," I warned. "Being shut up with you is not a punishment."

She nodded. "Oh, no, ma'am. I'll just tell him good night, then, and be sure he brushes his teeth and washes his face," she said. "He really needs a bath."

"Not tonight," I snapped.

"Yes, ma'am."

"And if you are in there with him more than five minutes, I'll keep him eight days, not seven," I warned. Of course, how would I know? Still, she'd be afraid I'd find out.

She nodded.

I started out. When I reached the top of the stairway, I could hear the piano in the ballroom. Garland really was making this a very special night. How would I harbor any anger with the prospect of so wonderful an evening ahead? Besides, it wasn't good for my complexion, I thought. I must put it all out of my mind. Frowning, just like too much smiling, could give you wrinkles. Tomorrow was soon enough to think about it. I framed my face in the expression I'd like in a portrait, regal and dazzling, and started to descend, for once following my mother's advice and stepping down slowly like a queen would.

Garland appeared in the hallway and looked up at me with the pleasure and pride he often showed the first year after Malcolm had been born. How dapper he was in his gray herringbone, three-button frock coat hemmed at the waist, high-sitting black trousers, Penworth red vest, black leather boots, and a high-collared dress shirt with a puffed black tie. If there was one thing I'd never be daft about, it was fashion, both for women and for men. He had a John Bull top hat in hand and put it on before taking a step forward and holding his arms out.

"That's all new," I said. "Down to your tie."

"Exactly. I needed new clothes for my upcoming business trip." He held up a nearly empty glass of champagne. "I started our celebration early. You look absolutely lovely, Corrine. You were right about your dress. It suits you."

He met me on the last step and held out his arm.

"Our own private ball, my lady," he said.

I put my arm through his, laughed at the way he postured and walked toward our grand ballroom as if the hallway was lined with adoring and envious people. His pianist was playing "Casey Would Waltz with a Strawberry Blonde." He was a bald-headed man with bubbly cheeks. His brown eyes caught the light when he smiled and nodded at me.

Garland immediately put down his glass, took my hand, and led me into the waltz. It was as if all the time between our first waltz at the Wexlers' anniversary gala and this day years later had been whisked away. I laughed at his enthusiasm as we danced on the grand ballroom floor that could easily cater to two hundred couples. Garland looked younger than ever and moved with grace and precision. When he was like this, there was such a strong positive energy about him. It was contagious. Every part of me was elated, happier.

At this moment I thought I should never be upset with Foxworth Hall and my new life. What was dark about it was my own fault. I should strive to be more accepting, more mature. How many women had a husband as sophisticated, wealthy, and charming as mine?

"You're wonderful," he said. "We'll capture everyone's attention tonight."

"Everyone?" I looked around and laughed. "Are you seeing your ancestors, those you spoke to in the attic when your father put you up there?"

"Only those who matter," he said, smiling. When the song ended, he poured us each a glass of champagne while Mr. LaRuffa played one melody after another. He kissed me on the cheek and then the lips.

"Maybe I should go with you on this trip, Garland. You'll be gone for weeks. I'll go mad here without you."

"No, no, no," he said vehemently. "You wouldn't enjoy a trip like this. Believe me. I don't linger in one place long, and I don't spend time smelling the roses. I visit the warehouses and offices, talk to boring businessmen, and get up very early every day, which you hate, too. Lots of smelly train rides. I want only certain things from these people and wouldn't dream of doing anything social with them. I spend a great deal of the time with dreary lawyers and then move on. Why would I take you through all that when you have everything at your beck and call here? Time will pass quickly."

Disappointed, I pouted for a few moments. He started to sing again to the music Mr. LaRuffa was playing. When he turned back to me, he laughed.

"You look like a spoiled little girl sometimes, but I love it," he said.

"If I can't go along with you, I'd like to join the Charlottesville Women's Club," I said quickly. Thinking about things he might refuse always made me hesitant and indecisive.

"Suffragettes? Most of those women have mustaches. I won't hear of it."

"They're not suffragettes, Garland," I said, smiling. "They sympathize, but they're doing nothing to promote it. It's a social club. Women gather to talk fashion, have lunch."

"How did you hear of this?" he asked suspiciously.

"At the department store earlier today, I met the wife of someone you know in business. Her daughter was with her."

"Who?" he asked, after sipping more champagne.

"Mrs. George Remington and her daughter Melinda Sue, who married Clarence Henry Carter. He works for George Remington."

"I know the clod. His father-in-law created a job for him. He is something of an assistant to the chief financial officer of the company."

"Melinda Sue isn't much older than I am. She's very sweet."

He was thoughtful.

"It's something for me to do while you're away. I feel locked away here. I haven't made any friends of my own, and the women you've introduced me to are all so much older. Melinda Sue is the first young lady I've met who's anywhere near my age."

"You have to be careful of clubs," he said. "These days they drift into suffragettes and embarrass their husbands. It could hurt my businesses if you're in any way associated with that sort of thing," he warned.

"I'm not interested in the women's vote. I'm interested in what you call idle chatter."

He smiled. "I do believe you wouldn't be interested in all that protesting and marching. Not good for the complexion and hair."

I stared at him. He was making fun of me, but I swallowed it back.

"Well, if you think you'd enjoy this sort of social club," he said.

"Melinda Sue said there's only really a half dozen who attend the meetings. They hold them at her home or another member's home. I could hold a meeting here if you give permission and tell Mrs. Wilson to prepare a garden lunch."

I wondered if I should tell him I once had my

own club as a girl, a club for my instructing other girls how to be more womanly. He'd like that, I thought, but still I hesitated.

"I'll think about it," he said.

"I'd like to have Lucas bring Melinda Sue here, maybe while you're still here so you can see how innocent and sweet she is. Actually, she's only five years older than I am."

"I'll think about it," he said again, but looked like he was giving in.

"Thank you, Garland. When are you leaving?"

"I have to go the day after tomorrow."

"That soon?"

"Get while the getting's good."

"How long is this trip?"

He drank the rest of his champagne before replying. "Not sure. Weeks," he said. "But it will go fast. You'll see. I promise."

He said that every time he left.

"Hey," he said, lifting my chin gently. "Don't despair. We'll get a head start tonight on my making up for missing nights."

Mr. LaRuffa began to play and sing "I Gave My Love a Cherry," and Garland joined him. He looked so young and handsome. I really would miss him. He saw it in my face, I think, so he took me in his arms, and we danced. We danced, drank, and laughed for almost another half hour before he decided he was hungry. Mrs. Wilson had stepped into the doorway of the dining room twice to signal her food was ready.

On the way to the dining room, he leaned in to kiss my cheek and whisper. "Invite her to lunch whenever you want. I'll let Mrs. Wilson and Mrs. Steiner know. I don't have to meet her. I trust your judgment."

"Oh, thank you, Garland," I said, hugging him.

Mr. LaRuffa followed us into the dining room and began to play his violin as soon as we sat and Mrs. Steiner poured us both some red wine from a decanter. Garland's enthusiasm and energy seemed to be contagious for everyone and not only me. We never had a more festive dinner. Everyone was smiling, and Garland was very generous with his compliments. The good food, the music, more wine, and Garland's continuous excitement about his business success and future were hard to interrupt with any sadness about what could be his longest trip away from home and me. As he had predicted, all that had happened to me earlier disappeared.

Before dinner ended, he leaned over to whisper. "I'll leave first. Come to my room."

There was that intent on romantic intrigue again. For whom were we putting on this act?

"Why don't I leave first this time and you come to mine? I've made some changes and additions you haven't seen."

He held his smile but didn't reply. Instead, he

finished what was left in his wineglass, thanked Mrs. Steiner, Dora, and Mrs. Wilson, and rose from his seat.

"Give me a few minutes with Mr. LaRuffa to pay him and arrange for Lucas to take him home," he said. "And then come up."

After Mr. LaRuffa said good night to me and told me how well I danced, he left with Garland.

I sat there feeling strangely numb. The women glanced at me and then quickly began attending to the table. At one point they realized how silly I felt sitting there by myself, and all disappeared into the kitchen. They didn't know Garland had asked me to wait a few minutes before following him. Maybe they thought he was returning.

I sat with conflicted feelings. It had been such a wonderful night, but it would have been even more wonderful if my husband had escorted me up the stairway and not had me behaving like some harlot sneaking around to his bedroom. It was almost as if he had another wife in the Swan Room and I was to tiptoe past her door. What did the women here think of us, of me?

I finished my wine, too, and then rose and walked out slowly.

Pausing at the foot of the stairway, I listened to the faint sound of the night breeze slipping over the windows. Some part of the house on my right creaked as if the entire mansion was leaning to the right. I could hear the women cleaning up more quickly now. In moments our wonderful dinner table would be naked and restored to its place as a piece of the antique world this mansion protected. It was as if time never passed for anything in this house. The rest of the world moved on, but Foxworth Hall held the hands of the clock from clicking forward. In years to come, I would slip dutifully alongside everything else. I wondered if my portrait would hang near any of the Foxworth ancestors or if I would be relegated to the darker inner belly of the mansion because I was too beautiful to be tolerated. My exquisite face would overwhelm them.

The very thought of it made me laugh. Or maybe it was the wine.

I started up the stairs. Every once in a while during the past few years, especially right after Garland and I had made love, I would wonder why I hadn't become pregnant again, not that I was eager to be. Sometimes I thought the angry ancestors had put a curse on me. There was a new Foxworth male, and that was enough. Garland never commented much about it. "When it happens, it happens" was more or less his attitude. He was certainly not going to criticize himself in any way. There would never be the possibility that he was responsible. My eggs were just "too squirrelly."

When I had ascended the stairway, I paused. The dimly lit hallway reminded me of the way it looked that first night Garland had brought me to Foxworth Hall. I had invited myself to my great-aunt Nettie's in Charlottesville and let Garland know when I would be there. He appeared after we had dinner and my aunt and her caretaker, Hazel, were about to go to sleep. I was berating myself for traveling all the way from Alexandria, apparently making a fool of myself because he hadn't arrived.

But when he did, all the depression and sadness evaporated. He was as charming and as handsome as he was at the Wexlers' gala. After my aunt had gone to bed, he made the surprising suggestion we go out to Foxworth Hall to see it in the evening. I would never forget how he described it as having one personality in the daytime and another at night. Now that I had lived here, I believed that was so true. It hadn't simply been a line to get me intrigued.

I would lose my virginity that night after becoming inebriated on his special Italian discovery, limoncello. It seemed to me at first to be nothing more than lemonade. Here I was, a girl who thought she was far more sophisticated than other girls her age, especially when it came to men, and I quickly fell into the most common male trap of all, alcohol. I was embarrassed and felt very foolish when Garland seemed to have stepped out of my life afterward, dispatching me and leaving me to my own regrets. Even so, I couldn't stop thinking about him.

And then it all happened quickly: my pregnancy, my marriage, and my Foxworth life. If I stood here now for a moment and closed my eyes, feeling a bit wobbly from all the wine, and then opened them, I might find myself five years younger, with the opportunity to turn around and flee before taking one sip of the drink. Would I do that? Would I give up all this? Had it been enough? Was every step I took on this stairway adding more regret? Who wouldn't want a chance to be sure?

But magic doesn't happen here for anyone but a true Foxworth, I thought. I laughed at myself for even dreaming of it, and then I started down the hallway toward Garland's room like a virgin bride presenting herself to her new husband the night of their wedding. I would just think it, and thinking so would make it real.

It had happened before, hadn't it? Although lately, that sort of lovemaking between us was more and more rare. Often, I came away feeling it was rushed, more like a husband's chore, something he checked off the way he checked off items on a profit-and-loss sheet, than it was a night of exquisite romance filled with the special kisses and caresses I used to tell my adoring girlfriends marked true sexual ecstasy.

Would tonight be one of those precious nights, another flower I could press into my memory? I so needed it. At times, with the gaps between us, I really did feel like I was fading. I'd stop to look at myself in the mirror more and more for reassurance. Part of the reason I went shopping so often was to garner the looks of other men, looks of appreciation and desire. Coming home with the vision of those was almost as important as the clothes, shoes, and hats I bought. Maybe, if I were truly truthful, I'd admit they were more important.

I needed to verify I was still Corrine Dixon, who had been one of the most beautiful young women in Alexandria, and who still was quite beautiful.

No woman who had been forced to marry before she wanted to could ever be certain of her husband's love, or at least that it would be lasting. Someday, somehow, one of us would throw it back at the other. Perhaps it would just be out of anger, but once it was uttered, it would linger like a terrible odor that no open window or stiff breeze could chase into a thinning memory. I lived like someone waiting for the second shoe to drop. Nights like this did so much to get me to forget my fear.

We would make love more passionately than ever.

Wouldn't we?

After all, a marriage without passion was like an orange without juice.

Hopefully, there was more to squeeze out of it and always would be.

# 5

I turned at the sound of footsteps on the stairway. Someone was hurrying up. I was surprised to see it was Lucas, who had left earlier to take the musician home. He couldn't have done so and returned this quickly. When he saw me standing there, he paused. I had changed in my room and was wearing only my nightdress, my hair down around my shoulders the way Garland liked it when we made love. I saw how embarrassed Lucas was. He lowered his head to keep his gaze on the floor and didn't take another step forward.

"What's wrong, Lucas? I thought you were taking Mr. LaRuffa home."

"I was, ma'am," he said. "A rider intercepted us on our way."

He held up an envelope.

"What is it?"

"A message for Mr. Foxworth, ma'am. It's marked *Urgent*."

I looked at Garland's door and then back at my own.

"Then deliver it," I said, and headed back to the Swan Room.

Lucas didn't move until I had entered and

109

closed the door behind me. I stood there, listening as he hurried past and then knocked quickly on Garland's door. After a moment, I heard Garland ask, "What's wrong?"

There was some mumbling between them. When I opened the door to peer out, Lucas had gone in, and the door had been closed. I stood there, waiting. Minutes went by before Lucas emerged. I closed the door softly until I heard him heading back to the stairway. Then I walked out and started again for Garland's room.

When I entered, he was dressing quickly and was up to putting on his boots.

"What's happened?" I asked. "What was the message Lucas had to deliver at this time of night?" He glanced at me and returned to his boots. "Garland?"

"I have an emergency," he said, standing. He reached for his coat. Whatever it was had clearly sobered him up quickly.

"What kind of an emergency?"

"Business. Everything in my life is about business! Don't you know that by now?" he added bitterly.

His sharp retort made me wince. What had happened to the man who had danced with me in the ballroom just a little while ago, the man who had been so happy and energized at dinner, his face filling with promises of love afterward?

I stepped back. There was something very

different going on here, I thought. He no longer looked flushed from his wine. He looked a little pale, in fact.

"Why are you so upset, Garland? You told me when you take it personally, you miss opportunities and make mistakes. You said your father taught you that emotional reaction shows weakness, especially when you are working in commerce."

"Yeah, well, my father's no longer here, no longer running all this. He never had these kinds of challenges. His empire was much smaller than mine."

"But where are you going now, Garland? It's late for business negotiations, isn't it?" I asked. "Who holds meetings at this hour?"

He paused and looked at me as if he thought I was a complete idiot. Then his demeanor changed as if something had clicked in his head, and he smiled. He walked to me and took my hand.

"I'm so sorry. I know what you were looking forward to tonight. But you really must get a better grip on your sexual hunger, Corrine. A woman has to be far less at its mercy than a man. You know what I think, what everyone of any quality thinks, of women who are unable to do that. You wouldn't have been the raging young mare you were when we first met if you had tightened the reins a bit, now, would you?"

"What?"

I stepped back, pulling my hands from his.

"What are you saying? Raging young mare?"

"My mother always warned me that women, especially the young women of this age, would aggressively set their sights on me. Every woman sets a trap for a man. It's simply in her nature. She makes herself as desirable as she can from the first day she realizes her sex. It's not unlike putting some cheese in a mousetrap.

"Don't look so outraged to hear me say these things. In your heart you know it's all true. It's just . . . life," he said. "A boy becomes a man when he realizes it."

"But you were the one who came after me, romanced me at the Wexler gala."

"A bit of flirtation . . . only natural. Actually, you were the one who followed up on it rather quickly."

"That's not true. Why are you saying these things now, years later?"

He held his smile. "I doubt there's a man walking the earth who would fault me for being so attracted to you. Don't misunderstand me. Of course," he said, stepping toward me again, "once it all happened, I realized how much I loved you and how it would all work out well for the Foxworths. Just look. We had a son immediately."

"What Foxworths? You're the only Foxworth, Garland."

He stopped smiling. "Don't be so literal. We were taught early in our lives that we should think of ourselves as generations and not individuals. I work as hard for my family's reputation as I do for myself . . . and you, of course. You should be proud of that, proud you bear the Foxworth name. You couldn't get into this house otherwise. Think of all those in this community who would die for that opportunity. They would overrun the estate. "

I stared at him, unable to think of anything else to say. The more we talked, the more uneasy I felt. *Let him go do his business,* I told myself. *He'll be different when it's over.*

I stepped to the side because he looked like he would charge right over me.

"When will you return?"

"Oh, it's late already, Corrine. Don't wait up for me. Just go to sleep. I promise I'll make up for it," he said, with that coy, flirtatious, and arrogant smile he could slip over his face instantly. Right now, it annoyed me. If I had the courage, I would slap him across his self-confident face. I didn't want him to "make up for it." I wasn't counting how often we made love. He made it sound like I had to keep a quota, deposit every instance in some wife's account.

He gestured toward the door. "I have to go."

I stepped forward, opened it, and walked out. The moment I did, he seized me at my shoulders, turned me, kissed me hard and quickly without much passion, and then started away. Whatever was driving him, anger, ambition, whatever it was in his body, hoisted his shoulders as he charged at the stairway. I stood there looking after him, feeling as if a sharp, cold wind had flowed in and out of the house, leaving me shivering and confused, confused because I had no idea why what had occurred and been said should make me so afraid.

But it had. I could feel it in my bones.

I returned to my room and slipped under my blanket. I let the lights flicker and watched the shadows dancing on the walls. They looked like they had emerged from somewhere within the mansion, little demons joyous at my unhappiness.

It was unlike Garland to be so critical of all women and throw me into the mix so casually. I was his wife. Didn't I deserve more respect? Right from the first time I had set eyes on him, he had struck me as flirtatious and coy. Especially during our first few years together, he never appeared terribly concerned about the warnings he now claimed his mother supposedly had given. He had never said anything remotely like that. In his heart he surely knew that I was certainly not a fortune hunter. My foolish young-girl mind was wrapped around an exciting romance, not an exciting bank account. He knew that.

Foxworth Hall and his immense fortune weren't even on my mind after we had met. I knew nothing about his businesses and property. Except for my father's references to Garland's financial success, I didn't think of him as someone so powerful and important in that world. Surely he had seen my innocence. It was almost as if his mother had been resurrected minutes ago and was whispering in his ear, saying things like *Just as I warned you, a fortune hunter. She has no respect for our money. As for our great heritage . . . look at how disinterested she is in your son. She'll never be a Foxworth.*

*That's unfair!* I shouted at the shadows. *I didn't demand a wet nurse. I didn't demand Dora be his nanny. He's the one who wanted to keep me like some precious sexual conquest, a jewel-laden wife hanging on his arm.*

I turned over and embraced my pillow like someone trying to squeeze the life out of it. My whole body was taut, in a rage. The mixture of emotions made me dizzy. There was no switch-back that could take me as high and then as low.

What business crisis was so critical this late at night that he had to turn me away from his bed and, on top of that, make it look like I was the one who was *so* disappointed? He had made it sound, or at least had made me feel, like he pressed himself into me with a golden phallus every time we made love. He practically had

115

said, *Be grateful for every thrust, every kiss and caress, and return to your Swan Room to drift into a pleasant sleep dreaming of my gift of love to come. You have made love to a Foxworth.*

The more I thought about it, the more I tossed and turned and ground my teeth with my building rage. I was tempted to get up, go down to his library, pour myself some of his precious whiskey, and sit there waiting for him so I could greet him with my indignation the moment he returned. I sat up, thinking I would do just that, when I heard a knock on my door. It was so gentle I had to listen hard to see if I had imagined it.

I definitely heard it the second time.

"Who's there?"

I watched the door open very slowly and saw Malcolm standing there. He had obviously gotten out of bed. Maybe all the noise had woken him.

"What is it?" I asked. I was definitely not in the mood to be soft and kind. What he had done was still fresh and painful in my memory. "Why are you out of your room?"

He took another step toward me and looked down. I stared at him. He was backlit by the flickering lanterns in the hallway, but I could see something curious on his left arm. I threw off my blanket and got out of bed. He looked up as I approached and quickly pressed his arm against his nightshirt. When I pulled it away,

I saw the bloodstain and the clear slice on his forearm. Fresh blood trickled down toward his hand.

"What is this? What happened to you?" I cried.

"I'm sorry, Mama," he said. Whenever he called me Mama instead of Mother, it was usually to pry some favor out of me.

"Sorry?"

"For what I did to you, to the album," he said.

I was still holding up his arm. "What about this?"

"I punished myself," he said.

"What? You deliberately cut yourself?"

He didn't reply.

"Oh, this is great. Your father is going to love seeing this," I said, but I didn't mean Garland would be angry at him. Somehow he would find a way to blame me. "Come on," I said, tugging him. "Where's Dora?"

"I don't know."

I took him to the bathroom and washed the wound. Not finding the medicine and bandages quickly, I started cursing under my breath. I gazed at Malcolm. He was staring at me. I saw no fear in his face, no pain from this deep cut he had inflicted upon himself. He seemed more intrigued with my reaction than anything. I began shoving things around in the cabinets. Finally, on the most obvious shelf, I located what I needed. I had never addressed any scratch or scrape he had suffered, so I wasn't familiar with the cabinet's contents.

He didn't take his eyes off me as I worked on his cut and bandaged it, hopefully as well as Dora would have. When I was finished, I led him back to his room and got him back into bed.

Ironically, I never felt as close to him as I did at this moment. He had been silent, helpless, and intrigued with me the whole time. I stood there looking down at him.

"Why did you do that, Malcolm? Why did you cut your arm? You could have caused a lot more bleeding if you had cut it lower down."

"Saying I'm sorry isn't enough," he said. He was reciting it, but somehow he still made it sound authentic.

I studied his beautiful face. As he grew he was capturing the best of both Garland and me with his cerulean eyes, perfectly shaped nose and mouth, and golden hair. I had no doubt that he would grow more handsome than his father and he would break more hearts. Ironically, I was both proud and sad about it. If I didn't do my duty and develop a respect for women in him, he would or could be more of a scoundrel than his father.

"Rather than punishing yourself to redeem yourself, Malcolm, think harder before you let your anger control you. Anger only leads to more pain and unhappiness. And you should be even more careful about what you do to girls and women. You're supposed to protect them, because men are stronger. Mothers and sisters, girlfriends, or just girls you meet will depend on you to be nice to them."

"Is Daddy nice to you?" he asked, his eyes narrowing with that Foxworth peer.

"He tries to be," I said. He looked like he understood my diplomatic answer. "The important thing is to try, try hard. You try harder, okay?"

He nodded.

"Go to sleep. Tomorrow, after breakfast, I'll let your father give you a present he bought you. You'll try again to be a good boy, okay?"

"Yes, Mother," he said.

I fixed his blanket. I didn't put him to sleep often enough. I leaned over and kissed him good night.

When I went to the door, he called to me.

"Thank you, Mother. I'm sorry," he said.

"Okay. Go to sleep, Malcolm."

When I closed the door behind me, I stood there. How terrible it was, I thought, that even after all that, I was still suspicious. I still suspected him of doing it all just to get me to relent. My son was not even five years old, and I didn't trust him, even after seeing him do such a dramatic and terrible thing to himself. Perhaps it was my fault. Perhaps I was simply transferring my suspicions of my husband to our son. Only time would tell whether or not that was true.

I started to return to the Swan Room and then stopped. Where was Dora? Malcolm would always go to her first when something unpleasant had happened to him. Normally, he would have gotten her to bring him to me. Maybe he had tried. Maybe she had told him to go to me directly. I knew how much she had wanted me to forgive him. I went to her bedroom, the room that had been the wet nurse's, and looked in. She wasn't there. For a moment I thought she had gone downstairs for something, and then it dawned on me. Of course, I thought, now really in a rage, and marched down to Garland's mother's bedroom. Angrily, I thrust open the door. There she was, asleep in his mother's nightdress.

*"Get up!"* I shouted at her. She sat up quickly. "He won't be needing you tonight for whatever voodoo-hoodoo this is. He's had some sort of a business emergency. Meanwhile, Malcolm deliberately sliced his own arm."

"Sliced?"

"He cut it and came to me. I've cleaned it and bandaged it. Don't bother going to him. I put him to bed. Just go to your own room. Now!"

I shut the door. My heart was pounding as I returned to the Swan Room. After I closed the door behind me, I leaned against it and caught my breath. Something inside me had changed or awoken. I was coming out of the shadows. I wouldn't be some ghostlike spirit moving expectantly from one place to another, following some role, pretending to be Mrs. Foxworth only anymore. Corrine Dixon would come back in her own way. I had spirit; I had personality of my own.

Earlier I had intended to go down and wait for Garland in his library. Why not do it now? That would certainly impress him. I spun around and walked out of the Swan Room to go downstairs. This was certainly something his mother would do, I thought, and stopped. For a moment it was as if I had been possessed. The idea simply burst in my mind like someone had tossed it into my head. I walked to his mother's bedroom. Dora was gone; she had left so quickly that she hadn't hung up Garland's mother's nightdress. I took mine off and put hers on. Like some magic coat of armor, it seemed to give me even more courage.

I went down quickly and settled myself into the soft-cushioned chair Garland used when he sat and read in his library, and I stared at the doorway to the entry, waiting. I doubted that a business meeting would take all the remaining night. He'd settle his problem and come charging back, and I'd be here just as I had planned.

That was my firm intention, but the hours

crawled forward so slowly, and after a while, the tension, Malcolm's dramatic apology, and his self-inflicted wound filled me with a deep and overwhelming fatigue. I was soon unable to keep my eyes open. Moments later, I was in a very deep sleep.

I didn't know what time it was when I awoke, but Mrs. Steiner was standing there looking at me when the sun streaked through the open curtains and the warmth nudged me awake. For a moment I didn't know where I was. Maybe I was still in some dream.

"Is there anything wrong, Mrs. Foxworth?" she asked. I imagined she was quite aware of what I was wearing. My mother-in-law's nightdresses were quite distinctly hers and quite different from my own more fashionable clothes.

I ground the sleep from my eyes and then looked at her. The entire night before came rushing back at me.

"Where is Mr. Foxworth?" I asked.

"He's gone on his business trip, Mrs. Foxworth," she said.

"What do you mean? He was here? He returned?"

"Yes, ma'am. Lucas told me he didn't want to wake you. There's a note left for you on his desk."

I rose slowly, incredulous. How could he have been here without my hearing or knowing?

"I heard nothing, saw no one."

"You must have been very tired, ma'am. Dora told me how Malcolm had woken you and you had to take care of his terrible cut. She's bandaged it again."

"What was wrong with my bandage?"

"Nothing. A cut like that has to be treated often or there could be infection," she said. She smiled. "Dora had a little bit of nurse training, you know. For when she took care of her parents."

"I know, I know. I know how competent Dora is." I looked at Garland's desk. "He left a note, you say?"

"Yes, ma'am. Would you like to take your breakfast in your room this morning?"

"I'll see," I said. "Thank you."

She nodded and left. I went to Garland's desk. There was an envelope. I sat in his chair and opened it to take out the note.

*Dear Corrine,*

*I'm so sorry but events occurred rapidly threatening business interests. I barely had time to come home and pack what I wanted to take with me to New York. I have to leave a day earlier than I had planned, but think of it this way: I left a day earlier so I'll be home a day earlier.*

*Please, when you've forgiven him, give*

123

*Malcolm the train. Perhaps you can spend time with him playing with it.*

*Do amuse yourself with having your new friend to lunch and going to one of their social meetings, if you like.*

*I shall hopefully return soon.*

*As always,*
*Love, Garland*

I sat back, stunned. He left a day earlier? Why hadn't he woken me to say good-bye? He'd be gone so long this time. Had he even noticed I was wearing his mother's nightdress? Wouldn't he have been a bit curious? This didn't seem right at all to me. I rose and went looking for Mrs. Steiner. She was just crossing from the kitchen toward the stairway.

"Mrs. Steiner," I called, waving the note like a flag.

She paused. "Yes, ma'am."

"Did you actually speak to my husband and see him leave this note on his desk?"

She looked like she didn't want to answer.

"Well, did you?"

"No, ma'am. I spoke only to Lucas."

"How did you know about the note?"

"From Lucas," she said, nodding.

"Is he back?"

"No, ma'am. He took Mr. Foxworth's things and left only about an hour ago."

"What do you mean, Mr. Foxworth's things? Where was Mr. Foxworth?"

"I don't know for sure, ma'am. I think waiting in the carriage. But I don't know for sure. It was very late, and the commotion woke me."

"Where's Dora?"

"She's seeing to Malcolm having breakfast. They're in the kitchen nook. He told her you said that was all right."

"He did, did he?" I walked past her up to the stairway. "Send her up to see me. Right away," I added.

"Yes, ma'am," she said, and turned to go to the kitchen.

I went into the bathroom and washed my face with cold water. For a few moments, I stared at myself in the mirror. I hated how I looked. Garland's compliments came only after he had drunk too much, I thought. Maybe he did see me as I was when I was younger, but he was looking through foggy eyes. This life, as effortless as it was for me, was aging me in subtle ways. When unhappiness gets into your blood, it deposits a darkness into your face. My mother unknowingly taught me that. The corners of my mouth drooped with self-disgust. My eyes had lost so much of their glow. I even hated my posture.

"Make changes, Corrine Dixon," I told the image in the mirror. "Make changes or rapidly become your mother."

125

I tossed the towel into the bathtub and charged out and to the Swan Room. Dora was already waiting there, oddly staring at the bed as if I were in it. She spun around when I entered.

"Were you up when my husband returned?" I quickly asked.

She shook her head.

"You were still asleep, too?"

"No, I was up, ma'am, but I didn't see Mr. Foxworth. I saw only Lucas and helped him gather Mr. Foxworth's things."

"Then he wasn't waiting out in the carriage?"

"I didn't see him, ma'am."

I sat on the chaise and fell back against it. My head began to ache. I knew part of the reason was how much wine I had drunk after drinking so much champagne. Events had sobered me but not cleared the poison from my blood. One of the things my father had told me after he had found out Garland had given me too much of his limoncello was "Alcohol will never be your friend, Corrine. You had a very bad introduction to it, and for the rest of your life, your body will remember."

"Bring me some coffee," I said.

"And some breakfast?"

"No, just some coffee for now. And the moment Lucas returns, send him up to see me. Immediately," I said, raising my voice.

"Yes, ma'am."

"As you obviously know, probably from him, I've forgiven Malcolm for now," I said, squeezing my temples with my thumb and forefinger. "Start his lessons downstairs in the library after breakfast as usual."

"Yes, ma'am. He said something about a present . . ."

"I'm not surprised he remembered that most of all. Tell him if he does his lessons well, I'll give it to him later today."

"I will, ma'am. I'll be right up with your coffee."

I nodded and closed my eyes again. *I've got to change my life,* I thought. *I've got to change it now.* I rose and went to my desk to write an invitation to Melinda Sue Carter, inviting her to lunch as soon as today, if she were so able to do so.

Before Dora returned with my coffee and, probably at Mrs. Wilson's insistence, some toast and jam, I put on my robe and fixed my oversized pillows so I could sit on my bed. Dora entered and put the bed tray over my legs.

"Lucas has just returned and is taking care of the horses with Mr. Wilson."

"Tell him I have a letter for him to deliver today. You can send him up as soon as he is free."

"Up here, ma'am?"

"It's where I am, Dora," I said sharply. I knew what she meant. It was quite unusual for me to have anyone other than Garland and her, and Malcolm, of course, in the Swan Room, especially when I was not fully dressed.

"Very good, ma'am," she said, and hurried out.

After I began drinking my coffee, I was happy Mrs. Wilson had insisted on toast and jam as well. Ten minutes or so later, I heard a very tentative knock on my door.

"Yes?"

Lucas opened it slowly and looked in timidly at me. Seeing me on my bed brought an immediate blush to his face.

"You can come in, Lucas," I said.

"Yes, ma'am."

He did, but he left the door open behind him. He stood there with his hat in his hands.

"When you returned early this morning to fetch Mr. Foxworth's clothing and whatever else he wanted, was he with you? Was he waiting in the carriage?"

"Oh, no, ma'am. It was a bit chilly this morning."

"But he wasn't in the house."

"No, ma'am."

"Then where was he, Lucas?"

He looked like he had swallowed his tongue.

"Did he tell you to keep it a secret?"

"Oh, no, ma'am."

"Where was he? Where did you take him?"

"The Caroline House, ma'am."

"You took him to a hotel for a business meeting at that hour?"

He was silent.

"Lucas?"

"It's where he wanted me to take him, Mrs. Foxworth."

"Did you go in with him?"

"No, ma'am."

"You waited in the carriage?"

He looked very guilty suddenly.

"Answer me, please, Lucas."

"I visited someone and then returned to the hotel."

"I see."

He was telling me he had a girlfriend, I thought.

"But you did go back to the Caroline House?"

"Yes, ma'am. When he told me to. When I arrived, he said that he had to stay there, but he had to leave on the early morning train, so I carried out his orders."

"Which included leaving his note for me on his desk?"

"Yes, Mrs. Foxworth. I didn't want to wake you, and I'm sorry if I did."

"You didn't wake me. I wish you had," I said. "Did he tell you any more about his emergency meeting?"

"No, ma'am. I wouldn't understand the ins and outs of his enterprises. I just deliver messages."

I looked at my coffee. Why make him suffer? I

thought. He was obviously quite uncomfortable standing in the Swan Room and being cross-examined.

"Okay, Lucas. Thank you for that information. I'd like you to deliver a letter to someone this morning."

"Yes, ma'am."

I held out the envelope. "The address is there. You might know it."

He glanced at it. "I do, Mrs. Foxworth."

"Good. Thank you. Oh," I said as he turned. "You can, if it is requested, remain until a response is written."

"I will, ma'am," he said.

He walked out and closed the door softly behind him. I glanced up at my swan.

"Something tells me I will need your protection and help after all," I whispered.

# 6

Melinda Sue was obviously excited about my invitation. She wrote out her response as soon as she had read it and handed it to Lucas, who hurriedly brought it back.

She would in fact come today.

I quickly informed Mrs. Wilson and Mrs. Steiner that I was having a luncheon for two. I decided the dining room would be too formal. Garland's mother had put in new windows in the kitchen nook years ago, so there would be more sunlight. I thought the room was far cozier. Facing southwest, it would not be over-whelmingly bright that time of day. Olsen, who had the magical gardener's hands, could provide us with garden mums in pastel tints to dress the table. I asked Lucas to tell him to do so.

"We won't be looking for a lot of food, Mrs. Wilson," I told her. "Finger sandwiches, perhaps chicken salad and cucumber. Afterward, we'll take tea in the library and have some of your applesauce cookies. For wine, we'll have one of my husband's Italian pinot grigio whites."

She looked a little surprised at my request for the wine.

"Anything wrong?"

"Oh, no, no. What else would you like, Mrs. Foxworth?"

"I'd like us to use the informal dinnerware. Also, we will use the cloth napkins with the Foxworth insignia on them. My husband is quite proud of that. Place our settings so that we're facing each other and neither has her back to the windows. Oh, and put out those salt and pepper shakers my husband brought back from Holland years ago."

Mrs. Wilson nodded, looking impressed with me and my attention to detail.

"Very well, Mrs. Foxworth," she said.

When I left the kitchen, I glanced back and saw Mrs. Steiner and Mrs. Wilson smiling at each other. I was never really sure about what they thought of me, but from what I had learned about their lives, I felt confident they saw me as quite spoiled and self-indulgent. Perhaps I should have been doing more before this to win their respect. After all, with Garland's devotion to his businesses and his traveling, I had spent more time with them than I had with him over the past few years.

But with my duties as a mother absorbed by Dora and with Garland's strict forbidding of my making any changes in the mansion, updating anything fashion-wise, what else could I be but self-absorbed? Nurturing my beauty and my own fashions and comfort, doing a little reading, taking walks on our property, and the small changes I could make in the Swan Room were all I had to fill my day. Whenever I accompanied Dora and Malcolm for his and actually my own exercise on walks and the occasional rowboat ride on the lake, I felt terribly extraneous. Most of the time, Malcolm behaved as if I wasn't even there, and if Dora was distracted or returned to the house to get us something, he peppered me with so many silly questions that my head began to spin and I was grateful for her return.

Maybe if Mrs. Steiner and Mrs. Wilson could see what a perfect hostess I could be without my husband present, their opinions of me would improve. Why that was so important right now puzzled me, but it was. It was as if I anticipated that someday soon I would need them to take my side of things. I would need their support. Goodness knows, my own mother wasn't going to give me any.

It was certainly long past the time to change things, to have a better relationship with my son and my husband, to garner the complete respect of my servants, and to expand and develop my own identity anyway. I had never been comfortable being known solely as Mrs. Garland Foxworth. I felt smothered at every social gathering we had attended, standing almost behind Garland and not being included in his political and business conversations. The other wives seemed vapid and meek. Their discussions of new tearoom china and the newest sanitary pads nearly nauseated me. I was almost always off to the side, ignored and grateful to be so. Their conversations reminded me of squawking geese. If I cleared my throat, they would stop, look at me, and then return to their conversations as if I weren't there.

Somehow, some way, I would bring back the independent and strong-willed young woman who had captured the imagination of most anyone who had spoken to or seen her before she had been married. I easily imagined her waiting outside the grand front doorway of Foxworth Hall, waiting to come in.

After Dora had completed a lesson with Malcolm, I told her she could bring him to the ballroom. I had changed and pinned up my hair for my luncheon with Melinda Sue. I found Garland's present for Malcolm near his desk and brought it into the ballroom, where Dora and Malcolm already were. She seemed almost as excited about it as he was.

"This is not a reward for your saying you're sorry about what you did, Malcolm. Your father was hoping we three could have a special celebration about his good business fortune, a family celebration," I added, eyeing Dora. "He was quite upset about what you had done to his and my wedding album and then what you had done to me, and he almost took this back to where he bought it."

Malcolm looked down. I doubted he was going to cry, but he could look like he was about to and tear the sympathy out of most anyone's vulnerable heart. Dora kept her hand on his shoulder, and I saw she squeezed tighter to keep up his bravery, not that he needed her to do it.

"Now, both Dora and I are upset over what you did to yourself. And of course your father will be when he hears about it. We hope you will never do anything like that again."

He looked up and shook his head. "No, Mama, never."

"Good. So now, you open this, and until we need the ballroom for an affair, you can set it up here so you have lots of room to play with it. Dora and I will watch you do it yourself to see how clever you are," I added, looking at Dora and clearly telling her that she should do nothing to help him. She stepped back a little when I handed Malcolm the box.

He sat down on the floor instantly and began tearing away the tape that kept the box closed. His eyes were lit with excitement. When he opened it up, he paused, looked at me and then Dora with that Foxworth confidence, and reached in to take out the train tracks. We watched him study them and then begin to put them together. Dora smiled at me just the way a proud parent might, seizing the moment before I could.

After he had the train tracks circle created, he inspected the engine. He reminded me of Garland whenever he was intensely into his paper-work. His face was tight with the same sort of concentration. A real train could come plowing through the house and Malcolm wouldn't break his absorption in what he was doing. He carefully lined up the cars and the caboose behind them on those tracks. There was a switch on the engine that kept the wheels from turning until he had wound it up.

"Don't overwind it, Malcolm," I warned. "I did that once with a toy, a figurine of a ballerina my father had bought me, and no one could fix it," I explained, mostly to Dora.

Malcolm nodded, his expression as serious as a doctor about to sew up a wounded soldier. After he was done attaching it all, he looked up at me, expecting a compliment. He deserved one, but I hated that he made his demand for it so obvious. Humility would starve to death in this house, I thought.

"That's very, very good, Malcolm."

He nodded, of course agreeing, and then he threw the switch and the train started around the tracks. There was a toy village in the box as well, and when the train stopped, he began to put that together before he wound the engine again. He was a picturesque little boy, totally into his imagination. He looked like he could be on a magazine cover. Why couldn't he always be this bright and sweet?

"I have some toy soldiers upstairs in my room. I might put them here, and I have horses and cows and pigs, too, Mama, and all those cars Daddy brought home from different places."

"Make it as big as you want," I said. "We're not having any parties in the ballroom for some time. Perhaps at Christmas as usual," I added. Dora nodded. "Mrs. Steiner didn't receive any plans for such an event?"

"I don't know, ma'am. She hasn't mentioned it to me."

"Nor to me. What's new about that?" I mumbled.

I looked at the clock and nodded at her.

"I have a guest for lunch," I said. "Remember, he should do his letters later today, too. You must do your lessons, Malcolm, or we'll put it all back in the box," I warned.

He looked up, saw I was very serious, and nodded. "I will, Mama," he said. "I promise."

"Good."

What man doesn't make promises he would easily break, I thought, even at nearly five?

I went out to the living room to wait for Melinda Sue. She was just a little late, and the moment she entered, she began with incessant apologies for it until I assured her I was often late myself.

"Besides, what woman isn't a little late when she's preparing herself to go out in public?" I said.

It was obvious she had, even in the short time between my invitation and her arrival, taken great care with her appearance. Perhaps, I thought, she was like a fireman, always ready on instant notice. On the other hand, she might have canceled another invitation to come to me or, more important, Foxworth Hall.

Her dark-brown hair was dressed fairly close to her head with curled fringe at the forehead and fairly high buns. She wore a triple-strand necklace and small pearl drop-bead earrings and what looked like an ostrich-feather puff aigrette. Whether she had her hair ready for an invitation like mine or not, I felt my hair was quite underdressed in comparison. Was it proper for a guest to outdress her hostess? I thought I looked more like one of the servants right now.

Like me, she did not wear a bustle. Her pink skirt was flared smoothly over her hips from a handspan waist and gradually widened at the hemline. After Mrs. Steiner, who had rushed to greet my guest, took her cashmere cloak, I saw that the sleeves of her blouse were far slimmer than mine, and she wore a cravat with a stick-pin bar brooch. Despite my keeping up with fashions in newspapers, I felt truly out of step with what was happening now. Half the time, I didn't trust the salesladies at the department store. They were anxious to get rid of what wasn't selling, and I was a prime possibility for sure.

"How pretty you look," I said. "Truthfully, I don't know how you did all this in the time you had. Only a man could do that. They have it so easy."

She laughed, her hazel eyes brightening with her soft, almost little-girl smile. Her small teeth were nearly perfectly straight. Her lips were thinner than mine and just a little crooked because of the way her cheek tightened on the right more than on the left when she smiled. Only someone who had been contrasting herself with other girls and young women all her life would be as quick to pick up any imperfections in her competition. But I had immediately liked her when we had been introduced in the department store. In some ways, she reminded me of my best friend at home, Daisy Herman.

Like Daisy, despite her social position and her being older than I was, Melinda Sue had the excitement of a farm girl brought to her first fair. Her eyes darted about the entryway in her ravenous effort to capture and memorize everything in and about Foxworth Hall as quickly as she could. I was sure, like my mother, who had been keen to request a report whenever I had visited a girlfriend, hers had told her to look at everything and take mental notes so she could report back. Or maybe the other members of her Charlottesville social club had given her that assignment. She'd probably have some negative things to say. Because of Garland's loyalty to his mother's choices and designs for Foxworth Hall, I was confident that my home was surely not as fashionable as any one of theirs. Changes here came as slowly as human evolution.

"I assume you've never been to Foxworth," I said.

"Oh, no, never, but I've always wanted to see it. Whatever my friends who have been to Foxworth tell me about it always makes me more excited about seeing it. It's so impressive when you drive up to it or look up at it."

"It is a house that cannot suffer exaggeration," I said, stealing one of Garland's frequent descriptions of his home to strangers.

"Yes, exactly."

"Let me take you for a tour of the downstairs," I said. Clearly, she was champing at the bit for just such an offer. "And then we'll go to our lunch just off the kitchen, where it is bright and cheery. Unfortunately, so much of this mansion, like most of them its size, has darkness and deep shadows practically painted on its walls. Well, maybe Foxworth has a bit more."

She looked up at the array of family portraits. "Who are they all?"

"Those are my husband's ancestors. As you can see, each one of them, even the women, must have suffered from gout at the time their portraits were done."

"Gout?"

After a moment she realized the sarcasm, laughed, and reached out for my hand. "Oh, how funny and probably true," she whispered, checking to be sure no one could overhear her. Her eyes were full of mischief and delight.

All of what I had left behind me when I was swept from my youth came rushing back as if my memories and not Melinda Sue's had accompanied her to rush through an opening in the fortress of Foxworth. In my mind I heard the laughter of my friends back then. A young girl's laugh was so innocent and underdressed. The subtlety of a smile, the awareness of her volume when she spoke, and the awkwardness she might convey were of no concern yet. We were all some dozen steps or so from feminine wiles, some more like a thousand.

I was the first in my group of friends to get there, and get there so quickly and completely the others were truly in awe. It was why I seemed so wise and aware of the sexual maze we'd all find ourselves in eventually. However, that might not have been the advantage I thought it was back then. It made me too arrogant and less cautious. Surely it was their unbridled adoration of me that had most to do with my super self-confidence and unfortunate foolish mistakes. I was too eager to accept compliments, which I learned makes you less able to see the truth.

"It takes two sets of stairs to get up there," Melinda Sue remarked, astonished when she looked up at the second floor. "How high. You have to go up there daily?"

"Yes, all the bedrooms are up there. There are thirty-six rooms in this mansion," I said. "Even after all these years, there are some I have barely seen myself. I mean, what would be the point of spending any time in a room that hasn't been used for over fifty years, if not more?"

She nodded, amazed. Her gaze moved quickly to the library.

"Are you a reader?" I asked. "We have hundreds of books, some first editions."

"It's the biggest I've seen in any home!" she cried, following me to the doorway. "We all read the latest popular novels. Myrtle Howard is the best reader in our little group. She's been reading a serialized story in the new magazine, *Harper's*, called 'The Simpletons,' but she says it's been censored. My mother doesn't want me reading it even though Myrtle says it's been hacked to death."

"Then I guess we should try to get the uncensored version," I said, and she laughed harder and squeezed my arm.

"Oh, you're so perfect for our club," she squealed.

"Sounds terribly improper. I don't know if I can risk my pure and angelic reputation."

"Fiddlesticks," she said, and giggled.

I showed her the dining room, which she said was the biggest she had ever seen, and then I took her to the ballroom. Her small eyes seemed to double in amazement. Malcolm and Dora were upstairs in his room for his schooling. I explained why the toy train and little village were there and then suggested we have our lunch before we saw anything more of Foxworth.

"Yes, we'll need the energy," she said. "How do you look after something as immense as this?"

"I don't," I said. "I've never touched a mop or a dust cloth and couldn't tell you where to find any."

She giggled and again claimed I was perfect for their club. "We're all quite spoiled."

"I wouldn't know any other way to be," I said. Her giggling was beginning to sound quite immature. Anything I uttered would bring it on.

Finally, she grew more serious when I led her to the kitchen nook.

"How pretty," she said when we sat at the table. "This is the Foxworth emblem, isn't it?" she asked, putting her napkin on her lap.

"Yes, Garland designed it himself, but he

wanted my opinion," I said, "before he confirmed it."

Now I truly wondered if he had or if he had asked just to impress me more that night that led to my being here. When I looked back at the details I recalled, so much seemed planned, contrived. I was quite gullible for someone who thought she was so sophisticated.

"What a beautiful flower arrangement. Everything is so perfect. Thank you. How happy you must be with all this at your beck and call."

I held my smile but didn't reply. Now she reminded me more of a little girl on Christmas morning, maybe myself. There was a time when I was like this, I thought, excited about everything and wide-eyed. Something deep inside me longed for that again. Was it normal to be so nostalgic so young?

Mrs. Wilson and Mrs. Steiner brought out the finger sandwiches and condiments, and Mrs. Steiner poured us glasses of wine, her face barely masking what looked to me to be disapproval. Then they left us. Melinda Sue was looking so intensely at the wine that I wondered if I had made some sort of faux pas by telling Mrs. Wilson to bring white.

"Something wrong? This is an Italian wine my husband brought back from one of his business trips. Would you like me to ask for red wine instead?"

"Oh, no. I just . . ." She leaned toward me. "We drink wine at our girls' social gathering, but otherwise I never have anything alcoholic without my father or my husband present. Naturally, we keep what we do at our club secret."

"How wicked," I said, half-kidding, mostly sarcastic.

"Our husbands have secrets, why not us?" she asked, pursing her lips like some debutante putting on her trifling indignation. I wondered if she used all this on her husband. Garland wouldn't even notice me doing it.

"Yes, why not us?" I parroted.

She smiled, and then she lifted her glass of wine. I did, too, and we toasted.

"To our secrets," she said, and tittered as though she had already drunk too much.

We drank, our eyes fixed on each other's. Which one of us would spill a secret first? I wondered. It did remind me of my younger days, when Daisy Herman and I squeezed the deepest, most tightly held ones out of our much less sophisticated girlfriends and even ourselves when we wanted to sound shocking.

We started to eat.

"Thank you for inviting me."

"Thank you for coming."

She looked more comfortable, comfortable enough to risk some intimate thoughts.

"You were so lucky to fall in love so young

with a man so handsome and so established," she said. "Your parents didn't have time to plan your life."

"Is that what yours did to you?"

She tilted her head to the right, obviously considering whether she should be candid or not, and then nodded. "My parents were afraid I'd make a terrible mistake. I was sort of seeing a young man who didn't come from a family on our level. His father was a plumber, and his mother worked in one of the Foxworth paper mills. He made enough money after a few years to go to college to become a lawyer, but my father didn't believe he ever would succeed and made me stop seeing him. Any note he sent was torn up at the door."

"How dreadful," I said, not denying to myself that my father would have done something similar.

"Yes. He brought my future husband to dinner at our home one night and encouraged our relationship until it was consummated in our marriage. Hammered and nailed in place. Now here I am, Mrs. Clarence Henry Carter. I often wake up hoping it was just a dream."

"So you're not in love with your husband?"

"Let's say I'm in like," she said, and laughed. Then she sighed. "I did complain to my mother before I took my vows, but she insisted that love is an illusion. 'You grow accustomed to

146

someone,' she said. 'That's the best you can hope for.' I'm sure that isn't true for you, not with a man as handsome and as charming as Garland Foxworth."

She probably thought my silence was curious, but she didn't pursue it. We drank our wine and ate.

"So beautiful here," she said, looking out the windows. "How's your little boy? What is he, about five?"

"Yes. He's fine. A handful, or two handfuls," I said, deciding that was all I would say about Malcolm.

"We're going to start a family this year. Clarence plans everything we do like it's part of my father's accounting records or something."

"He uses protection?" I asked.

She wasn't shocked by my question. She looked happy that I had asked it, in fact. "Yes. When we do it, I mean. I find it all quite unromantic, not that we're ever that romantic anyway. I never told this to a soul, even my girlfriends at the social club, but for some reasons I can't describe, I don't mind telling you."

"What?"

"My husband makes love the same way for the same amount of time every time as if he has a stopwatch for a heart. He often does it leaving most of my clothing on."

She took another long sip of her wine. It was

147

giving her courage, that and my expressionless face. She could see I wasn't someone easily shocked.

"I know I'm not unpleasant to look at, but he doesn't seem to need any additional encouragement. I'm sure your lovemaking is quite different."

"Yes, my husband can be quite romantic, and usually it's somewhat different each time," I told her, because it was what she wanted to hear. Besides, I didn't want to in any way suggest my marriage was anything but as spectacular as they all seemed to think, listening to her.

"Mr. Foxworth is always quite debonair. I wish my husband kept in style the way yours does. He has a half dozen suits and never looks to buy anything new. Your husband does. He keeps up with fashion."

"He does that, yes," I said. I smiled at her. "How do you notice him so often?"

"Oh, it's not that often," she said, looking as guilty as a little girl caught shoplifting.

Mrs. Steiner came in to pour us each another glass of wine.

"Everything all right, Mrs. Foxworth?"

"Yes, thank you, Mrs. Steiner."

She smiled at Melinda Sue and left us.

"I was thinking of having Lucas, our driver, take you and me for a ride on the estate. We'd end up at the lake. I wouldn't attempt to take a rowboat out. One of us would develop calluses quickly."

She laughed. "Perhaps Mr. Foxworth will be home by then and he could take us?"

"No. I'm afraid he left on the train for a business trip very early this morning."

She held her glass on her lips and did not sip her wine. Then she lowered it slowly. I saw the way she was avoiding looking directly at me.

"But . . ."

"But what, Melinda Sue?" I sat back, smiling.

"But on my way here . . . I saw him going into the Caroline House. That couldn't have been more than an hour ago," she said.

I held my smile and stared at her. "Are you sure you saw him?"

"Oh, you couldn't make a mistake when it comes to your husband, Corrine."

"Maybe something happened with his travel arrangements," I said. She was holding back something more. "Was he with some people?"

"How difficult it must be for you to have him gone so long," she said, rather than answering.

"Well, I don't know exactly how long, but yes, it is difficult, but my husband has a great many successful business enterprises." I stared at her. "You saw him with other people?"

"Not people," she said, so low that I almost didn't hear.

"Do you know who was with him?"

She looked just like someone who had been knocked over a bit by the wine and who had uttered something she now regretted. As my father would say, the horse was out of the barn. No point in closing the door.

"Do you?"

"Mrs. Catherine Francis," she said. "She's a widow. Her husband died in a carriage accident two years ago. They were only married four years. She inherited a lot of money." She smiled. "I doubt your husband would be interested in her for any reason other than business. He's probably courting her to invest in one of his enterprises. Has he mentioned her?"

"I don't recall," I said, "but I don't pay attention to business talk."

She nodded but kept her gaze lowered.

"However, I'm sure," I continued, "that my husband meets with rich women as well as rich men. To him money is money regardless of whose pocket it comes out of."

"Oh, of course."

I studied her a moment. The silence was thunderous.

"But that's not what you were really thinking when you saw him earlier with this Catherine Francis, was it?" I asked sharply.

"Oh, I swear, I . . . didn't mean to imply anything . . ."

"Of course not." I dabbed my lips with my

napkin and smiled. "Tell me more about your women's social club. When and where do you meet next?"

"My house next Tuesday. Everyone is hoping you'll be there. I mentioned seeing you at the department store, and we had a meeting at Bessie Lawrence's home that night. I must say you were the main topic of conversation. Few have seen that much of you, and only one had attended your wedding, Lillie Chester. Her father is president of the Charlottesville National Bank."

"I don't remember her. There were so many at the wedding. What exactly do you do at your club meetings besides sneak in glasses of wine?"

"We discuss fashions, food, some of the new entertainment. Very little politics, if you're worried about that."

"And gossip?"

"Oh, I won't deny it. My father always says, 'A woman's work is never done if there's one more rumor to spread.'"

"Maybe you should tell me all the rumors about me before I meet with your friends, before I walk into the lion's den, Melinda Sue."

I heard the sharpness in my voice. She sat back as if I might sting her like a bee.

"Oh, dear, I've somehow upset you. I'm so sorry."

"I'm not upset. I'm curious," I said, smiling but with a chill in my eyes for sure. "My father used to say, 'There are two mirrors, one in which you see yourself and one in which you see yourself through the eyes of others. Best to know how others see you before you meet them if you can.'"

"How wise."

"I agree. So?"

She looked down. I poured some more wine into her glass, and she looked up.

"Oh, dear, I think it's going to my head."

"Stomach first," I said, and she laughed as if she would never stop.

She reached for her glass of wine and sipped. "Well, most think of you to be like the Lady of Shalott imprisoned in a tower of sorts, Foxworth Hall. No one has seen you alone anywhere except the department store. Like the lady who sees the world only through a mirror, you, especially you, see it only through your husband. Although I'm sure he's seen enough for two. You're such a mystery," she quickly added.

"Maybe it's better we leave it at that," I said, and her smile faded. I squinted. "More interesting, don't you think? I'm afraid I'd spend most of my time at your club meetings answering questions about my private life and what my husband does or doesn't do when he's not at Foxworth Hall."

She was speechless.

I stared out the window. "It looks quite breezy

suddenly. Perhaps we should postpone the ride around the estate and going to the lake. It might not be pleasant."

"Of course. Whatever you think."

"It's something we can do another time."

"Oh, I'd like that very much."

"Perhaps in the spring," I said.

Mrs. Steiner came in quickly. "Did you want me to prepare your tea, Mrs. Foxworth?"

"No," I said. "Thank you. Maybe later," I added. "Could you inform Lucas that I'll need him to take Mrs. Carter home soon?"

She looked as stunned as Melinda Sue. "Very good, Mrs. Foxworth," she said, and left.

I turned back to Melinda Sue. "I've suddenly developed a headache. I hope you don't mind."

"Oh, no. I'm so sorry. This is entirely my fault. My mouth goes like a steamboat sometimes."

"No need to blame yourself. I just need a little nap," I said. "I've been quite busy with family matters lately. I'm sure you understand how trying that could be."

"Yes, of course," she said, her chin quivering like someone who was about to cry.

I stood, and she did, too.

"I do hope I haven't upset you, Corrine."

"Of course not. I might look dainty, but I assure you I am not."

We started out.

"I really do appreciate your inviting me to

lunch. Foxworth is so overwhelming. Everyone talks about it."

"I'm sure."

"You do have something of a unique bedroom, don't you?" she asked.

I paused. "How exactly did you hear about my bedroom?"

"It's just something people who know Foxworth Hall mention."

"No one but our servants and my husband and I have seen my bedroom these past five years."

She laughed thinly. "I don't know, really. Someone in your house said something to someone, I'm sure. Charlottesville is a much smaller city than people imagine. My mother says, 'Someone can't sneeze without someone on the other side of the city saying God bless you.'"

"Yes, I can see now how that might be true."

Mrs. Steiner was waiting at the door to help her on with her cloak.

"Thank you," she said. "Please tell the cook I enjoyed everything."

Mrs. Steiner nodded and left. I opened the door and, folding my arms across my breasts, stepped out with her. Lucas had brought the carriage to the front. He stepped down, opened the door, and held out his hand to help her up.

She turned to me. "Thank you so much for everything, the tour, a wonderful lunch."

"We'll see each other again."

"I do hope so. And our little club . . . won't you reconsider and join us?"

"I might," I said. "Thank you."

"I do hope your headache gets relieved quickly."

"Thank you."

She leaned forward, and we hugged. Lucas helped her in, glanced at me, and got up to start away.

I stood there and watched her being driven off. She looked back once and waved. I waved back like I imagined the Lady of Shalott might, lifting my hand slowly, tentatively, with an obvious longing, a wish that I could, like Melinda Sue, ride off to pursue her romantic dream.

Mine was fading in ways I hadn't imagined, but, as my mother frequently told me, young girls don't have the vision they will have when they are older and can see much further.

I went into the house and went to the ballroom to watch Malcolm playing with his train set. True to his plan, he had brought down every figurine, soldiers, toy houses, and cars to create his imaginary world. Dora sat off to the side doing some needlework and looked up at me quickly.

"He did very well with his lessons, ma'am."

I nodded. I had no illusions about my son. He didn't do very well because he loved reading; he did very well so he could get back here to play. Maybe he would grow up to be just like his father and create new and profitable businesses.

"Be sure he washes up for dinner when it's time, Dora."

"Yes, ma'am."

Malcolm looked up, that Foxworth irritation visible in his face. "Can I play after dinner, Mama?"

"For a while," I said. "If you don't rush your food."

"He won't," Dora said.

If he could have her follow him through his life, he would never need a lawyer, I thought, and left them to wait for Lucas to return. When he did, I sent Mrs. Wilson out to get him as soon as he had unhitched the horses. She told him to come to me in the library. I decided I would look more authoritative sitting behind Garland's desk. Lucas was very surprised to see me there.

"Ma'am?" he said, approaching.

"You said this morning that you took my husband his things to go on his long journey and he was still at the Caroline House, correct?"

"Yes, ma'am."

"And to be sure, this was where he had a meeting very late last night?"

He stared at me a moment. Confessions were raining down like sleet.

"That was where I had taken him, yes."

"How could his meeting go on through the night?"

156

"I don't know, ma'am."

"I'm a bit confused about what happened after that. Didn't you take him from the Caroline House to the train station?"

"No, ma'am. He was going with someone else in their carriage, I think."

"Who?"

"I don't know, ma'am. Perhaps someone from his business meeting."

I stared at him. He shifted his eyes from me.

"Someday you and I will tell each other the truth, Lucas. I envy my husband for commanding so much loyalty."

He looked down at his hat and twirled it in his hands.

"Okay, Lucas. Thank you," I said.

He nodded, looking grateful for being dismissed. I watched him go and then turned and looked out the window. The sky was graying. I recalled the surge of fear that had passed through my body on my wedding day.

It was returning.

But peering over its shoulder was the face of loneliness, its eyes filled with threat.

"You will not live any longer in this house," I said.

Anyone hearing me and seeing me would think I had gone mad.

# 7

I had underestimated Melinda Sue Carter. Any other young woman I knew or had known would surely have been intimidated by the abrupt manner in which I had ended our luncheon shortly after she had made her rather suggestive comments about Garland. She wrote a few days later to say that despite my reluctance, she was still sponsoring me to become a member of the Charlottesville Women's Club.

Included in her letter was an invitation to their Halloween party occurring in a week. It was going to be a costume party, so I was advised to wear a mask or find a costume. She compared it to a Mardi Gras in New Orleans. They were having music and punch, *punch* double underlined so I would understand it would have something alcoholic in it. It was being held at the home of Amanda McKnight, who had "the biggest grand room but nothing in comparison to Foxworth Hall's ballroom." There was no mention of Garland. The invitation was addressed only to me. It was as if she knew Garland's travel schedule. I had never told her exactly how long he'd be away, so that renewed my suspicions.

Nevertheless, during these years married to

Garland I hadn't attended any social event without him. Many occurred while he was on one of his frequent business trips, but I didn't even reveal that an invitation to one had come to us. They were left on his desk in the library, and only by chance did I notice any. I did nothing about them. He never had told me not to go anywhere without him, but when I mentioned it once to my mother when she visited and saw one of the invitations, she declared it would be highly improper for a married woman to do so. She had never attended any social event without my father.

"The very thought of it puts ice on my spine," she told me, to clearly drive home that I shouldn't even be contemplating such a thing. It was another nail in the door keeping me feeling like a prisoner in my own grand mansion.

I was torn between defiance and embarrassment. Still smarting from the innuendos Melinda Sue had left behind like bread crumbs, I decided to go into Charlottesville a few days later. I had Lucas drop me off at the department store just so he wouldn't have any suspicions concerning my true intentions for the trip. I thought it was just possible he would send a note to Garland if I did anything he thought Garland wouldn't approve, not that he was obviously spying on me or even that Garland had asked him to do so.

However, I suspected Lucas probably knew

more about where my husband was traveling and where he would be on any given day than I did. Surely there were often messages from one or more of the Foxworth businesses that had to be delivered, and I had no doubt he had been given that responsibility.

As he dropped me off, I gave Lucas instructions to return in two hours. He wanted to wait, but I told him that would make me nervous.

"I don't like drawing unnecessary attention, Lucas, especially in Charlottesville. And that's what would happen if you sat out here waiting."

He nodded and started away. When he was gone, I began walking down High Street to the Caroline House. For a few moments, I stood outside working up my courage, and then I entered the lobby. It was large enough to feature two long settees, side tables, and two brown-leather cushion chairs, with a beautiful gilded candle chandelier. On the wall to my left, there was a large painting of a Confederate officer with his sword raised, pointing ahead, and his face lit with that sort of mad excitement that overrides any fear.

The hotel clerk, a balding dark-haired man of about forty, short with what looked like bifocals slipping down the bridge of his bulbous nose, sat behind the high counter reading a copy of the *Virginia Star*, his head barely above the counter. He was so absorbed in what he was reading that he didn't see or hear me enter. The building itself was three stories high, and off to the right of the lobby was clearly a dining room. There were at least a dozen tables, some set for four and six and three set for two in a room with large windows with ruby drapes.

The receptionist finally noticed me.

"I'm sorry," he said, standing. "How can I be of some assistance?"

He was wearing a black vest, a white shirt with a black bow tie, and black pants. When he smiled, he revealed he was missing quite a few back teeth on both sides. His soft, pale lips seemed to sink into his mouth in the corners.

"Thank you," I said, approaching. "I didn't realize how nice the Caroline House is. Is the restaurant open for lunch?"

"For dinner and breakfast only. Breakfast is free for our long-term guests."

"What is a long-term guest?"

"Usually a week or more," he said. "We currently have two," he added proudly. "Are you looking for a place to stay in Charlottesville or looking for a hotel for someone, a visiting relative perhaps?"

"No. I was shopping nearby and realized I had never been to the Caroline House. My husband has been here often for meetings," I added.

"Meetings?" He held his smile. "Oh, dinner meetings."

"Not just dinner meetings. Perhaps the better word is *rendezvous*."

"I'm afraid I don't understand," he said, his eyelids twitching nervously. "Our establishment holds the highest esteem."

"That's probably why my husband comes here."

"Who is your husband?"

"Garland Foxworth," I said.

His smile faded like a nearly empty gaslight trickling dead.

"Do you recall him?" I asked, after his lips seemed to seal closed.

"I . . . not lately," he said. "I'm here only during the day and rarely on weekends."

"Yes, he is away on a business trip," I said.

He nodded, his smile returning but looking forced. Why beat around the bush? I thought.

"Is Mrs. Catherine Francis staying here?"

He shook his head, again pressing his lips together tightly as if he thought words might bubble out.

"She has, though, hasn't she?" I asked, holding my smile.

Again, he nodded, but with obvious reluctance.

"When was she here last?" I asked, with more authority.

His face reddened, his cheeks reaching a dark crimson at the crests. "I'm afraid we've been told to never give out the personal information of our guests unless the police ask us," he said.

"That's personal information?"

He didn't reply, but I continued to stare and wait.

"We've been told by the management that—"

"Thank you," I said abruptly. You didn't have to be a genius to understand what was being said between the lines. He sat the moment I turned to leave, as if talking to me had exhausted him. Then I spun back around, and he popped up again as if he had sat on hot coals.

"Ma'am?"

"Please give her my regards whether she's here or not," I said, smiling.

He looked absolutely terrified. I was boiling inside, but no one could tell. My smile was inscrutable. As I walked away, I didn't look at anyone or hear anything but my own thoughts.

How indiscreet was Garland? How much more did Melinda Sue and her friends know about all this? Was I the only stupid one? Were they all laughing behind my back, mocking the beautiful but young and naive trophy bride? Could Dora know, or Mrs. Steiner? Both she and Mrs. Wilson went to Charlottesville often. How thick and free was the gossip? Was Garland so arrogant about it that he didn't care? What did this Catherine Francis look like? How could he choose to be with an older woman rather than me? Where was all this going? How many more women was he seeing? Was he really on business trips?

I felt like such a little idiot, shut away in my castle. Yes, yes, I was the Lady of Shalott. Melinda Sue and her hens had pecked me right.

Whom could I confide in? Certainly not strangers or that pack of gossipmongers in Melinda Sue's social club. I had to go home to Alexandria for a day or so, I thought. I had to talk to my mother or my father, maybe both, about this. I knew how they felt about my marriage and life. My mother's infamous "You made your bed behind my back, now sleep in it" haunted me, as well as my father's favoring Garland's business skills and his votes over my future happiness, but how would they react to this? Wasn't this different? In a real sense, weren't they being insulted, too?

I spun around and started toward the train station. I would buy a ticket today for tomorrow morning, I thought, but first send a telegram.

How ironic. Almost five years ago, I had been in this telegraph office to tell my father I was coming home from my great-aunt Nettie's because Garland had disappointed me. Garland had sent a message that he wouldn't be coming to get me the day after I had drunk too much limoncello and he had taken advantage of me. We were supposed to spend the day at Foxworth. He was shocked to discover I was a virgin at the time. I had no one to blame but myself, I had thought. Any man would have found me quite sophisticated for my age. I never admitted to being otherwise.

Nevertheless, even after all the disappointment in him, I hadn't been able to clamp down on my feelings for Garland. My heart had been softened for forgiveness, and he had been so sincere when he proposed I could do nothing else but accept if my parents did. When I thought about it while I was walking now, it was as if I was thinking about a girl completely different from the woman I now was. I would never have admitted it at the time, but I was as vulnerable and as naive as any of the girls my age whom I had ridiculed. Fools all.

The man who had taken my telegraph message back then was still there. I wasn't sure he remembered me, but when he saw me enter, his eyes brightened, and he certainly looked like he knew who I was now. He still had a thick black mustache but with strands of gray. I remembered he looked like he had almost no chin. Nearly bald then, he was completely so now. When he smiled, he revealed he had lost more of his teeth, one prominently in the front.

I nodded, picked up the pen, and wrote out the telegram. It was simple and quite unrevealing.

*Visiting tomorrow. I'll be on the early train.*
*Corrine*

I had it sent to my father's bank office. They'd both be surprised. I hadn't been home since they had their open-house party in their new home. After that, they had always come to see me, Garland, and Malcolm. After all, how could they pass up an opportunity to visit Foxworth Hall? My mother gathered as much as she could to describe and enthrall her catty friends with when she returned home.

"You're Mrs. Foxworth, ain'tcha?" the clerk asked when I handed it to him.

"Yes, I am."

"I seen your picture in the paper from time to time and saw you go past in that fancy carriage a few times."

"I'm glad you're so observant," I said. "How much for that?" I asked, nodding at the note.

I gave him the coins and then watched him start to send it.

After he finished, I started to leave, then paused and looked back at him.

"Are you from Charlottesville?"

"Yes, ma'am, born and raised, as was my daddy."

"Did you know the Foxworths back then?"

"Everyone knew the Foxworths, ma'am. And the Foxworths knew you one way or t'other."

"What does that mean?"

"You were either on the good side or bad. There was no in between. That's what my daddy use-ta say. But you, ma'am, you brung 'em somethin' nice, somethin' they didn't have far as I knew."

"What's that?"

"Beauty, ma'am. Pure and simple," he said, smiling like a pumpkin set out for Halloween.

"Maybe it's not enough," I mumbled to myself, and left.

After I bought my train ticket, I returned to the department store to shop for something I didn't need and meet Lucas at the appointed time.

When we arrived at Foxworth Hall and he was helping me out, I informed him of my intentions to visit my parents and what time I'd be leaving.

"Yes, ma'am," he said. Especially when Garland was gone, Lucas tried hard to avoid looking directly at me. The second he finished a sentence or just a word like *yes,* he would look down.

"Where exactly is my husband right now, Lucas? Don't tell me you don't know, either," I said sharply.

He looked up, glanced at me, took a breath, and said, "On his way to London, ma'am."

"London? He didn't say he was going to London."

"That's all I know, ma'am."

"Somehow I doubt that's all you know, Lucas," I said, and went into the mansion, walking quickly before he could offer to open the door.

If I had to venture a guess, I thought, I'd say Catherine Francis was in London right now, too.

I raged back at the wall of portraits, what I now thought was more a wall of rogues. *None of you can look down on anyone else,* I thought. *This is a family of scoundrels.*

I went upstairs to pack a small overnight bag. Dora and Malcolm were down in the ballroom, Malcolm playing with his trains and toy people, houses, and animals. The seeds of the godlike Foxworths were being planted and exercised. His fingers and his imagination gave him the power to move families, cause accidents, save lives, and change day to night. It was a rehearsal for the day he would sit on the throne and really affect how people lived. How bitter I suddenly felt, and how guilty over how easily it could spread to my son.

I stopped packing for a moment and sat on the swan bed, gazing around helplessly. From the day I had first seen it, seen this fantasy room, I thought it would be perfect for romance. I wondered, of course, why it had been kept as more of a museum piece and never used. The little changes I had made in lamps and pictures did nothing to diminish the wonder of its colors and the wonderful dreamlike atmosphere the graceful and beautiful swan projected.

Who wouldn't want to make love beneath her? What made Garland avoid it? Why, in fact, had our lovemaking become so mechanical, quick, and far between these past years? Why did he feel so much guilt, enough for him to create this dark fantasy with Dora? Would I mention it to my parents? I should, I thought, and yet that trembling returned, the trembling that began inside me every time I planned on revealing it or asking him direct questions about it.

I had no doubt that Dora knew more than she was telling me. Even after all this time, any reference to it put her in a small panic. She stuttered, looked for ways to escape, and answered my questions as vaguely as she could. The implication was clear. She had actually come right out with it once: if she said too much, Garland would send her away and take revenge on her brother.

Occasionally, I would make a vague reference to Mrs. Steiner or Mrs. Wilson by mentioning Garland's mother's clothes and how he guarded them like gold. My comments were always met with silence or a shrug, sometimes just a nod. Once Mrs. Wilson said, "It's through the possessions of your dear departed ones that you hold on to memories. Once someone is forgotten, he or she dies a second death."

I recalled that was something Garland had told me, almost word for word. Did loyalty to the Foxworths go so deep as to affect the words these servants used or thought?

And yet how could I complain about that idea, that way to preserve the memory of someone you had loved?

However, I was sure there was more to it; there had to be. Garland was certainly not a religious man. He had no older brother or even a sister to confide in now. He had little contact with the more distant relatives. As far as I could see, he shared some of his most intimate or most secret thoughts only with Lucas, who moved about him like some shadow, turning where he turned, following where he went, and going wherever he wanted him to go. Lucas kept Garland's words as sacrosanct as a priest in a confessional kept a sinner's.

A man who carried heavy guilt and had no place to go or no one to go to in order to relieve himself quite understandably invented or resurrected the one person he might have trusted in his life, his mother. I certainly, even after five years, couldn't fill that role. It was painful to realize that I probably never would. Yes, in so many ways, I had married a stranger and remained one, even to my own child and especially to all the servants.

I finished packing and went down to inform Mrs. Wilson and Mrs. Steiner of my trip to visit my parents.

"That's very nice, Mrs. Foxworth," Mrs. Wilson said. "Too many young girls forget their parents when they marry. It's truly like the bird leaving the nest. Birds fly by their mothers without so much as glancing or waving a wing at them."

"And then there are those who never stop

circling them," I muttered, loudly enough for both of them to hear. I watched their eyes. They looked at each other quickly and then back at what they were doing.

I left to look in on Malcolm and Dora. Dora was sitting off to the side, reading, and Malcolm was totally absorbed with what was becoming his toy city, his own little Charlottesville. It looked like he had doubled the width and length of it from when I had seen it the last time.

"You build things as fast as your father," I said, and he looked up.

"Mama, the train can go backward, too!"

"It can?"

I looked at Dora.

"He discovered how to do that himself," she said.

I couldn't believe how much I resented her taking pride in him, but at the moment, I felt like slapping her. I didn't need his achievements pointed out. Or did I? Maybe I should be slapping myself.

Instead, I went over to Malcolm and lowered myself to the floor beside him. His eyes widened with surprise and glee.

"Show me," I said, and he went about doing it.

The more joy I took in watching him explain and do, the more I felt the tears falling inside me. How could I love my son if I lived in a house without love for me? He was, after all, an integral part of this house and this family. He was first and foremost a Foxworth.

Later I made sure to have dinner with him and described the real train rides I had taken and the one I was going to take tomorrow. He surprised me by asking if he could come along. I looked up at Dora. I didn't want her going with me on this visit, but without her, Malcolm could distract my parents and take their concentration and interest away from my purpose.

"It's only going to be an overnight trip this time, Malcolm," I said. "I'll take you on a longer trip."

"When?" he asked, with those Garland eyes that focused so hard on you that you couldn't make a general, noncommittal response.

"We'll take the train to Virginia Beach and maybe do some cycling along the water on the boardwalk," I said.

His face exploded with excitement. He turned to Dora. "Dora, too?"

"Maybe we'll give Dora a day off," I suggested. "She has one coming."

He looked at me suspiciously. "You won't change your mind, will you, Mama?"

"Not as long as you don't do anything bad," I said.

He still looked skeptical. "Pinkie promise?" he asked, holding out his hand.

"Who taught you that?"

He looked at Dora.

"Something I did with my mother," she confessed.

"People who demand you make promises already show they don't believe what you say," I told him, but he didn't take away his hand.

I did the pinkie promise, and we went back to eating. He was full of questions about our prospective trip now. Would there be a bike his size? How far would we pedal? What if it rained? Would we also go rowing in the ocean? Would I buy him more toy people and houses? What about the rides? It was as if I had opened a dam. I barely had time to chew and swallow.

Afterward I was happy to send him back to the ballroom with Dora and go up to rest for my trip and plan on what exactly I would tell my parents. I had to make them see this wasn't simply conjecture. To me there was clear evidence my husband had been and was unfaithful. It was a restless night for me, but I was up early to prepare. I wasn't going to look like some house-wrecked wife. I wasn't going to arrive with my tail between my legs.

Because I knew how I hated train travel now and how nauseated it could make me, I made sure to have a small breakfast. My departure occurred before Malcolm was up and Dora was getting him dressed, but when she came to bring down my overnight bag, I left instructions for him, something I ordinarily didn't do. Most of the time I permitted Dora to design his activities.

"I don't want him spending all his free time in the ballroom with those trains. He needs to be out in the fresh air, too. Make sure of that," I said.

"Yes, ma'am." She avoided my eyes. She always did when I spoke to her sternly. Nevertheless, her fear was palpable.

"When I return, I want to have a real heart-to-heart talk with you, Dora."

She looked up. "Have I done anything wrong, anything to upset you?"

"I don't know. Yet," I added. Let her worry about it, I thought. She'd be more truthful when I wanted her to be. I nodded at the door. "Lucas should be waiting for me."

She walked ahead. I checked my appearance one more time and followed her down the stairs and out where Lucas was indeed waiting. He looked nervous and moved quickly to help me into the carriage, making sure I was comfortable.

*They're all walking on tiptoes today,* I thought. *They sense something is very wrong. Good.*

When we arrived at the train station, Lucas wished me a good trip. I made sure Lucas knew exactly when to be back to greet me on my return. From my seat, I watched him hurry back to the carriage. Would he go right home, or would he go right to the telegraph office to inform Garland I had left Foxworth Hall? My telegraph operator would certainly be curious. I wondered how Garland would react. Would he be angry, frightened, and worried about his precious reputation?

I sat back to close my eyes and think. My parents' house opening was almost four years ago. I felt a mixture of emotions returning now, but for some reason, fear was the strongest. What if my parents didn't support me, weren't at all outraged for me, and sent me home feeling more alone than ever?

I was disappointed when I arrived at the Alexandria station. My father wasn't there in person to greet me. He had sent a carriage with my name on a placard. I waved to the driver, who hurried to get my bag. He looked like Abraham Lincoln with his beard, his height, and the rather sad expression Lincoln was depicted and photographed wearing throughout the Civil War. Bad omen, I thought, and boarded the carriage.

So much of Alexandria had changed since I had gotten married and moved to Foxworth Hall. It obviously hadn't lagged behind when it came to streets and lanterns, storefronts and sidewalks. We actually had to pass my father's bank on the way, but I saw no point in stopping to see him there. Privacy was what we needed now, and I wanted my mother and father together when I spoke. Checking the time, I saw he would be home in an hour if he followed his usual schedule. I was confident he was as intrigued as my mother about why I was making this sudden visit.

She was at the door when we drove up, obviously sitting near the front windows, waiting and watching for me.

"What's happened?" she demanded before I reached the entrance.

The driver carried my bag behind me. "I can take that now," I told him, and reached for it. He nodded and left.

"Well?" my mother asked when I entered.

"I'd like to freshen up first, Mother, if you don't mind. The train ride was quite tiring and dusty."

"You know where the guest room is," she said. "I'll be in the kitchen. Tonight is your father's night for a pork chop and applesauce. I assume you'll have the same."

"Whatever. I'm not that hungry."

She looked at me askance. My mother was aging faster than she had hoped she would, I was sure. I would never deny that my mother was an attractive woman with nearly perfect features. How could I be pretty if she were otherwise? She was tall and regal and had hands as pretty as mine. When I was younger and would catch her sitting quietly by herself, I thought her face was like one carved in ivory, a cameo, and her blue-gray eyes, not stained with anger or disgust, were strikingly attractive.

Gray strands had invaded her hair with a vengeance. I was surprised at how she was letting it just go whichever way Nature decided. In my mind Nature was not gentle or forgiving. Her features were corrupted somewhat by the way her skin was starting to sag and her pallor losing whatever hold it had on a youthful, healthy look with soft crimson in the crests of her cheeks. Her lips looked thinner and her eyes tired. I never noticed until this moment how her shoulders had begun to sink and her back to rise just below the base of her neck.

I didn't feel as much pity for her as I felt fear for myself. Would I age as quickly? What would I be without my beauty? I despised the thought of my being stodgy and irritable, my posture gone, my arms hanging like two branches drenched in ice. Standing there, I realized that we see the changes in our loved ones more clearly the more time we are apart. It was as if during the days, months, and years you were separated, age had a freer hand. Was this how it was and how it would be between Garland and myself, no matter what? After each of these long business trips, when he set eyes on me, would he see more and more of my faults and less of my beauty? Unless your love for each other was deep and powerful, time would sweep away affection. You could grow to despise the very sight of each other without those immortal moments of warmth and fondness.

"I do hope this isn't some overly dramatic crisis in your life, Corrine. Your father has enough to burden him in these difficult financial times."

"I'll wash up," I said, and, without further comment, turned and walked down the hallway to the short stairway that led to the guest room.

When I stepped in, I simply stood there looking around for a moment. Every room in every house looked like a cupboard to me now. Whenever I left Foxworth Hall, it was as if the world had shrunk. Even my thoughts could be crowded in a bedroom this small. I put my bag down and sat on the bed for a moment. My mother's instant reluctance to permit me to complain told me this was not going to be the place where I would find sympathy easily. I framed my words, planning on how I would make my parents feel more abused than me.

By the time I had washed and changed and started down, my father had arrived. They were both sitting in their living room anticipating what had brought me home so suddenly. Despite being less than a quarter of the size of my living room, or the Foxworths', I should say, their room struck me as far more cozy and comfortable. My father still had his favorite soft-cushioned chair with his footstool. My mother sat in another, and I was obviously to take the settee across from them.

Unlike my mother, my father hadn't aged as quickly. He had some gray hair, even in his eyebrows, but his face was as robust, and he was, as always, obviously dedicated to his physique. He was certainly not as muscular as a laborer, but he didn't look as soft and pudgy as most bank executives his age or even younger.

"Hello, Daddy," I said. I approached him as he leaned forward for me to kiss him on the cheek. "You look well."

"Thank you. You're taking good care of yourself, too, Corrine."

He glanced at my mother. Was that a small reprimand for the way she was letting herself go? I sat.

"Well, let's not waste time," my father continued. "For you to come rushing here would take something serious. Are you sick? Is Garland ill, or Malcolm?"

"I'm fine, and so is Malcolm. Garland is not ill unless you consider adultery a disease," I said. I waited. Neither spoke or stopped staring at me with stolid faces.

My mother shifted in her seat and sighed.

"And you know this how?" my father asked.

I told them about Melinda Sue, her women's club, the gossip, and crowned it all with a detailed description of the exchange between myself and the hotel clerk at the Caroline House.

"A widow?" my mother said, looking almost amused. "And wealthy?"

"I doubt that money would be Garland's prime reason anyway, Mother. Although I know he likes to get people to invest in his enterprises."

I glared at my father.

He sat back. "Have you confronted him?" he asked.

"No. He's not home. I suspect he's traveling in England with her as we speak."

Both were silent.

"I think it's a terrible act of disrespect to drag our family through the muck," I said. "Eventually," I added, when that drew no response, "it will seep into the Alexandria social world, if it hasn't already, and you will be embarrassed, too."

"When one enters the world you're in and the world we've been in for most of our lives," my father said slowly, speaking just the way he did when he was going over a financial issue at the bank, "we expect gossip behind our backs. For most of these people, that's all there is. Perhaps you're blowing this out of proportion. It might be just that, gossip."

"Well, how do you tolerate it?" I demanded.

He shrugged. "Most of what happens to us in our lives can be overcome by ignoring it. It's like a terrible icy rain. You wait, and eventually it's a memory, sometimes not even that."

"Men of that stature and wealth are prone to such things," my mother said. "Your father's right. That comes and goes like a bad day. It's far worse to harp on it and destroy your marriage. These dilettantes are throw-away napkins," she said. "What sort of a future will they have, rich or not?"

"I don't care about her future. I care about my own. I care about our family's reputation."

"You didn't care about that the night you conceived Malcolm," my mother said.

"Now, now. No reason to rake up past errors," my father said. "You are the mistress of Foxworth Hall, Corrine. You have a position almost all women would envy. This will pass. Perhaps Garland suffers his own passing regrets. Even if your worst suspicions are true, he'll realize it's a waste of his time to chase some widow, and he'll come back to you stronger and be even more dedicated to you and Malcolm."

I stared at him a moment and then looked at my mother. What was he really saying?

"Did you . . ." I lived with some suspicion whenever I considered how indifferent my mother seemed to passion. "Why do you say these things?"

"Let's not get into such a discussion," he said. "We appreciate your coming to us for advice. Let's have a wonderful dinner together and talk about happier things. The future bodes well for us all. Things are improving in the country, although I'm sure you don't lack for anything."

"Maybe everlasting love," I said in almost a whisper. If they did hear it, neither responded.

I looked at my mother. She was complacent, satisfied with my father's rationalization. This was who she was her whole life, I thought. No wonder it was always deep inside me and strong to become someone she wasn't.

My father slapped down on the arms of his chair and rose. "Your mother makes the greatest pork chops," he said, smiling.

Were they deaf? Hadn't they heard a thing I had said?

She rose, too. "The table's set," she said.

"I have this wonderful French rosé," my father said. "A gift from a client. That alone will be worth your coming to see us."

He held out his hand.

Somewhere, deep in the chambers of my mind, I could hear the cry.

*You are alone. Whether or not you will be forever is entirely up to you.*

# 8

My father, either to avoid me or simply to keep to the schedule he lived by, was gone by the time I went down in the morning for coffee. He had left no message except to have my mother tell me he hoped I would have a good trip home.

I wouldn't eat much more than a slice of toast and jam. My mother looked so nervous without my father there that I didn't even suggest again the real reason I had come. Afraid I would, she talked, really babbled, about some of the new things she was doing with their house, a new piece of needlework she had started, and some gossip about her neighbors, none of which interested me. She barely paused for a breath. Her life seemed built on a foundation of trivialities. Would this be my life in a few years, too? It was almost that now.

I finally interrupted her to ask if she had either seen or heard anything about my best friend, Daisy Herman.

"Daisy Herman? You haven't heard at all from her?"

"Not because I didn't want to," I said with clear bitterness.

"Daisy married a railroad man two years ago. They moved to New York. Odd that she didn't invite you to her wedding. You two were inseparable."

"She wasn't invited to mine, you'll remember. My husband wanted me to cut all contacts with my friends so I would not look as young as I was. Neither you nor Daddy opposed that idea at the time."

She picked up a dish and went to the sink. I watched her hovering over it.

"Remember?" I pressed.

"Marriage is like a rebirth," she began, not turning to look at me. She reminded me of someone just speaking her thoughts. "Especially for a woman in 1895, Corrine. You enter your husband's world, and the door closes behind you. People often say a man's home is his castle. They don't say a woman's home is her castle, do they?"

She turned around, folding her arms around herself as if she was afraid she would come apart.

"What they also don't say, but it's there clearly, is that the man is the king, the emperor. I warned you of that many, many times. I knew that it was never as true as it was for you living in a mansion built by a family with all that heritage and power. I'm happy for you and sorry for you, just the way I was for myself, but whatever has happened to me has and will happen ten times to you. Make your peace with that reality, Corrine, or you'll never enjoy one moment of happiness despite all your wealth and privilege."

"Swallow down the sour milk and smile?"

"Yes," she said.

"Maybe I won't," I said. "And whatever happens will happen to me because I chose it so and not because my husband deemed it so with a wave of his hand."

She looked at me for a moment and then nodded. "A man and a woman have a child, and in that mix, someone totally different emerges. Maybe that's good; maybe it isn't. It's too late for me to do anything about it. I'm sure you don't believe it, but I did my best bringing you up. I wish you well. You've made me angry, at times very angry, but in my heart I want only good things for you. That's all I can do now for you, wish you the best."

She turned back to the sink. I sat there a while thinking about her. I had the deep and terrible feeling that this good-bye might be a forever good-bye. I almost didn't utter it.

After I thanked her for breakfast, I went to gather my things and meet the taxi carriage to take me to the station and home, for where I was going was home whether I liked it or not. The ride home in the morning seemed to take twice the time and was twice as uncomfortable for me, perhaps because it was crowded and noisy.

Lucas was right there waiting when the train pulled into the Charlottesville station. He looked more timid than usual, leaning over and staring down at his feet, avoiding anyone's glance. The moment I emerged, he hopped off the carriage to get my bag.

"Welcome home, ma'am," he said, as if I had been gone weeks or traveled across the country to get here.

"I was away barely more than a day, Lucas."

"Yes, ma'am."

"How long is Mr. Foxworth to be in London, Lucas?"

"Only a few days." He stood there a moment, deciding whether he should say more.

"And? When will he be home, then?"

"The crossing normally takes seven to ten days depending on the weather, but he's taking the SS *Majestic*, a double-screw steamship. So it will be sooner than normally, I'm sure. He's sailing out of Liverpool."

Alone? It was on the edge of my lips to ask, but I didn't ask it. I sat back, and we were off. It wasn't until Foxworth Hall came into view that I made up my mind. I would attend Melinda Sue's group's Halloween party at Amanda McKnight's, but I wasn't going to let her know. I was simply going to appear in some costume and mask and be their mystery guest for a while. The very thought of it brought some excitement and glee.

What a fool I had been to sit back and wait for my husband to complete his mix of business and pleasure all the time. What an obedient little wife, denying herself her own pleasure. I had been more like my mother than I had ever wished I would be. That would end now, end forever, I vowed.

The moment Lucas opened the grand doors for me, Dora appeared. The way she clutched her hands and pressed them to her bosom and the look on her face told me she was a model nervous Nellie. My father often called particular customers at the bank that name, explaining it came from "old Nell," an expression for a high-strung nag. Dora's teeth looked like they were chattering. I had forgotten my telling her that we would have a heart-to-heart talk on my return. She had probably been grinding her thoughts and fears about it the entire time I had been away. She hurried to take my bag from Lucas.

"Welcome back, ma'am. Was your journey pleasant?"

"It was horrid," I said. "Smelly and bumpy, noisy and crowded. How can so many afford the train, and why do they permit all that smoking? How is Malcolm?"

"He's fine, ma'am. He's been doing his lessons proper and is playing in the ballroom. Should I fetch him?"

"No," I said. I turned to Lucas, who was still

standing behind me in the doorway. "Thank you, Lucas. I will need your services Saturday at seven p.m."

"Yes, ma'am," he said, and quickly stepped out, closing the door.

"Just take my bag up to my room and then bring up some cold water. Ask Mrs. Steiner to look in on Malcolm while you and I talk," I said.

All the color left her face. She nodded and rushed ahead of me to the stairway. I went into the library and sat for a while to catch my breath and gather my thoughts. The impact of my parents' indifference to my plight really hadn't sunk in until I had stepped back into Foxworth. Despite the vows of matrimony and the authority I had over the servants here, the mansion remained a foreign world. The very house itself, with its size and its antiques, kept me subordinate, timid, and helpless. How small I could feel in the darkness of its shadows, shadows cast by all of its oppressive history. I was afraid to raise my voice here. I was as terrified of breaking something old and Foxworthy as any guest might be. I saw myself now as the servants probably always had: just another possession Garland had brought home and put in its proper place.

The fires that had simmered under my breast from my wedding day until now flared up. I actually could sense the heat rise through my neck to my face. When I touched my cheeks, the tips of my fingers felt singed. Because of my weakness and indiscretion that fateful night, my limoncello night, my mother believed I had sentenced myself to a fate I had to accept. My father evaluated it the way he would any investment. My life had become another profit-and-loss statement. A little sadness here and then some happiness there. Subtract the sadness, and you have net happiness.

So if I followed his thinking, I was destined to search every corner, take a candle to every pool of darkness, and explore every cupboard to find some crumbs of happiness and delight. Be satisfied with that, I told myself, or suffer regrets until like rust they weakened your heart and turned you into some wrinkled and broken woman not even worthy of self-pity, much less the compassion of strangers.

I would not remain complacent, I thought. I would resurrect Corrine Dixon in this house, in this life. I would walk straighter, firmer, challenge every scorning ancestor and especially Garland, until like some wild, untamed animal, all that was Foxworth would cower before me. Either that, or I would destroy it. If anyone or anything was going up in flames, it would be Foxworth Hall and not me. Oh, no, not me, I vowed, and rose.

I walked up the stairs slowly and so unlike that first day, my wedding day. Every step I took this time was firm, the gait of a true mistress, a lady so unlike the Lady of Shalott that no one would dare compare me to her again.

Dora had brought up my water and was waiting in the Swan Room. I paused for a moment. She was looking at the image on the headboard as if she thought it was real. She was reaching out as if to touch it for luck or something. How often, I wondered, had she been in here before I had married Garland? Could she be so clever and conniving as to study everything there was about his mother and then deliberately do things to get him to think of her that way? Had she put on his mother's dress that day knowing he would find her in it?

I knew Arrogance walked these halls, but was Paranoia right behind it?

"Sit," I said.

She instantly brought her hand back, spun around, and guiltily moved to the chair. I realized it would be more effective for me to stand over her. She continued to look down at her hands in her lap like some child about to be reprimanded.

"I have had a difficult two days, Dora. I don't have to explain any of the details to you to convince you. Just know that my patience has flown out the window like an escaped canary. I want straight, honest answers now. Do you understand?"

"Yes, ma'am." She looked up and nodded.

"I knew you were expecting my husband the night Malcolm deliberately hurt himself, but when was the last time before that when you dressed in my dead mother-in-law's clothes and waited in her room for him?"

"Oh, weeks and weeks ago, ma'am." She saw that I was expecting a better answer. "Five days before Mr. Foxworth left on his previous trip. I always check the room, service it as he wishes, and that day saw his mother's dress on the bed."

I nodded and paced a moment, reviewing the time, Melinda Sue's innuendos, and Garland's recent behavior. I turned back to her, feeling more like a prosecutor in a courtroom.

"You have told me he cries and confesses. Five days before his last trip, did he confess to being with another woman, maybe being with other women since we've been married? Well?" I followed up quickly so she couldn't think of any vague answers.

"I really can't say, ma'am."

"I warned you about my patience, Dora," I said, stepping back up to her and glaring down at her.

"It's not that I don't want to tell you; it's that I can't, ma'am."

"Whatever threats he made I will double. You will be out of here tomorrow," I said. "No, I'll have you gone today."

My hands were clenched. I could feel the strain in my neck.

"I can't!" she cried. "Because . . ."

"Because what? Damn you, woman."

"Because I really don't remember what he said that last time, ma'am." She started to cry, flicking the tears off her cheeks.

"You can't remember exactly what he said last time?" I stepped back, grimacing. "What sort of an answer is that? You recalled other times, other things he had said." I thought a moment. "Did he get you drunk? Is that why? Did he give you some of that limoncello?"

"Oh, no, ma'am."

"Well, how do you account for this lack of memory for that particular night, then?"

"I once told you that I said things and I didn't know from where they came. But I also . . . I think sometimes I swoon because I suddenly realize where I am and that Mr. Foxworth is gone. That last time something like that happened and he'd left the room before I was conscious again."

I looked at her askance. "You want me to believe that?"

"It is the truth, ma'am."

I was beginning to think I was right about her. She was not innocent and helpless. She was conniving and clever.

"I'm starting to wonder if you know what the truth looks like, Dora."

"Oh, I do, ma'am."

I stood there with my hands on my hips, staring at her.

She hesitated, took a deep breath, and then rolled up her right sleeve and turned her arm.

"What is that?"

"I don't know, ma'am. It wasn't there before I came to Foxworth Hall."

I reached for her hand and lifted her arm. A cut across her wrist had scarred. I couldn't tell how deep it had gone, but whatever had been used to cut it had been jagged enough to prevent a good healing. I let go of her hand and stepped back.

"Who knows about this?"

"My aunt knew. Mrs. Wilson knows, I'm sure, although I was never to mention it, and neither has mentioned it to me."

"Who did this to you?"

"I don't know, ma'am."

"What are you telling me, Dora? After one of these sessions with my husband, you woke up and found you were bleeding?"

She took a deep breath and nodded.

"You don't believe Mrs. Foxworth's ghost did it, do you?"

"I don't know, ma'am."

"Of course my husband did it. No ghost did it."

"Yes, ma'am."

I thought a moment. A possible realization frightened me, but I didn't reveal my alarm. I wanted her to keep talking. This cut, this ugly slice, was dangerously close to where leeches drained people of their blood to drop a fever or where people deliberately cut themselves to step out of this world.

She wore his mother's dress. She was in his mother's bed, and he was talking to her as if she was his mother. How much did he want that to feel true?

"Did his mother attempt to . . . what do you know about her?"

She looked even more terrified.

"I'm ordering you to tell me and tell me now, Dora."

"My aunt says she did, but fortunately, Dr. Ross was here with Mr. Foxworth at the time. He had just returned from a hunting trip, and they were celebrating his kills. That's all I know, ma'am. I swear."

She raised her hand as if she indeed thought we were in a courtroom. I studied her. I was wrong to be so suspicious. She really was too simple to make all this up, I thought.

"Who treated your arm?"

"Just my aunt. It wasn't as bad as it could have been, but unfortunately, there's this scar."

"So she saw you in Mrs. Foxworth's dress?"

She nodded.

"Did she ask you about it?"

"No, ma'am. My aunt is one of those people who don't want to turn over a rock and look at the ants. I'm probably more like her than I think."

Something even more chilling occurred to me.

"Did Malcolm ask you about this? I'm sure he's seen it?"

"Yes, ma'am, but I told him it was an accident when I was a child. I was playing with my father's tools, and I shouldn't have. I hoped it would be a warning to him."

"Odd that he cut himself in almost the same place on his arm."

She didn't seem to grasp my point. I paced and nodded and then stepped in front of her again.

"Okay. This thing you do with my husband will end now. You won't do it again, Dora. I've never meant anything as much as I mean this. After he comes home, if there is a dress on the bed, you will come to me first. Just leave that dress on the bed."

"But he'll—"

"Do nothing. I assure you," I said. I straightened up, glanced at the swan and then at her. Right now Dora looked small and as afraid as an eight-year-old child. "Okay. Let's not talk again about this. I promise no more questions if you do what I told you to do. Will you?"

She nodded.

"Go prepare my bath. I'm actually hungry tonight. I've barely eaten anything all day. Tell Mrs. Wilson I fancy having her chicken stew.

Then get Malcolm ready for dinner. Go on, Dora. Carry on as usual," I said, "and tell no one about this conversation, not even your aunt. Maybe especially your aunt," I added, thinking. I never did trust Mrs. Steiner. She was here too long. The Foxworths were like an insidious rash crawling up and into your body, demanding loyalty. That was probably why she hadn't asked Dora any detailed questions about her wound.

Dora nodded, wiped her eyes, and left.

I turned and looked at the swan again. Sometimes I imagined it raising its head and that eye looking right at me.

"It's going to change," I promised. "It's all going to change."

I glanced at the party invitation. I knew exactly where I would go to find a costume. I'd bring Dora along with me this time. I would go up to the attic. I had new courage. We'd go up there tonight with candles, and let rats and other vermin be damned. I vowed that this house would not rule me. In time, it would fear me and not vice versa.

I told Dora my plan right before dinner. She didn't look frightened; she looked surprised and then almost happy about it. Maybe Dora knew more about what was in my heart than I did.

At dinner Malcolm greeted me with "When are we going on our trip to the beach?"

It was as if he had never noticed I had gone to

see my parents and thought I had just come down from the Swan Room.

"How are you, too, Malcolm?" I said. Then I imitated him in his sometimes whiny voice. "And how was your trip, Mama? How big was the train? Were my grandparents okay? I missed you, Mama."

He looked at me askance and then clenched his fist around his fork and jabbed it into his tomato, his lips curled and his eyes full of rage.

"It's already dead, Malcolm," I said.

Mrs. Steiner laughed. I looked up at her and then at Dora. I smiled and returned to my salad.

After dinner, I forced Malcolm to sit in the library with me and do his reading. Dora sat next to him to help him pronounce words. He thought he was going to be able to play in the ballroom, but by the time he was finished, I saw he was fighting to keep awake.

"You'll go to sleep now," I told him. "Dora will take you up, help you with your bath, and put you to bed."

"I wanted to play."

"If you go to sleep, you can play in the morning right after breakfast. We'll give you a day off from your lessons."

He looked at me suspiciously. Skepticism was rampant in the Foxworths' blood. Eyes always narrowed, and corners of mouths always tightened into smirks. I could see it in one of the portraits of great-great-uncles and aunts.

"When I tell you something, Malcolm, I mean it. I don't lie or trick you. I'm your mother." I almost added, *Not your father.*

His narrowed eyes softened. Someday he might understand why I was constantly reinforcing that fact, but I feared it might be too late.

Dora stood, and he followed her out, looking back only once to be sure I wasn't smiling after fooling him.

Garland's little boy, I thought. For sure.

Later I went up and met Dora in the hallway. She had two lanterns ready.

"What are we looking for, exactly?" she asked.

"Something fit for Halloween. Shouldn't be hard when we go through the things that belonged to this family."

She fought back a smile and led the way.

It suddenly occurred to me. "Have you ever been to the attic, Dora?"

"Yes, ma'am. I had to go up to get Malcolm. I bawled him out for going there, but he was intrigued by the old things, swords, and old toys. I was the one who asked Olsen to put the key in the lock. I'm sorry. I forgot he had done so and I didn't just return, lock the door, and take the key."

"Knowing Malcolm, he would have found another way to get up there," I said, and she nodded.

When we reached the door to the attic stairway, we paused. Without any stars or moon sending some light through the tall windows, it looked like a pit of dark hell.

"We could go up tomorrow in the morning," Dora said.

"It's fine. I might want to work on the costume during the day and, if I don't like it, go back up there to look for something different."

I went forward, opened the door, and started up the stairway. The boards beneath us complained as they had done when I had gone looking for Malcolm. I could hear some scurrying about, but, probably because I was motivated by more than anger now, I never hesitated, and neither did Dora. She followed, the two lanterns now throwing enough light to see around clearly. We walked past some Confederate uniforms hanging on a rack and stopped at two black trunks.

"Let's start here," I said. "Just hold the light for me."

I opened the first trunk. Dresses and pants were stuffed in randomly as if someone had been hurrying to escape. Nothing was properly folded, and, like opening Pandora's box, I had freed some stale odors. There was nothing particularly interesting for me in it anyway, so I closed it and opened the second trunk. After I lifted away what looked like an old tablecloth, I paused.

"Is this what I think it is?" I asked, lifting some of it.

"Don't know, ma'am."

I brought up the material and then stood holding it before me. There was no doubt. It was a nun's black outfit. It consisted of a headdress made of a stiff coif that would frame my face, a white wimple that would run from under my chin down my chest, and a long black veil I could attach to the top of the coif. It would extend down my back. There was a black dress and even the stockings and a woven belt that held the rosary. When I dug farther, I found a pair of black shoes, but they looked too small for my feet.

"This is perfect," I said. "What an idea. I'll find one of Malcolm's highwayman masks that go over your eyes, and then with this much over me, I won't be easily recognized."

I laughed.

"How ironic to dress like a nun for Halloween. I knew people who were afraid of them, who thought they whipped children for forgetting the exact words of the Lord's Prayer."

"Yes, ma'am," Dora said, so firmly I was convinced she had once harbored such a fear.

I looked at it all again and wondered. "How could there have been a nun in this family, Dora?"

"I don't know, ma'am. Maybe a daughter who had married the church years and years ago?"

"Well, I'm marrying the church for a night," I

200

said. "Help me take it down. We'll wash it and do the best we can to restore it. Then we'll take it in where it needs to be. I'll find a pair of my own shoes that would work. You and I will do it all. We don't need your aunt's help," I emphasized.

"Yes, ma'am. But why, again, are you wearing this?"

"I'm going to a costume party. To scare a few gossips to death," I said. "They'll be sorry they told lies or spread evil stories."

She helped me fold it all, and then we carried it down. I insisted we do all the work in the Swan Room the following day and went to sleep dreaming of the effect I would have when I entered the party of snoopy gossips.

Dora was actually very good with tailoring and told me she often had to do it for her brother. We shortened the hem and took it in at the waist and bodice.

"You are good at this, Dora. Did you do it professionally?"

"Oh, no, ma'am. We didn't have the money to send things out. My father would say, 'Necessity is the mother of invention.'"

"Yes, I've heard that."

"I tailored some of my mother's clothes for myself, too," she said. She tried to say it simply as a statement of fact, but I could see the waves of pride flushing through her face.

It really didn't surprise me that Garland had

manipulated and molded her to do whatever he wished her to do. She had a child's simplicity packaged in a grown woman's body, and, like that child, she was totally unaware of her feminine powers. She had her limp, but spending more of my time with her, I realized Garland was wrong about her. If she was out there, even doing menial work in some pub or some other public place, she would find her man, and she would have a fuller life. I put it in the back of my mind: someday I would find a good way to send her off to a life without a Foxworth.

Ironically, Dora found a pair of my mother-in-law's black shoes that fit the nun's outfit better than any pair of shoes I owned. She even found a better pair of stockings for me. In the days that followed, I thought she was taking more pride in perfecting my costume than I was. We both laughed at the figure I presented, and as strange as it seemed, nothing had bonded us any closer than this.

She was more nervous than I was Saturday night when I dressed and descended the stairway. The look of shock on Mrs. Steiner's face brought laughter to both of us.

"What in all tarnation . . ." she said. She looked to Dora to explain, but Dora bravely turned away and led me to the front door.

When I appeared outside, Lucas's mouth fell open.

I could almost feel his imagination stampeding to wild conclusions. Had I become so disgusted with Garland that I had I decided to go to a convent? He looked to Dora, whose smile gave him some relief.

"Wipe that worry off your face, Lucas. I'm off to a costume party, and to get into my part, I want you to treat me with religious respect."

He looked at Dora to see if I was serious, and she gave him a firm, grim face.

"Here's the address," I said, handing him the invitation.

He read it and nodded. "I know the house," he said. "It's just on the other side of Charlottes-ville."

"Then let's be off. There are souls to save. Thank you, Dora," I said, turning to her. She curtsied and hid her laugh behind her hand as I turned and got into the carriage.

Nearly a half hour later, we turned into a long drive that led to an impressive house.

"Don't go all the way up to the house," I told Lucas. "In fact, stop here."

He pulled the carriage to the side and jumped down to open my door.

"Are you sure, ma'am?"

"It's fine," I said firmly. "Go wait with the other drivers."

I started away. I didn't want him seen bringing me up to the front of the house. Too many people knew who Lucas was, and my surprise would be ruined. Confused, he got back onto the carriage and headed toward the area where other carriages were parked. I walked slowly up the rest of the drive. Two carriages ahead were dropping off guests. I could see the women were in elegant dresses and wore only small masks that covered their eyes and noses. Being fully disguised was not going to be anyone else's choice but my own, I thought, and walked more quickly to the marble stairway.

The house wasn't as large as the Wexler mansion where I had met Garland, but it was designed after the Queen Anne shingle style, with quite picturesque elements on the exterior, including asymmetrical gambrel gables, a soaring chimney stack, and an eyebrow dormer. The large main foyer led to a beautifully curved staircase. I followed the two couples to where there was music and laughter and entered a circular ballroom area with stained-glass windows, a large fireplace, and eclectic but elegant furniture that looked like it had been pushed to the side to make for a more open main floor. There were two violinists playing softly, the conversations overpowering them.

Groups of men and women were forming, but it looked to me like most everyone knew everyone. I saw more elaborate masks on the men, some of ghouls; a few were quite frightening, in fact. There was a man in a clown's outfit who was attempting to juggle something. The woman beside him, who I assumed was his wife, looked like she wanted to keep her distance. He was embarrassing her, apparently, but to me she looked like she had the personality of someone easily embarrassed who giggled incessantly.

Melinda Sue and a man I assumed was her husband were off to the right with two other couples. When I entered the room, everyone paused and turned to me. Even the violinists lifted their bows from the strings of the instruments for a moment. Who would dress in a nun's garb and consider it a costume? Wasn't that blasphemous? Instantly, everyone was questioning everyone else about who I could be. I walked directly toward the punch bowl. The two women and men standing in front of it parted to make a clear path for me.

"Do nuns drink alcoholic beverages?" the taller man asked. They all laughed.

"Have you not heard of the blood of Christ?" I asked without a smile.

Their smiles quickly faded. Was I serious? I served myself a cup. They turned to look at the woman hurrying toward me. I imagined she was Amanda McKnight and they were wondering if she had, for some religious reason, invited a real nun.

"I'm sorry I didn't greet you at the front door,"

the short, light-brown-haired woman said. She was wearing a purple mask with a bird's beak. "I'm Amanda McKnight."

She held out her hand. I took it and nodded.

"I'm afraid I can't recognize you," she added when I said nothing. Now she was wondering if I really was a nun.

"Well, isn't the fun of this built around our keeping our identities secret?" I asked.

She held her smile but was quite surprised I didn't reveal who I was.

"Definitely is the purpose of the costume and masks," the tall man said.

"Then let us continue to have fun," I said.

Everyone laughed except for Amanda McKnight, who turned away to talk to someone else. Feeling more confident now, I crossed toward the table with the hors d'oeuvres. As I put some on a plate, two women stepped up beside me. They smiled when I turned to them.

"Are you Betsy Winningham?" one asked. "No one has seen her for years, but we did hear she might be attending without her husband."

"Hardly," I said. "Nuns don't marry mere mortal men anyway."

"What?" She looked at the woman who had accompanied her.

"Well, you have everyone guessing. Amanda McKnight just said that everyone who was invited is here," she said.

"True," I said. "I was invited." What I didn't add was I hadn't returned an answer about whether or not I would attend.

They looked at each other and, obviously frustrated, stepped away. I hadn't had as much fun since I had my womanly talks and with vivid sexual references stunned the girls who attended.

As I turned from the table of food and started across the room, intending to stand beside Melinda Sue to tease her, a rather handsome man wearing a black eye patch over his right eye started toward me. He wore a velvet cape with a black vest and black slacks. What looked like a pair of a woman's red knickers was stuck inside the leather belt, worn supposedly to be some sort of romantic trophy.

He was taller than Garland and had a nicely trimmed coal-black chevron mustache. His facial features were chiseled to perfection, with firm full lips. He smiled at me as if he knew me, knew what I looked like beneath this nun's outfit. His eyes moved over me so intently I felt like he was undressing me. It was not unlike the smile Garland had once sent my way, only this one seemed somewhat more intense. He didn't look amused so much as appreciative.

Before I could say a word, he took my hand, did a short bow, and said, "Forgive me, Sister. I am a poor sinner."

He stood inches away, his eyes fixed on mine, but kept holding my hand.

"You might be a sinner, but you don't look poor," I said, and he laughed. It was a manly laugh, not the short hee-hee or little giggle some of these friends of Garland's uttered. They either did that or roared loudly, guffawing and choking when they were drunk.

"Can I assume you chose this costume because you are not married?"

"No," I said. "Tonight we are all supposed to be someone we are not. I am certainly not a nun."

He widened his smile and looked at my hand in his. "Not the hand of a woman who labors."

"Depends on what you mean by labor."

"Ah," he said, and let go. "Well, I'm not a firm atheist, but I'm happy to hear you're not a nun." He leaned in closer to whisper. "However, I'm really who I seem to be, Beau Dawson, a thief of beauty."

"And how, pray tell, do you steal beauty?"

"I paint it," he said, smiling.

Apparently, his talking so long to me raised the temperature of curiosity. Melinda Sue, accompanied by Amanda McKnight, approached us. Melinda Sue was wearing a glittery half mask, as was Amanda.

"It's you, isn't it?" Melinda Sue asked. "We reviewed all the invitations sent, and you were clearly the one outstanding."

"I cannot deny that I am who I am," I said.

I glanced at Beau. His startlingly golden brown eyes were glittering as much as Amanda's mask. I turned to her.

"I'm sorry I didn't respond quickly to your invitation. It was a last-minute decision, and this was the best I could do. I hope I haven't offended anyone."

"Oh, no. It's a wonderful idea. It has everyone buzzing," Amanda said. "I'm so honored and pleased you decided to attend, Mrs. Foxworth."

"Call me Corrine now that I've been unmasked," I said.

"Please," she said. "Permit me to introduce you to everyone. You've already met Mr. Dawson, I see. Have you convinced her to have her portrait done yet, Mr. Dawson?"

"Not yet, Mrs. McKnight. Perhaps you'll convince her for me."

"Perhaps," she replied. "Shall we introduce you now, Mrs. Foxworth?"

"Thank you," I said. I nodded at Beau Dawson. "You're forgiven," I told him, and drew the cross in the air. His laugh was harder, louder, as we started toward the others.

"What did you forgive him for?" Melinda Sue whispered.

"I'm sworn to keep that secret like any nun would," I replied.

She smiled and squeezed my hand. "You should

have him do your portrait. He's an up-and-coming artist. Everyone agrees he will be quite famous one day."

"Really?"

"He's doing my portrait at the moment," Amanda said. "He's not inexpensive. When it comes to his art, he's quite arrogant."

"Arrogant? How surprising," I said. They didn't hear my sarcasm.

"Oh, he's worth it even though he's not yet that well known. Melinda Sue is right. He will be," she assured me. "Everyone who's anyone is lining up to have him do theirs. But mine will take a while longer. He's quite the perfectionist, and he sees the same quality in me. However, I'm sure whatever he will do will be quite surprising to me as well as my husband and our friends."

I nodded.

It wasn't surprising for that reason, I thought, but didn't say. It was surprising because he had called himself a thief of beauty.

She wore a half mask, but that didn't matter. It was easy to see.

What would he steal from her?

Except her money.

# 9

The party turned out to be more fun than I had anticipated. Despite being there without Garland, I was treated like royalty once everyone knew who I was. I was, after all, even though only through marriage, a Foxworth. I saw how my dressing like a nun first had offended some. They grimaced like people with stomach pain, but once they learned my identity, what was at first so distasteful became "so clever."

Most of the women worked their way to the front to be sure they had introduced themselves almost before I had gotten across the room. If I moved left or right, the clump, which was what they seemed to me, moved right along. At times I really felt like I was surrounded by a flock of geese pecking away at me with their questions about Foxworth Hall and the life I led: "Why would you ever leave those grounds?" "How long is your lake?" "How many servants are there really?" "Are there really hundreds of works of art?"

I gave vague answers to questions about Garland, basically stating he was a man dedicated to his work.

"I know what you mean," Louise Mason said.

She was a woman in her late thirties who I thought looked on the verge of turning sixty. She had wrinkles my mother didn't have. She looked back disapprovingly at her husband, who ran an export-import business, and said, "There is such a thing as a 'married widow.'"

Heads nodded in agreement, but eyes were searching to see if I was going to say something more sensational about my husband. I sensed that a good gob of gossip about him and me surely had been spread like butter on bread before I had arrived, since no one had expected to see me. Melinda Sue kept her gaze on the floor when questions about Garland were asked. She looked afraid I would mention her innuendos and find confirmation.

"Yes, well, not everyone and every marriage is the same." I looked at Melinda Sue when she raised her gaze. "Didn't you tell me at lunch never to judge a book by its cover?"

"What?"

"Surely you all know that what seems to be true often is not."

Eyes widened, heads bobbed. I smiled gleefully. Most had no idea what I meant.

"Nevertheless, we can't live in our husbands' shadows," said Adelaide Wiley, who liked the theme we were on. "We'll wilt like flowers if we just hang on their reputations and never have one of our own."

"Yes, poor us, striving for some identity and more of the attention we deserve. Our husbands are so busy it's almost as if we have to make an appointment to see them," I said.

I watched their faces go from shock to smiles.

"You sound like a suffragette," Adelaide said cautiously.

"Politics is boring. I can't even spell the word," I replied.

Some continued to smile, but there was clear disapproval from a few.

"You don't have to be in politics to enjoy the company of other women," Amanda McKnight said.

"Socially?" I asked, teasing her.

"Yes, of course. Few of us see you alone anywhere but the department store. We enjoy a 'ladies' day lunch' occasionally at one of the finer restaurants in Charlottesville, just as our husbands do. I believe you would be pleased if you attended."

"Yes," most parroted. "Please do."

"I'll see," I said.

"I'm working on her," Melinda Sue declared. "There's hope. She came here, didn't she?"

They smiled and nodded, talking about me as if I were not right in front of them.

"Yes. We were all hoping to see your husband here," Mrs. Moccasin said. I gathered she was like the informal president of their club. When she spoke, she eyed the way those clinging to our conversation reacted. How clever she thought she was to bring up Garland, I thought, and how naive she thought I was.

"One never knows where or when he'll turn up. He likes to surprise me."

Some of the women nodded in such unison that I thought their necks were connected.

"But then, I do like to surprise him as well." I leaned into her but whispered loudly enough for everyone around us to hear. "Makes for more romance, don't you think? A marriage that lacks spontaneity can become dull. A kiss too properly prepared lacks . . . passion."

There was a pregnant silence as everyone anticipated what Edna Moccasin's retort might be. It was a tennis match with words instead of balls. She looked too frightened to speak. We were treading on that thin ice called sex.

"I'll say," Melinda Sue blurted, nervous at the silence. She barged in between Edna and me. By now, maybe because of her fear concerning what I would reveal we had discussed at my luncheon, she had built her courage by drinking more punch than any of the others. She giggled, raising eyebrows that nearly flew off faces when she added, "Now I just have to convince my husband to look it up in the dictionary."

Although no one actually did, I heard them gasp in their thoughts and then look around to be sure no man had heard the remark, especially Melinda Sue's husband.

I smiled at her to indicate how clever that was, and, like the company of flatterers who clung to the shadow of the queen, they all laughed.

Feeling a little liberated, they all chirped an agreement that they had to do the same with their own husbands—all except Mrs. Moccasin, that is.

Men were drawn to our conversation when the women laughed so loudly. Obviously, they thought we were having more fun. I suspected, however, that some feared their wives were somehow being infected by the outgoing and far too independent young Mrs. Foxworth. Perhaps I was saying too much, a good deal of which would find its way back to Garland. I knew I was drinking more of the alcoholic punch than I should. I had even accepted two glasses of champagne by now.

However, I held on to my faculties and was surprisingly bright when it came to any questions from the men about Garland and his enterprises. My answers brought more husbands to our circle. Thanks to my father, I knew how the stock market had started and what sorts of investments led to making more money. He would go on and on about it at dinners when, according to him, I was finally old enough to understand.

The women were quite disinterested in anything

I had to say about business and investments. Their eyes and interest began to wander, but the men listening looked like they were taking mental notes for future transactions. They were like bees drawn to nectar now. Any other woman here would be quite intimidated, I proudly thought.

"You're obviously a great asset to your husband," William McKnight said after I had explained, as my father had taught me, why you don't buy stocks when they are climbing in value but wait for them to hit a low, knowing they'll begin a bounce back if it's a stable company. It was very obvious that he and the other men listening were quite astonished at my intellect. They had made their assessments of me either through gossip or simply through my appearance. Maybe they wouldn't come out and say it, but in their minds they believed beauty diminished brains.

"Thank you. I do try to be."

The more serious the conversation became, the more women drifted away from me. I was soon left with only a few who stood by their husbands. Perhaps Melinda Sue's friends wouldn't want me in their social club after all, I decided. They'd be bored to death. I was laughing so hard inside at how quickly they had lost interest in me that I was afraid I would spill my glass of champagne. Melinda Sue stood off to the side smiling dumbly. She'd still take credit for my being here,

I thought. After looking at her quite homely husband and how dull he appeared, I realized she needed any compliment and any excitement she could get. I felt generous and directed myself at her whenever I had anything to say that a woman might enjoy. I wanted her to feel special. Truthfully, I wouldn't have been here if not for her. She should take credit.

Once in a while, I saw Beau Dawson talking animatedly to one of the wives, but I caught the way he was watching my every move. Whenever I looked his way, he nodded or smiled, even when he was talking to more than one woman at a time.

Meanwhile, the food and the punch, as well as the bodies surrounding me, reinforced the one thing I had forgotten about my costume: it was too heavy and too warm for such an occasion, especially with all these people around me in a rather closed-in area. I felt the sweat building, and so, as the evening continued, I discreetly took off the headgear of the nun's outfit completely. It felt so relieving to let my hair fall loosely, which I could see astonished some of the other wives and especially most of the admiring men. It was almost as if I had bared my breasts.

As delightfully appointed as it was, another thing I noticed about the McKnights' grand room was that it didn't have the cross breezes we enjoyed being so high up at Foxworth Hall. After a while, I was actually beginning to feel a little faint despite my disrobing. Maybe it was too much alcohol as well. The talk seemed more like a buzz near my ear by now.

Suddenly, as if he had been waiting to see the flush appear on my face, Beau Dawson swooped in and whispered in my ear. "You look like you could use a breath of fresh air. I'm going out to smoke an expensive thin Italian cigar I received as a gift this week. Care to join me? Perhaps inconspicuously?"

"Inconspicuously? Show me how to do that," I whispered back, and smiled at a Dr. Beezley, who was describing an uncle who had made a killing on the stock market. He drooled a bit when he spoke excitedly. Seeing that and his crooked, tobacco-stained teeth was churning my stomach.

"I'll leave first. I'll be outside, off to the right," Beau said, and walked off.

I let another five or so minutes go by, signaled to Melinda Sue, and asked her to show me the closest loo.

"Loo?"

"Bathroom," I said.

"Oh, sure."

Leaving with her drew no special attention.

"Everyone is so happy you came," she said as we walked out. "The men are raving about you, and my envious friends all want to walk in your shadow."

"Really? I was beginning to think they thought I was quite boring."

"Oh, no. They're quite impressed."

"Even the ones who thought of me more as the Lady of Shalott?"

She laughed. "I'm so sorry I told you that."

"It's fine. Maybe it was true . . . then. But it won't be true anymore."

"Oh?" She smiled. "Then you'll join our social club now, won't you?"

"Most probably," I said, even though I couldn't imagine sitting in a house, sipping wine or tea, and listening to these women gossip and spread nasty and ugly thoughts about other women while never holding up a mirror to look at themselves.

"I'm so happy. I'll have you to my house for lunch first and give you all the details about each and every one of them."

"I don't need to be prepared. Let's wait. I'll have you and your friends over at Foxworth once I get our schedule from Garland. I'm sure they want to see Foxworth Hall."

"That would be wonderful," she said, pausing at the door. "Want me to wait here for you?"

"No, please, don't," I said. "That makes me nervous. I know my way back."

I don't know where I came up with that, but it sounded right. She nodded, big-eyed, obviously eager to tell the others what I had said and take credit for it. She started away to return to the party. I watched until she was gone, and then I hurried down the hallway and out the front entrance. There were two doormen there, but neither said anything. They glanced at me and looked away as if I really were the queen and staring at me was forbidden.

At first I didn't see him. He was leaning against the side of the house, and then the thin little cloud of cigar smoke rose up and floated off into the darkness. I glanced at the doormen, who avoided looking at me, and stepped carefully over to him. He glanced at me, smiled, and looked into the darkness again.

"Warm for October here, isn't it?"

"Where are you from?"

"New York. Manhattan."

"What brought you to Virginia?"

"Work. Money. Opportunity. My mentor, Jean-Paul Vitton, an older man, an artist from France, schooled me in how to . . ." He smiled. "As you might put it, invest in my career. Speaking of investing, I caught some of your lecture back there."

"Lecture? It was hardly that."

"Whatever you call it, you had quite the male audience. You appear to know a great deal about financial matters."

"Maybe I sound like it, but I'm not that brilliant when it comes to business. My father is a banker and wanted me to appreciate what makes the world go round."

"What does?"

"Money. At least to him."

"Makes sense. A banker. I'm talking about a different sort of investment as an artist. Yes, I need to make money to continue practicing my art, but you have to invest in people who can invest in you first, if you know what I mean?"

"Get an introduction to the high society of a city like Charlottesville, paint the portrait of one of the women in that house, and she tells a friend who tells a friend?"

"Yes, exactly. You are quite amazing, Mrs. Foxworth."

"For someone my age?"

I studied that sly smile in which his eyes twinkled even though we were both in the darkest part of the front of the house, now without a chance of moonlight or starlight pouring through the surrounding hemlock and white pine trees. The breeze was cool, but I could sense that colder air was on its heels. For me it was refreshing at the moment. However, talking to him while dressed in nun's clothes was making me feel silly now.

"Wisdom comes in all sizes, shapes, and ages."

I nodded. His compliments stirred my suspicions about him. "Despite this . . . disguise, you knew who I was before Melinda Sue Carter and

Amanda McKnight approached me, didn't you?" I asked, practically making it sound more like an accusation. "Isn't that why you came over to me so quickly?"

"How could I know that? Apparently, no one at the party knew who you were immediately, and most, if not all of them, appear to know anyone they would consider worth knowing."

I thought about it for a few moments. He was right. How could he have known? Why would he think I was a better opportunity for him than any of the others? This nun's garb certainly hid my best attributes. There had to be something, though. Although I didn't know him, he seemed quite cunning. And then it dawned on me.

"You were out here having one of your cigars when my driver stopped the carriage to let me off so I could walk part of the way. Am I right?"

He smiled. "Do you work for the Pinkerton Detective Agency?"

"Probably could. So you recognized my driver, didn't you? He's been with my husband for years and years. And by now you certainly know who the Foxworth family is."

Before he could reply, I added, "You do your research for your investing, Mr. Dawson. I'm not blaming you for it. If I were in your position, I'd do the same."

He laughed and looked away for a moment, probably debating whether or not to tell the truth.

"I saw you being driven into Charlottesville the other day. I was on my cousin Beverly Morris's front porch. I'm staying with her for a while. She's nearly seventy, before you ask."

"Would I?"

He laughed. "I was outside, having one of these cigars, and saw you go into the Caroline House. When you came out, you went to the telegraph office and then to the department store before your driver returned."

I was speechless for a moment. It frightened me and yet intrigued me that some stranger would watch me so closely, in fact, follow me, especially when I was doing something quite surreptitiously.

"Why would you do that? Track after me and watch me come and go? I've never seen you before tonight."

"I'm like a gold miner, I guess, who can recognize an important vein in the rock. When I see something, someone who could inspire me to do my best work, I'm drawn to her. I had no idea who your driver worked for then. I didn't know who you were until those two identified you in front of me earlier this evening."

"And so despite your beliefs," I said, "you do eventually confess, Mr. Dawson."

He looked at me a moment, and then he laughed the hardest he had.

"Nice talking to you," I said. I wanted to stay

with him longer, but alarm bells were sounding inside me.

I stepped forward and turned toward the entrance of the house. Melinda Sue was surely looking for me by now anyway, I thought.

"You going back in there?"

"Not for long," I said. "I do wish you good luck with your work."

"Thank you. And you?" he cried out when I turned to walk away.

I turned back. "Me? What sort of work do I do?"

"Now that I know you're Mrs. Foxworth, I know your position carries a great deal of obligation. I've seen your home from a distance. The queen couldn't have more to do overseeing the care of Windsor."

"Oh, she does, Mr. Dawson. Believe me, she does," I said, and returned to the Halloween party. Before I stepped in, I asked one of the doormen to ask my driver, Lucas, to come to the front entrance. The room felt even warmer on my cool face now. I went directly to Melinda Sue and Amanda McKnight.

"We were just going to send out a search party for you," Melinda Sue said.

"Yes, I'm afraid I chose the wrong costume. A little too warm for this evening. I stepped out to get a breath of cooler air, but I'm a bit tired anyway. I had a big day today," I said, and left it mysterious.

"I'm sure every day is a big day for you," Amanda said.

"Yes," I said. If they wanted to romanticize who I was and the lives the Foxworth family lived, let them, I thought. "From morning until night there is so much to do. Thank you for thinking of me."

"I hope we'll see you soon," Melinda Sue said, almost sang, and winked.

I nodded, smiled, and left. When I walked out, I looked for Beau Dawson, but he was no longer standing there. Lucas helped me board, and we were off. I sat back, not sure now if I was happy about the impression I had made at the party or not. Had I sounded too confident? I wondered what the men there would tell Garland when they saw him. I hoped it would all be laudatory and he would regret having done and doing anything that would displease me. Maybe now he really would know how lucky he was to have me, I thought. He would regret anything that jeopardized our marriage. I thought back to my youth and wondered if I was still a dreamer.

My feeling that I had made a good impression at Amanda McKnight's was reinforced the following day when a note from Melinda Sue was delivered.

*Dear Corrine,*
*Everyone was so impressed with you at the party that your leaving didn't*

*stop the chatter and all the questions I was asked just because everyone knew you had invited me to Foxworth Hall. Amanda wanted me to be sure to tell you she hoped you enjoyed yourself. In fact, all of the members of the Charlottesville Women's Club look forward to seeing you again. I'm hosting the next social club meeting two weeks from today, unless, as you insisted, you want to have something at Foxworth Hall.*

*In the meantime, I am at your disposal for anything, even a walk on the grounds of Foxworth Hall. To talk, intimately.*

*Your dear friend (I hope),*
*Melinda Sue*

I immediately liked the fact that she signed her given name and not *Mrs. Carter* as she had done when she had responded to my invitation to lunch. Maybe it was my doing. I had made her think more about her own identity. It all made me quite cheerful. I decided not to send for her immediately, however. I didn't want to give anyone the impression I was desperate for friends or lacking in anything anyone else had. It was better that I didn't respond at all for now. Except for how I had behaved toward my husband after we had first met, I had always played hard to get, whether it be a friendship some girl wanted to have with me or a romance some boy dreamed of having.

My father would say, "We cherish more that which took us longer and was more difficult to possess."

I couldn't help fearing that was not true for Garland and his possession of me.

Nearly a week later, Lucas told me that Garland's ship had pulled into port. The next day he sent a telegram informing me that he would be home in two days, but I thought he mainly wanted the servants to know. He listed what he expected to be done in preparation for his arrival: his room aired, the bedding changed, and his office cleaned and polished. After all, it had been weeks. I was feeling more like a personal valet than a wife. There was nothing in his telegram about his missing me or looking forward to seeing me. Being greeted properly by his servants was the thrust of his telegram. I couldn't imagine a king or a prince being treated any better. Once I dictated Garland's wishes to Mrs. Steiner, she almost went into a panic to get everything to Mr. Foxworth's standards, as if my standards were lower. Everyone was at work from sunrise to sunset. Dora was given extra duties. I felt sorry for her and took over most of the work with Malcolm, especially his lessons.

Dora had taught him well when it came to breaking down new words to pronounce, and when he knew he had done so correctly, he would get that sharp, self-satisfied smile that made me wish he had gotten it wrong.

I knew it was unnatural for me to feel this way about my own child. What I was doing more and more was transferring my anger at Garland to his son. Was it because Malcolm had never really come to me for reassurance, for comfort, for love, unless it was to manipulate me and get something he wanted? Did he even truly desire any affection from me? Was it my fault he was afraid to ask, to hug me, to want to kiss me good night or crawl into my bed and embrace me if he had a nightmare?

Dora must go, I thought, again placing the most blame at her feet. Eventually, soon, she must go. I must become a mother whether I liked it or not. Maybe there was still time to make him into a decent young man who had sympathy for poorer people, treated the people who worked in his businesses decently, had sympathy for women who were abused or violated, and, most of all, had sympathy for me.

When I looked at him now, I wondered if I could affect any of this. Did he have any real respect for me? What did he really think of me? I should praise him more, I thought. My main contact with him was either to bawl him out, spank him, punish him, or hound him to do his lessons. He could probably count on the fingers of one hand how many times I truly had smiled at him, embraced him lovingly, and kissed him with any affection.

But was this really my fault entirely? Garland had forcefully insisted Dora be his nanny and tutor.

"Dora is used to looking after a male, Corrine. You have no brothers, and your father is quite self-sufficient. If we're honest about it, we'd both admit you were and are quite self-absorbed."

"That's—"

"True, my dear," Garland said, and smiled. "That's fine. I'm glad you looked and continue to look after your beauty. The wives of the men I know, many of whom you have seen at our dinners, either were plain to start with or have neglected themselves so badly that they practically beg their husbands to have wandering eyes.

"No, you remain as you are, almost a goddess, and let Dora do the day-to-day upbringing of Malcolm. Children can exhaust you and age you faster than anything. We are lucky to have someone so qualified that we don't hesitate to give her the heavy weight that a child like Malcolm can load on your shoulders. And mine, for that matter!" he added.

From the little I had deduced about his father, I thought he was thinking and behaving as he would. I didn't argue. At the time I thought that maybe he was right. I could love my child from some distance, as it were, and protect my youth and beauty. What I didn't anticipate was how much my son would resent me for it. When I really thought about it all, deep in my heart I knew that he longed for my love and bitterly accepted Dora's affection as a substitute. Was it too late to change any of that?

At the moment, he was looking at me intently, more like someone three times his age would, as I reviewed his math papers. He was thinking about me too hard, judging me. It made me quite self-conscious.

"You can do very well with your studies when you want to, Malcolm," I said.

"When I want to," he agreed. Maybe he didn't hear the warmth in my voice. Maybe he was immune to it.

"You should always want to," I said. I couldn't help falling into the role of stricter disciplinarian. Dora really was better at this. "Only someone lazy and foolish wouldn't want to, Malcolm. You don't want to be either. No matter how much money you have, people will look down on you when you turn your back. Respect is very important."

He grimaced. I recalled my mother's lectures, how I had always smirked or had closed my eyes and dreamed I was somewhere else. Eventually, she would stop, and I could breathe again.

"When are we going to Virginia Beach like you promised?" he asked.

I shook my head. My words went in one ear and out the other, I thought. Why bother? Malcolm was already asking questions in the same tone his father used, which was more like demanding responses.

"We will. Your father is coming home. First we'll see what his plans are. Maybe he would go with us. You'd like that, wouldn't you?"

He thought about it and nodded, but not with the enthusiasm anyone would expect a son to have.

"So then let's keep it on hold until everything is decided, okay?"

He shrugged. Then he looked longingly at the doorway. "Dora would let me go play by now."

I sighed. "You want to grow up and be as successful as your father, don't you, Malcolm?"

"Daddy says I will be."

"He assumes that you're doing your lessons and behaving."

He stared. Just like Garland, when he made a firm statement, he would hear nothing to contradict or qualify it.

"All right," I said. "We'll practice your letters later. Go play. I'll check on you soon."

He said nothing. He slipped off his seat and started out. And then he stopped in the doorway as if he had been told something.

"Thank you, Mother. You are a good teacher, too," he said, and ran off.

I shook my head and smiled. Was that the best sort of compliment I could hope to get from him, or was it his way to get me to give him what he wanted?

There would never be a Foxworth man in this house who wouldn't know how to get what he wanted, one way or the other. Every smug male ancestor glaring down from his portrait so much as reassured me of that.

Two days later, Garland arrived. He could have had horns blaring and flags flying at the front entrance. Mrs. Steiner had apparently been watching for the carriage to approach the house. I heard her yell to Mrs. Wilson and then to Dora. I wondered how long it would take me before asking him who Catherine Francis was and why he was with her right before leaving.

Or did she go along?

He didn't hesitate to ask me questions as soon as he was able to do so. I was standing in the entryway just where and as he would expect when he entered. Lucas carried his luggage in behind him.

"Corrine," Garland said, almost as if he hadn't expected me to be there.

I stepped forward, and he kissed me and then held me at arm's length for a moment.

"Absence does make the heart grow fonder. At least for me."

"Does it?" I asked. I saw the look in his eyes change quickly, and I glanced past him at Lucas, who immediately looked away.

"Just take it all upstairs, please, Lucas," he told him. "Where's Malcolm? Why isn't he here to greet me?"

"He's been absorbed in the gift you gave him. He's at it every moment he can be. Wait until you see the toy city, the toy world he's built in the ballroom. Should we show him you're back now?"

"Later," he said. "I want to wash up and change. It's been quite a trip. I'm sorry it took so long. You were anxious for my return, were you not?"

"Yes. Did you come directly from the train station in Charlottesville just now?" I asked.

He hesitated and then said, "Of course. Why would you think otherwise? I've been well informed about the Foxworth enterprises here. I'll start on those inspections tomorrow. After we reintroduce ourselves to each other, I mean. It must feel so long."

He stared at me. Sometimes I believed he could read my thoughts.

"Everything has been prepared for you, Mr. Foxworth," Mrs. Steiner told him when our conversation paused. "Mrs. Wilson is preparing a roast with the purple potatoes you like."

"Very good. Thank you, Mrs. Steiner. I shall get refreshed then."

He started for the stairway and then stopped, turning back to me.

"You didn't even ask how successful my trip was, Corrine."

"I'm sure you'll give me the details at dinner."

He nodded and then smiled. "From what I hear, you'll understand it all."

Garland loved dropping explosive little remarks. He quickly turned and started up the stairs. Lucas was already getting his luggage into his room. Either he had given Garland a detailed report or, as I strongly suspected, he had been in Charlottesville for at least a day earlier. Maybe even longer, and he was lying about that now.

I glanced up at the portraits.

How my imagination loved to run away with what I saw in them.

But to me it wasn't so far-fetched. His father, standing by a fireplace and leaning against the mantel, looked like he was smiling.

"That's my boy," he could be saying. "Keep 'em in their place."

# 10

I gave Garland time to bathe and change. I was angry and nervous but had never felt more defiant. After I had knocked on his bedroom door and had entered, I saw he was in what was apparently a new velvet robe with a furry black collar. His eyes seemed to be even more strikingly blue, more like sapphire. I wondered if there would ever be a time when I would look at Garland and not feel a flutter in my heart, no matter what he had done to me. He was so handsome that mirrors sighed.

I tried to push down any of my dark suspicions and chase my questions away. I longed for those moments when we had first met, when every color around us was brighter, and when after either of us began to speak, the voices and sounds around us could barely be heard.

But the laughter and the ridiculing smiles that I was sure were behind Melinda Sue's innuendos at my luncheon with her here at Foxworth squirmed and slipped in around me, washing away my memories of our most romantic times. I lived in a mansion high on a hill and seemingly was the envy of so many, and yet if the whispers were true, how could I ever feel more foolish parading

235

about like some deaf and blind queen? For days I had dreams of the entire group of partyers at Amanda McKnight's home bursting into laughter the moment after I had left. Everyone had merely pretended to be impressed with me when, instead, I was the laughingstock of Charlottesville.

"I see you had time to buy yourself something new," I said.

He smiled and ran his hands down the sides of his beautiful robe. "Yes, and to buy something for you, too."

He nodded at two gift-wrapped boxes on his bed, one very small and one large.

"I was going to bring them to dinner," he said, "but now that you're here, I do prefer we have our privacy when we do something intimate."

"Intimate?"

I looked closer at the boxes.

"What are they?"

"Open and see."

Children and women are so distracted, so mesmerized, by surprise presents that they'd ignore being in a burning building, I thought. I was disappointed at how excited I was and how quickly my pride and indignation had weakened, my fury and determination along with them. I had stepped in here ready to demand answers to questions I knew would stir his rage. I was more than willing to do that than I ever had been, but right now all I could think was *What's in those boxes?*

"Go on," he urged when I hadn't moved.

I opened the small package first and took out a bottle that had a fancy label with the words *Au Fil de l'Eau.*

"Use it only for special occasions," Garland said. "That is one expensive bottle of perfume. Of course, I managed a discount because I worked with the owner of a company who's best friends with Guillaume Lenthéric, who manufactures it in France."

"Where did you buy it?"

"In New York at quite the fancy new department store."

"What does it mean?" I asked. I had learned little French even though my mother had urged me to do so, especially after my marriage to a Foxworth. She thought I would do so much more traveling than I had and meet many international entrepreneurs.

"English translation? *With the Current* or *With the Tide.* Sounds a little mysterious, eh?"

I sniffed the opened top. "It's interesting," I said. Truthfully, I had never smelled a scent like it.

"Which when you wear it will make you more interesting. The saleslady told me that it was designed specifically for the tsar of Russia and is one of the favorite fragrances of the queen of

Spain. It has a nice floral bouquet. Lily of the Valley."

Indignation began to flood into me again.

"When did you do this shopping? I thought you said you would have no time to stop and smell the roses and that was why you didn't think I'd enjoy being on your trip."

"I make time when it's something for you, and as I said, it comes from a business relationship, but by no means did I have time to go on shopping sprees. I happened to be passing this new store. If you had gone with me, you would have unpacked and packed again practically the same day. Go on, open the next, please. I've been anticipating these moments for days."

Now more intrigued, I put the perfume aside and began to open the bigger box. For a moment I stared down at its contents, and then I drew out the silk lace garment and held it up. It was so sheer. It would hide nothing.

"What is this? Something to wear under a dress?"

"No, no," he said, laughing. "You wear nothing under it or over it."

"What?"

"I met this young fashion designer who thinks that will become very popular soon as a nightdress. He calls it a negligee. Right now he's hand-making every one, and his customers are mainly women who make money being women, but wives of some very important men are beginning to order them secretly."

I felt myself blush. "Women who make money being women? Was this . . . ?"

"No, no. That's brand new. I didn't buy it from any woman, if that's what you're thinking."

I continued to hold it up and look at him through it. "No, what I'm thinking right now is you were right to give it to me without anyone else around. As you know, I'm not easily embarrassed, but this might have done it."

He laughed. "I'm looking forward to you putting it on and coming here after dinner."

"Why don't I just come naked?"

He shook his head. "There's a bit of a scent on that, too. Very nice. Something the French call *séduisant*, seductive. It's more exciting than nudity, I think. I have learned that the suggestion of something is far more enticing than the object itself. In my deepest thoughts, I believe you knew that instinctively, Corrine. You have a way with your eyes, your shoulders. You can set a man's imagination on fire; you did mine. That new fashion will be like feeding coal to the fire," he added. "*Tu es chaude.*"

I put it back in the box. "What does that mean?"

"*You're hot.* Nothing more."

"I'll have to have a French tutor to stay up with you."

"I just get by with *Combien*? That's usually

my only question when I'm in France or with a French merchant: *How much?*" He deepened his smile. "So? Do those gifts please you?"

"Yes," I said, but with a little uncertainty perhaps only I could hear in my voice.

He stared at me a moment and then leaned back and folded his arms across his chest. "All right. Now it's your turn to please me."

"Meaning?"

"I have some questions for you. First, what's this about you going to a party dressed as a nun?"

Even though it was the least of my expectations, I suddenly felt defensive.

"It was a Halloween party. Melinda Sue Carter was here for lunch, you'll recall. You said it was all right to invite her and get to know these women in the Charlottesville Women's Club. She had me invited to their party. I've been quite bored with you gone so much and so long, Garland. As hard as it might be for anyone else to believe, despite its size, this mansion gets tiring, even with all that's yet to be discovered. Four walls are still four walls."

"I see."

"Do you? How many walks to the lake can I do and how many trips to Charlottesville to shop? With Dora and all the servants doing everything but brush my teeth, there is not much more for me to do than care for my own personal needs.

240

And as much as that might surprise you, it's not enough."

He nodded. "All right. Let's not start on all that again. I can't help how busy I am. Back to my question . . . so you dressed as a nun for Halloween? How odd. You did frighten Mrs. Steiner, though." He laughed. "What a weird idea. Where did you get such a notion to dress like that for a Halloween party of all things? Did a nun frighten you?"

"I went up to the attic to look for something fitting for the occasion. There's enough up there to supply a theater company. Dora came with me, and I discovered the nun's habit in a trunk, buried under something else. Whose was it?"

His smile faded. "Up in the attic? You should have asked my permission to use that clothing first."

"Why? What's so special about it? There isn't much change in style for a nun. So? What Foxworth meaning could it have?" He looked hesitant. "I think we've been married long enough for you to tell me the story behind it, Garland."

"My mother's youngest niece had an incident with an African man and became pregnant. The child was given to a Negro family, and she was . . ."

"Condemned to a nunnery?"

"Something like that. It didn't end well."

241

"Didn't end well? What does that mean?"

"Figure it out. We never saw her again. All her clothing was sent here and put up in the attic."

"To put in another Foxworth cemetery, as you said. I suppose everything in this house has some history tied to it one way or another, the darker history hidden away."

"Not unlike other great families," he said, unfolding his arms. "How did you explain it when you were asked at the party?"

"I didn't."

He smirked and shook his head. "I don't care how bored you've been, Corrine. You should have sent for my permission for it all, attending that party as well as using that nun's habit. Your social activity is my responsibility now. Frankly, I'm surprised Dora went along with it."

"Are you? Why? Did she know the story behind the nun's habit? Does she know that much more than I do about the Foxworth family? How does she know so much?" I followed when he didn't respond but looked away instead.

"It's not the point," he muttered. "My wife should behave as a wife."

"Really? Then tell me why you left so quickly that night and then just sent a note. You didn't even deliver it yourself. Was that how a husband should behave?"

All the softness in his face was gone. He was

as chiseled in granite as his father was in his portrait.

"There wasn't time for anything more. One of my enterprises had gone bankrupt," he said, speaking through clenched teeth. "I had to salvage what I could before I left for Europe. And I don't have to explain it to you. You should trust I'm doing the best I can for our family."

"But that late at night?"

He looked like he was about to return to a smile but formed an even darker, arrogant sneer instead. "My lawyers make a lot of money off of me. They'll meet whenever I want, wherever I want, Corrine."

I took a breath and held it. Time to stand straight and be Corrine Dixon again. "Even the Caroline House?"

Now he did smile, but it was a cold smile, the traditional Foxworth smile. "I understand you went there and cross-examined Murphy Branson at the desk. The poor man has a heart condition. You could have murdered him."

"If he told you that, he told you what I had asked."

"He did."

He went to his table between the windows and opened the drawer to take out a box of what looked like strange cigarettes.

"These are from Turkey," he said, plucking one from the box and changing his tone. He didn't sound at all angry now or worried. He looked just as relaxed as ever. "They have a very nice aroma."

He lit it and leaned against his table, puffed, and nodded as he looked at me.

"So was that why you went running home to your parents in Alexandria the next day?" he asked.

"Is there anything Lucas hasn't told you?"

He shrugged. "I don't depend entirely on Lucas. He's loyal, but he has a fondness for you. I'm sure he doesn't tell me everything I should know. Just know that this is my town, Corrine. Many ears and eyes belong to me."

"Does that include Mrs. Catherine Francis?" I shot back.

He took a long draw on his cigarette and blew the smoke toward the ceiling. It did have an unusual aroma.

"I don't know what you've been told by the local gossips, but Mrs. Francis is merely an unfortunate investor."

"What does that mean?"

"She bought a partnership in the company that went bankrupt." He shrugged. "My father was the one who taught me never to invest more than you can afford to lose. She didn't have a wise father or husband. I managed to get her back twenty cents on the dollar. She may have to tighten up on her expenses as well as her corset. She was quite frantic, but my compassion for financial stupidity is quite limited."

He put his cigarette out.

"I don't mind your checking up on me. It's kind of amusing, sexy in its own way, actually."

"Sexy?"

"Yes. That beautiful fury I first saw in your face the first time we met still arouses me when I see it again. You don't have it that often these days. But you have it now." He smiled and gazed around. "I know. Why don't we do it differently tonight? You've really riled me up with your suspicious eyes. I have appetite for nothing else but you at the moment."

"What?"

He dropped his robe and stood there naked. He wasn't lying. He was obviously aroused.

"Put on your Parisian gift. We'll have dinner afterward for a change. I mean, you're here already. Why waste such a passionate opportunity?" he asked, bringing his hands down and turning them as he framed his loins and his erection.

I didn't know whether to laugh or be angry, but he kept his lusty smile and, when I said nothing, crossed to me, reaching into the box to pluck out the negligee and hold it up.

"Go on," he said. "I'm turning my back so it will be something like a surprise. In fact, after you put it on, go to the door and step out and then step in. I love the role-playing we can create sometimes."

I stood there, speechless. Everything was happening so fast.

He walked away and remained with his back to me, staring out of a window. He'd never looked as muscular, and the firmness in his hips and rear did stir me.

I glanced at the negligee and began to undress, feeling just as stunned by what was happening and as sexually excited as he was. I had no idea how it had come to this when I had come up to his room with an entirely different set of goals. There was so much more I had expected to ask him.

I slipped on the negligee and smelled a fragrant aroma coming from it. To me it was like putting on someone else's garment, however. I used to put on my mother's things when I was very small and always detected the scent that had clung to her blouse, her skirt, anything. *Was* this brand new? How could I tell?

Nevertheless, when I glanced at myself in his full-length mirror, I did feel sexier and could easily imagine capturing every ounce of his desire wearing it. Suspicious of the scent, I had expected to feel cheap, a woman of the street, what he had called a woman who makes money being a woman, when I gazed into the glass. Instead, I felt more powerful, more beautiful. It was only now, through this, that I could command him. Why not do it? How stupid other wives were for being ashamed of their sexual selves. If only my mother had been given a negligee, I thought, her marriage might have been more pleasing. I stepped out of Garland's bedroom, feeling as he had described, playing a role, but one I had, after all, cast myself to play.

It occurred to me to tease him. I did not immediately open the door and step back into his room. I could hear the seconds ticking by, and as if I could see through his thick oak door, I imagined the surprise and then the panic and disappointment gripping his face, widening his eyes, straining his lips. He was caught between waiting and rushing to the door to see if I had defiantly gone to the Swan Room.

Maybe I should, I thought. So aroused, what would he do then?

I had started to turn toward it when the door was thrust open. Before I could take another step, he reached for my right wrist and clamped his fingers around it like an iron cuff.

"You dirty little tease," he said, and yanked me to him, slamming the door quickly behind me before he embraced me so tightly that he nearly knocked the breath out of me. He kissed me hard, pressing his tongue into my mouth. When I gasped for breath, he laughed and lifted me in his arms, and dropped me onto his bed.

I started to turn to get more comfortable, but he pressed down on both my shoulders, pinning me where I was. Then he reached down and lifted the negligee up, rushing so hard and fast to pull it over my head that the motion rubbed the material into my back and nearly burned my arms before he had it off, practically ripped away. He then tossed it to the right as if it were ugly.

"Why . . ." I started to ask. I wanted to know why he would make such a big thing about my wearing it if he was just going to tear it away in seconds and toss it like garbage. He had barely seen me in it. Was he imagining someone else he had seen in it?

But before I could speak much more, he lifted my legs and drove himself into me, practically nailing me to the bed so he could press and thrust while he arched his back. He had his eyes closed, and lifted and twisted me to make himself more comfortable and drive himself toward a frenzied finish. At that moment I wondered if we were making love out of our passion for each other or some underground stream of rage that had twisted its way through his veins and now snaked itself around his heart.

It was certainly feeling that way to me. He was gritting his teeth and handling me rougher than he had during these past years. I barely had a chance to enjoy any passion for him. Now I really was feeling more like one of those women who he said made money being women. Like a thin icicle shooting through my mind, I suddenly suspected he definitely had been with such women and thought of me in a similar way.

He was turning me into his whore.

I pushed up on his chest, digging my nails into him until he opened his eyes.

"What the . . ."

"Stop!" I screamed.

"What?"

"You're hurting me." I struggled to turn away, and he retreated.

"What's gotten into you?" he demanded, his anger turning his face crimson, his eyes into hot coals, and his lips into an ugly twist. He reminded me of a head of wax melting.

"Me? What's gotten into me? You're full of rage, not love," I charged. "Why are you so angry? I thought you were filled with love, tenderness, and passion at the sight of that French thing you tossed away. Why did you want me to wear it? You wanted me to be one of those women, that's why. Am I right?"

He sat back as if I had just thrown a bucket of ice-cold water at his face.

"That's not so," he said, practically in a whisper. He looked like he was considering the possibility, something that might be surprising even to him.

"You didn't even kiss me after you tossed

me onto your bed like a bale of hay, Garland."

I turned to get off the bed and grab the clothes I had taken off and draped over a chair.

"That's . . . nonsense," he said, regaining his composure and his characteristic superiority. "I won't be accused by my wife of such a thing. Recant that charge. It's ridiculous."

I would not be bullied. "No, it's not. You made me feel cheap, unwanted for anything but your sexual satisfaction." I reached for the doorknob. "And you didn't even ply me with your precious limoncello first," I added, and walked out, closing the door quickly behind me.

Fortunately, everyone was downstairs anticipating dinner. I ran to the Swan Room, which had become more and more my sanctuary, closed the door, and, despite my determination to be strong, to be Corrine Dixon, I began to sob, standing there, looking at the swan, clinging to my clothing, and waiting for my blood to stop boiling and drain away from my face. I felt like I had a fever. After a few more moments, I stopped holding my breath and leaned against the closed door. Slowly, my fear and pain turned into anger. I welcomed it and quickly regained my composure. The swan seemed to smile. I went about changing into my clothing, mumbling to it, assuring it I was all right. I had finally taken a firm stand in this marriage.

Garland was downstairs by the time I

descended. He was in the ballroom with Malcolm and Dora, listening to Malcolm explain the little city he had built around the tracks and train. When he saw me, he nodded and then without looking at me said, "Malcolm says you wanted to take him to Virginia Beach but were waiting to see if I would go, too, and make it a family outing."

"Yes," I said.

"Perhaps next week. I'll check my schedule early in the week or next weekend. Is that okay with you?" he asked. It wasn't something he had ever done, seeing if I agreed to any event or travel before he planned it, especially in front of anyone else.

"Yes."

He smiled. "Of course, we'll take Dora with us," he added.

It was on the tip of my tongue to say, *But this is supposed to be a family outing.*

I didn't. I'd leave that for later, I thought. Dinner was ready.

During it all Garland behaved as though nothing terrible had happened between us a little over an hour ago. He talked about his business trip as if he had a big audience of strangers at the table, describing some of his achievements with details that could bore even a man like my father. As usual, he lectured about the government, taxes, and politics.

He looked at Malcolm, who was as disinterested as ever, and said, "I hope you're paying attention. You're never too young to learn about all this, son. Someday you will be in charge of Foxworth Enterprises. I'm happy I always listened to my father, even at your age."

Malcolm looked at me and then, almost bringing me to laughter, asked, "When will we know about Virginia Beach?"

The frustration in Garland's face was obvious. He couldn't wait to finish eating and go to his library to have one of his cigars and brandy. He made no effort to include me. I told Dora to take Malcolm up to bathe and get ready for bed. I even offered to read him a story.

"Dora has to finish the one she's reading to me first," he said. Dora kept her eyes down as if she had been caught trying to steal away any ounce of affection my son had for me.

"Go on, then," I told him.

Dora took his hand, and they hurried away.

When I looked in on Garland, I saw him sitting at his desk, bent over papers. I waited in the doorway, but he never looked up. I had never felt as dismissed and as much like just another servant. Although it was quite cool outside, I put on my jet-beaded black velvet cape and went out to walk and think. I hadn't gone more than one hundred yards from the house toward the lake when I heard a cough and turned to see Lucas about halfway between me and the building.

"Lucas. What are you doing?" I asked, stepping toward him.

"I was at the stable, ma'am, and saw you. I just wanted to be sure you were all right."

"That's kind of you. I'm fine."

"Okay, ma'am." He started to turn away.

"Lucas."

"Ma'am?"

"Did you tell my husband about the Halloween party, what I wore?"

"No, ma'am. But . . ."

"But what?"

"He asked me, so I had to tell him."

"But he knew about it?"

"Yes, ma'am. He didn't seem angry. I thought he laughed about it."

"Then," I said, more to myself, "how long was he back before you brought him to Foxworth Hall?"

He looked like he wasn't going to answer. I took another step toward him.

"Well?"

"Maybe two days, ma'am."

"He was at the Caroline House, wasn't he? Don't worry. You don't have to confirm it," I said. "The look on your face is as good as an answer. Thank you."

He nodded and walked away.

I gazed up at the mansion, at the dark attic

windows. I didn't really believe in ghosts, but it looked to me like something gray and shapely flowed across a pane and retreated to the darkness. I walked some more and then, growing tired, returned to the house. The lights were off in the library, and all was quiet, so I went upstairs and to my room to undress and go to bed. Tonight, I thought, I would read myself to sleep.

I had just opened the cover of the book to begin when there was a gentle knock on my door.

"Yes?"

Dora opened it slowly, her eyes avoiding me.

"What is it? Something wrong with Malcolm?"

"No, ma'am."

"Then?"

"There's a dress of Mrs. Foxworth's on the bed. I'm telling you just as you had asked me to do, ma'am."

"Go to your room," I ordered, and reached for my robe.

She backed out slowly.

"Now!" I cried at her. "Go!"

She closed the door.

I was trembling. I was afraid, but I started out for Garland's mother's room. When I entered, I saw the dress spread out on the bed. My mother had a dress like it, a dress that had what they called a false yoke, the fitted portion of the dress cut above the bosom. Like my mother's, this one had pleats and was corn-colored silk. I stared at it a moment. From the way it had been laid out, one could easily imagine a woman dressed in it and lying back on the pillows of the bed, I thought.

I approached it slowly. My first thought was to take it off the bed and hang it back in the closet, but that wasn't what I wanted to do now. It was time to kill a secret in Foxworth Hall, to bury it along with so many others. I slipped out of my robe and my nightdress, and as quickly as I could, I put on Garland's mother's dress. For a moment I stood there looking at myself in the mirror, and then I sat on the bed, my heart pounding. I remembered how Dora had described herself after she had put on one of these dresses, and I lay back, my head sinking into the soft, oversized pillow, and stared up at the ceiling.

The clock on the dresser was working and ticking loudly. Garland had left instructions that it was to be wound always. Would I soon hear his mother's voice?

# 11

Minutes seemed more like hours after Dora had left. My heart was thumping so hard I thought it would shatter my chest. I almost couldn't hear the footsteps in the hall and the door being opened. I didn't move a muscle but lowered my eyes to see Garland standing there in his nightdress, staring at me, first with obvious confusion and then with anger rising up his neck and into his face, turning his complexion crimson. His eyes widened and filled with fury. I could easily imagine sparks flying out of them. His neck tightened as he hoisted his shoulders before he raised his arms, the palms out like someone trying to keep something away from him or like someone who wanted to deny what he saw.

"What are you doing here?" he shrieked, and then repeated it in a voice just above a whisper, his words raspy, grinding their way up and out of his throat, sounding more like the words of a ninety-year-old man.

I sat up slowly and looked around as if I had just realized where I was. I'm sure I looked baby-innocent, confused. He waited, his eyes wide, his mouth opened but twisted to the right.

"Oh," I said, with as much casualness and control as I could muster. "I saw Dora go in and out and questioned her. She looks after the room sometimes for her aunt. They know how important it is to you to keep it as clean and as tidy as it was when your mother was alive. I thought maybe that was something I could do every night before I went to bed. Dora has so much to do with Malcolm and all, so I dismissed her and assured her I would. Then I saw this dress lying out on the bed."

I leaned toward him to whisper.

"I think from time to time, Dora tries on your mother's clothes. Poor thing. She dreams of being a woman of means someday." I pulled back and raised my voice as if I was reprimanding him. "It's not a terrible thing, Garland. You must not think ill of her," I quickly added. "In fact, I was curious about this dress myself and tried it on. It's an interesting color and fabric."

I stepped off the bed and turned around and then looked at him.

"What do you think?"

He stared quite in disbelief, quite unsure of himself. It gave me more courage. I was so convincing that I half-believed what I had said myself. He looked unable to find the right words, perhaps afraid of what he might reveal. I smiled. It felt so good to have him at a disadvantage.

"Why are you here anyway, Garland? Were you

checking on Dora's work? No worries. As I said, from now on I'll look after it, especially when you're away on business."

I stopped talking and stared at him, this time forcing him to speak.

He lowered his arms, the redness in his face receding as he came back to himself like someone who had been possessed for a few moments. Perhaps he had been.

"No, you don't look good in that dress," he said. "You're right to stay with what's fashionable and not use my mother's clothes. Put that dress back where it was hanging," he added, and walked out of the room without a word about my now caring for his mother's room and her things, my promise to be in here every night.

I stood there staring after him a moment, listening to his footsteps die away, and then I widened my smile.

"I think your mother can now rest in peace, my darling husband," I mumbled, and took off the dress.

Afterward, I had one of the most restful nights in a long time and woke up quite refreshed. I was excited about facing Garland and seeing what he remembered and how, at the start of a new day, he would react to my assuming control of his mother's room and wardrobe. Would he have regained his superiority? Would he still be more angry than surprised? What if he was?

He couldn't say much in front of our servants. I thought I wouldn't mention a word. I would treat the confrontation as if it hadn't happened. Let him, if he dared, be the first to bring up what had occurred.

I had never felt more confident and self-assured and eager to face him, but by the time I went down to breakfast, he was gone. He had left for his offices in Charlottesville. Lucas had not yet returned. I felt frustrated and considered following him to the Foxworth offices, forcing him to face me, and maybe asking more detailed questions about his business trip and that company he said had gone bankrupt. I was that emboldened. Of course, I knew the business with Catherine Francis had been a giant lie. I was eager to tell him so. It would be like tossing salt on the little cuts I had made in his ego.

When I arrived, if I went, he'd be shocked again. I had been to the Foxworth offices only twice and was bored silly each time. He had an accountant, Herman Daly, who tracked Garland's day-to-day business, and he employed a secretary, Louella Whipple, a fifty-four-year-old unmarried woman with a heavily pockmarked face and thin, dull, gray-streaked dark-brown hair. I thought she was months away from being bald. When I remarked about her to Garland, he told me he deliberately looked for unattractive women to hire.

"A woman who has no appealing features will rarely think about herself. She is more efficient. That's why," he said, smiling at me, "I can't see you doing anything for Foxworth Enterprises."

It sounded like a compliment and a criticism at the same time, but I didn't try to find out which one was really what he meant.

No one could tell when I sat at the table for breakfast, but I was quite disappointed Garland had left so early, and yet it felt energizing and strengthening to have him on the run from anything, ever. As a consequence, I had a fierce appetite and ate nearly double what I usually had for breakfast. Mrs. Steiner even remarked about it. I half-suspected Dora had told her I had gone to Mrs. Foxworth's room to await my husband's arrival. Although neither she nor Dora knew what had transpired, she could tell I was happy. It was the perfect morning to be gleeful.

It looked like it was going to be a beautiful fall Virginia day, even though it was quite a bit colder than it had been until now. I had been so absorbed in myself and what was occurring at Foxworth Hall most of the time that I rarely took a few cherished moments to gaze out the window at the beautiful trees that surrounded the property. In the distance I could see the way the Blue Ridge Mountains were rapidly changing color. Too soon, the yellow and brown leaves would be gone, and there would be only the dull gray and brown tree skeletons asleep, waiting for the spring and their green resurgence.

I was sipping my third cup of coffee and so absorbed in thinking about everything I had missed these past five years that I didn't even notice for a few moments that Dora had brought Malcolm down. Her eyes were drowning in her nervous and fearful curiosity about last night. I could almost hear the questions. What had I told Garland about her? What had he said? Was he enraged? Were her days here limited? What about her brother?

"Good morning, Malcolm," I said, practically singing it. He glanced at me through his still sleepy eyes. "How did you sleep?"

The joyfulness in my voice stirred his curiosity, too. I could practically hear his thoughts. He was so distrustful. Was I setting a trap? He was raking through his memories, trying to recall something bad or naughty he had recently done.

"I don't know," he said. "I woke up."

"He means I woke him up and made him dress so as not to miss his breakfast," Dora said, giving him her best effort at a face full of reprimand.

"Dora is right, Malcolm. Our loyal servants work hard to please us. You can't have them at your beck and call. They have other duties to fulfill. There's a proper time for breakfast, and the least you can do is prepare for it."

He grunted and looked down. Then he looked up quickly.

"It's nice out. Are we going to Virginia Beach today?"

"You heard your father. We have to wait for him to tell us when we can all go."

He thought a moment. That Foxworth face was a window on the gears that turned in his mind, conniving, plotting, and inventing something that would give him pleasure or get what he wanted.

"I know," he said. "Let's you and I go, and then we'll go again with Daddy."

I glanced at Dora. It so annoyed me to see how proud and pleased she was with him at times. Right now she was surely thinking he was such a clever little tyke. Yes, for himself, he was, I wanted to say. Foxworths first, and the rest of the world be damned.

Mrs. Steiner put his plate of eggs and toast in front of him with a glass of orange juice.

"Eat your eggs while they're still warm, Master Malcolm," she said.

He looked up at her disdainfully. Even at this age, he wore an expression that said, *How dare you tell me what to do? I'm the heir.* Arrogance, not blood, flowed through Garland's son's veins. I used to think that because he had suckled a stranger's breast and not mine, he was so much less my child. The truth was, I fought seeing anything of myself in him. I was grateful every time he was compared to Garland as if I hadn't even been a part of his birth. And every time I thought it, I felt terribly guilty.

"Yes, please eat," Dora said.

"If you finish your breakfast properly, I'll consider what you suggest," I told him.

His eyes nearly exploded with surprise, but it occurred to me that neither he nor I, but especially not I now, should be at Garland's beck and call with his whims and wishes so arbitrarily tossed at my feet. What a surprise it would be for him to learn I had decided to take Malcolm to Virginia Beach myself. Well . . . maybe not by myself, I thought, glancing at Dora.

"Would you be so kind as to fetch me the train schedule, Dora? It's usually at the right corner of Mr. Foxworth's desk."

She nodded and left to get it. Malcolm began to eat quickly.

"Don't gobble your food, Malcolm," I said, glancing at Mrs. Steiner, who stood off near the doorway to the kitchen watching us. "Mrs. Wilson works very hard making your eggs just the way you like them."

He nodded and slowed, his face now glowing with excitement.

Dora returned with the schedule.

"Would you see if Lucas has returned yet, please, Dora?"

She nodded and hurried out. I glanced at

the train schedule. There was a train we could make in an hour, and there was a return that would bring us back a little after our usual time for dinner. I would have Mrs. Steiner and Mrs. Wilson delay it a bit. Garland would be home before us, I thought, and quite shocked and surely quite upset.

"Okay, Malcolm. We'll go for the day. The way the weather changes, we might not have as pleasant an afternoon for a while. Maybe not until the spring."

He nearly exploded with happiness in his seat. "We're going!" he shouted to Dora as she was returning.

"Lucas has returned," Dora reported.

"Inform him that he will take you, Malcolm, and me to the train station in twenty minutes," I said. "Then get Malcolm ready for the journey. I'm going to go up and change into something sensible for a day at the beach. We'll take him on the rides and have a wonderful lunch. You can build us a sandcastle after that," I told him. "We'll have a picture taken with the ocean in the background, too. And if you behave, I'm sure we'll find a good souvenir."

He nodded with such an unusual look of affection toward me that I thought he would lean over to kiss me on the hand, perhaps hoping I would kiss him. His face was splashed with Garland's smile. After all, he had gotten what he had wanted.

"Okay, Mama," he said. "I promise I'll behave."

"Don't promise. Just do it. Finish, and do what Dora tells you," I said, and rose. I paused and looked at Dora. "Do you have something proper to wear?"

"I do, ma'am. Thank you."

For the first time, I really and truly felt like the mistress of Foxworth as I ascended the steps to change my clothes and fix my hair. I was giving the orders that would affect everyone. Surely I was behaving in the manner Garland's mother would behave, with similar stature and dignity. Perhaps a little of her spirit had crept into me when I had put on her dress. I smiled, realizing that I was beginning to think like Dora.

Twenty or so minutes later, I was just finishing up dressing and preparing for the trip when she knocked on the door.

"Master Malcolm is waiting in the entryway, ma'am," she said.

I looked at her and nodded, but she didn't move. She didn't have to come up to tell me that. Her face was still riddled with questions. This was perhaps her best chance to ask them. We might not be alone again for some time today. It was cruel to hold back any longer anyway, I thought.

I gazed at myself in the mirror as I spoke. "He was surprised. Shocked is probably more accurate. I had put on the dress."

"Did you, ma'am?"

"Oh, yes," I said, smiling at her look of astonishment. "I thought it might stop him cold. I was right. Then I told him it was my understanding that you had been instructed to look after his mother's room nightly, but from now on, that would be my responsibility. I said I suspected that from time to time you did put on Mrs. Foxworth's clothes because you wanted to feel like the mistress of the house. He was speechless. The only thing he said was I looked better in more fashionable dress, and then he left. Ran away, I should say. I'm sure he won't be bothering you with it again, and he blames you for nothing. I made sure of that and will continue to do so."

"Thank you, ma'am."

"Thank you for your honesty, Dora, and especially for keeping your promise and confiding in me. It will continue to be our little secret."

"Yes, ma'am."

"I'll be right down. Get Malcolm into the carriage."

"Yes, ma'am," she said, and left. I knew she was quite relieved.

I had handled it all well, hadn't I? I asked my image in the mirror. And now look at me, planning a trip without Garland's stamp of approval. It was probably something his mother would have done to his father.

Did I prance down the stairs a few minutes later? I certainly felt like I was glowing, floating. Weeks ago, anticipating the possibility of a beach visit, I had bought myself a cotton piqué seaside dress consisting of a middy blouse, a blouse with a sailor collar, and a flared skirt. The collar was red, as was the belt, and the blouse and skirt were an off-white. I had a beautiful pair of robin's-egg-blue kid leather boots with milk-glass buttons that had caught my fancy four years ago. I didn't have that many occasions to wear them, but I thought this trip was perfect for them.

Lucas was waiting to help me board the carriage. I gave him the time for our return train. Dora had dressed Malcolm well for a seaside visit. He had on a dark-green jacket, a waistcoat, and short trousers, with buckled shoes. She had his hair brushed neatly.

"You look very nice, Malcolm," I said.

He sat back proudly. The words *thank you* almost didn't exist for him, no matter how many times I reminded him to say them.

Dora looked as excited about our trip as he did. She had brought along a book to read to him for the journey, but he was far more interested in what he would see, especially on the train. He was full of endless questions about the train, what he saw, and where we were going. For some reason, he didn't want Dora to answer any. Most mothers would be happy their child had an endless curiosity about the world around him, but I kept thinking how lucky I was to have Dora to absorb most of it most of the time.

When we arrived at the beach, he wanted to go directly to the kiosks to buy a souvenir, but I told him we'd do so on the way out.

"Why carry all that around now?"

He nodded, determined to be obedient, but he did look like he didn't trust me. When we stepped on the boardwalk, his eyes went everywhere to support another endless cascade of questions. There were donkey rides and cycle rides and a merry-go-round. I stood off to the side while Dora took him on each. I paid for a photograph of the three of us. It would be delivered to Foxworth in two days. Once the photographer heard the address, he was quite a bit more accommodating, offering to do another for free.

At the continually expanding boardwalk, there was a nice hotel, the Princess Anne. It had a restaurant where I decided we would have lunch. We sat and looked out at the sea and the boardwalk of wooden planks where there were already dozens of tourists and families walking, the women with parasols of various colors. The sky was nearly cloudless, and the breeze, although cool, was fortunately calm. On the horizon we could see a steamboat making its way east.

Malcolm cried to get right down into the sand to build his castle. I had bought him a pail and shovel, but I insisted he sit down to have something to eat first. Actually, I wanted Dora to have something. She was doing all the work, and I feared she'd be too exhausted and I would soon have to take over. Every time I told Malcolm to slow down and not gobble his food, he gave me his father's look of rage. *It won't be long,* I thought, *until he is totally defiant.* Maybe then his father would take more interest and control.

I ate very slowly, so I wasn't done when they were. I told Dora to take him close to the water but not close enough to get wet. Malcolm practically flew off, with Dora following and shouting warnings. Garland was right, I thought. Bringing up a child could age you, especially a boy like Malcolm who drained almost all Dora's energy every day and, thankfully, not mine.

I sat and had a cup of tea and a scone, watching them. Dora had gotten right down on the sand with him, something I was not keen on doing, which was my real reason for taking so long to finish my lunch. When it comes to boys, mothers have to be more like older sisters sometimes, I thought, and for the first time really, I regretted not having a daughter. I would have so much to tell her, to teach her, and I was convinced a girl would look more like me. She'd be dainty and quiet, and even though she would be a Foxworth, too, she wouldn't be so obviously condescending. A woman in 1895 had to know how to be subtle if she was to keep anything of herself alive.

I was so deep in thought about it all that I didn't hear my name until it had been repeated.

I turned, surprised, and faced the artist, Beau Dawson. He wore a navy-blue blazer and a blue striped shirt and trousers, but right now had his blazer over his right shoulder and looked quite casual and relaxed, which I thought added to his good looks.

"Oh. Mr. Dawson."

"Please call me Beau. When you didn't respond, I began to wonder if it was indeed you," he said.

"Why are you here?" I asked, mainly because of the shock of seeing him. I think I even sounded angry about it.

He laughed. "I'm not tracking you again. I happened to be staying at this hotel. I finished the portrait I was doing and returned to my true love."

"Oh?"

"Not a woman," he said. "My true love is landscape painting, especially the sea. And why are you here? Is your husband here, too?" he asked, gazing about the restaurant.

"No. I brought my son and his nanny. It is a trip I've suggested we'd do for a while, and with the weather so magnificent, I thought it was a good day to do it. That's the two of them," I said, nodding toward the beach.

He looked and stepped closer. "Cute boy."

"Yes, most fall in love with him the first minute or so."

"And then?"

"How long are you going to be here?" I asked instead of answering.

"A few more days, I think."

"Where do you go after that?"

"I have a couple of inquiries for portraits in Charlottesville, so I'll return to my cousin's home. I'm just debating whom to do first." He leaned toward me to whisper. "Neither is a very inspiring subject to paint."

"But each has the money to employ you."

He laughed.

I locked my eyes on his. Neither of us spoke for a very long moment, and then he took a deep breath and looked out at the sea.

"I really prefer being at the sea," he said. "Someday I hope to return to the Côte d'Azur."

"Where is that?"

"The French Riviera, a small village known as Villefranche-sur-Mer."

"Oh, not another would-be Frenchman," I muttered. He raised his eyebrows. "My husband adds more French words to his vocabulary weekly these days. I don't know whom he's trying to impress, certainly not me," I said. "But I might be forced to get a tutor."

"*Je peux le faire.*"

"What?"

"I can do that, tutor you," he said. "But, to be honest, I'd rather paint your portrait."

He swung his blazer around and put it on.

"Have to get back to my work. It calls. My canvases have no patience or tolerance for procrastination. To sum it up, I'm driven. *Au revoir*, Madame Foxworth," he said, laughing with his eyes. "I hope to see you again when it's part of my job to stare."

"Yes, *au revoir*," I said, but not loudly enough for him to hear.

I watched him walk off.

But I didn't notice until I turned away that my heart had been racing the whole time we had been talking. I finished a glass of water, rose, and walked out to the beach. The breeze had strengthened. I felt the air threading through my hair. Dora looked up. Malcolm had built an impressive castle. He anticipated my coming to suggest we start on our way, stopping to buy him a souvenir. But first, he had to run down the beach and tempt the tide.

"Bring him back up, Dora, before he gets those shoes soaked," I told her. "We'll begin to make our way home."

"Yes, ma'am. What," she asked, looking at Malcolm's creation and shaking her head, "is more temporary than a castle built on the beach?"

Youth, I thought, but from where that wise

answer came I did not know, and didn't want to know. I just nodded and turned away, looking to see if Beau Dawson was anywhere in sight.

He wasn't.

I felt as if he had been a figment of my imagination, a wish so strong that it had the power to satisfy itself, if only for a few moments.

On the way home, Malcolm made up for my silence. I don't know how many times I reviewed my conversation with Beau. Dora looked so happy and looked to me to be happy about Malcolm's exuberance, too.

"You'll have to be sure to tell your father every little detail, Malcolm," I said.

"Yes, I will."

I smiled to myself, imagining Garland trying to express his anger while his son raved about his trip. The moment we pulled up to the front entrance, Malcolm was out, leaping to the ground before Lucas had a chance to lower the steps. Both Dora and I shouted at him, but he was clinging to his new sailboat and rushing to the front door, deaf to anything but his own excitement.

We followed him in. The house was frighteningly quiet. I glanced into the library and Garland's office, but he wasn't there. We continued toward the dining room from where we now heard Malcolm's voice. Sitting at the head of the table, Garland, dressed for dinner, had

273

his hands clasped and resting on the table. He was sitting back with a familiar expression of anger. Malcolm, standing beside him, ignored it and rattled on and on about the rides, the tide, the pictures we had taken, and the castle he had built on the beach. When he put his new sailboat on the table for Garland to see, Garland finally exploded.

*"Take that damn thing off our dinner table!"*

Malcolm did it and then looked toward Dora and me.

In a calmer tone, Garland explained why it was an improper thing to do.

He looked at Dora. "Take him up and prepare him for dinner immediately. I will not wait much longer."

"Yes, Mr. Foxworth," she said, and hurried to guide the shocked and disappointed Malcolm Foxworth out of the dining room and up the stairs.

Mrs. Steiner had heard his burst of rage and stepped into the doorway to the kitchen.

He anticipated her and turned. "We'll eat in ten minutes regardless of who is and isn't at the table, Mrs. Steiner."

"Yes, Mr. Foxworth," she said, and retreated into the kitchen.

"I'll just freshen up," I said. "No need to change."

"How dare you do this? How dare you go

to Virginia Beach and keep me waiting on my dinner?"

"Oh, it was such a beautiful day. We're not that late," I added, smiling. "And with how busy you've been these days, who could anticipate when and if you'd be home for dinner? You're at the Caroline House so often for dinner."

His face blanched as if he had been in the blazing sun. I turned to leave and then turned back.

"Actually, this was your son's idea. He suggested we go today because of the beautiful weather and then again as a family when you had the time. Already, he thinks so cleverly like you do, Garland. You can be proud of him."

He opened his mouth to speak but said nothing.

"Wasn't your mother proud of you? Isn't that why you miss her so dearly?"

He looked like someone who was being nailed to a cross.

I knew what was going to be now, what our lives would be like.

He would never again make love to me tenderly and passionately. His rage wouldn't permit it.

Perhaps he would never look handsome, charming, and sexy to me again.

Perhaps in these recent months and days, we had become just like his parents.

It wasn't so difficult to believe that the austere mansion with its ancestors lining the walls in the hallways and rooms, looming with their condescending eyes, demanded that we surrender to its darkness.

Garland had called the attic another Foxworth cemetery, but that wasn't the whole truth of it. However, only someone who navigated its corridors and passed through its shadows would know that the house itself, this grand mansion, was the Foxworths' true cemetery.

For me the only sanctuary was the Swan Room. It was meant to be an escape, which was probably why Garland wasn't fond of being there.

For he, now more than anyone, was afraid of the Foxworth curse. There were too many tragedies in the past. There was so much honor and power with the name but so much envy surrounding it, waiting to pounce.

I should feel sorry for him, I thought, as I went to freshen up for dinner.

I should.

But first, I had to feel sorry for myself.

# 12

As usual, but especially tonight, Garland couldn't wait to retreat to the library and his office after dinner. Malcolm hadn't stopped talking about our trip and thankfully had directed his endless questions about the ocean, boats, even beach sand, at his father. "How did it get there? How was it made? Why isn't there beach sand here?"

Dora helped serve and then went to eat her own dinner in the kitchen with Mrs. Wilson, so it was left to me to give Garland any relief. I gave him none, offered no answers. Garland didn't have a chance to talk about business or politics. He had to swallow back his usual diatribes and lectures about stupid politicians. Thanks to the excitement our trip had developed in him, our nearly five-year-old son dominated almost every minute.

I didn't rush out after Garland had left, flashing his anger and frustration at me as he did so, still smarting from my taking Malcolm on a trip without his knowledge, but I had only smiles for him. Sometimes a smile can be sharper than a whip lashing.

Dora, who as usual had been standing near the doorway after she had eaten dinner, hurried over to take Malcolm upstairs to give him his bath and prepare him for bed. He had finally shown signs of fatigue, fighting to keep his eyes open.

I sat for a few moments, reminiscing about the day at the beach. Visions of Beau Dawson, standing there with his jacket over his shoulder, his smile sexy but also clearly kinder than Garland's, dominated my thoughts. It was almost as if nothing else had happened.

As usual, no one took anything off the table until I rose to leave, even though they hovered about me like buzzards. When I finally stepped out, I walked through the hallway and looked at the artifacts, statuary, and paintings as if for the first time, and just as I had the first time, I felt intimidated, felt those austere, condemning eyes following me.

Suddenly, an idea burst, not in me but all around me. The result of this thought would surely please me, but, more important, it would change the very air that clung like moss to these somber walls and turned the echoes of footsteps into the dire sound of someone pounding in coffin nails.

I turned and headed for the library. Garland was at his desk, sorting through some papers, when I burst in so forcefully that I could feel the air between us separate like the Red Sea Moses had parted.

He looked up surprised and, I thought, a bit fearful. His brain was churning. What was I here so determined to do? Surely it wasn't destined to be good. The way I rushed in quickly and not timidly convinced him I had come to make trouble. Perhaps now he was wondering what I really did know about his extramarital affairs. What would I say? Whom besides my parents would I tell? How would I threaten him? He sat back, looking like someone who was expecting a blow, his arms slightly off the table. I stopped right in front of his desk.

"I don't want to get into any nonsensical female arguments," he declared before I could speak. "I have a lot of work and need to concentrate. P-and-L statements have come in from an investment in a train system that's begun in New York and—"

"Oh, I'm not here to argue, Garland. Not at all," I said, giving him my best smile, pure and without any visible underlying anger. I could almost hear his sigh of relief. Since he had come upon me in his mother's bedroom, I believed there would always be new insecurity and hesitation in his eyes whenever he confronted me, especially now with everything so fresh.

He lowered his arms, his eyes still filled with suspicion. "Good. What is it you want, then? I have another early-morning call and a full day tomorrow."

"I want something for the house. It doesn't involve any changes," I quickly added.

"These rooms don't need any more furniture, including your bedroom, Corrine. It would just mean more for the servants to dust and polish. Amuse yourself another way," he said, with a dismissive wave of his hand. He started to look at his papers.

"I agree. No more furniture."

He looked up slowly, relaxed a bit more, and sat forward, now legitimately curious. "Then what is it? Some new thingamajig for the kitchen? I think it's best Mrs. Wilson request it, since she has to work with it and—"

"I don't know anything about our kitchen, Garland. I couldn't even tell you where the mixing bowls are kept."

He dropped his pen and clasped his hands as he leaned on his forearms. "You have a more than adequate charge account at the department store and a generous allowance for anything else. If you want some new linen or clothes, go get them. When Lucas is free, he's at your beck and call. I'll make sure of it."

"And for all that I am truly grateful."

"Then what is it?"

"I walk through our halls often and look up at all your ancestors, even your parents, and I've realized something about these portraits."

"Which is?"

"They're all done when the individual is along in his or her years, in some cases very, very old, and despite the skill and talent of the artist at the time, they look . . . unattractive."

"Unattractive?"

"None of them even smiles."

"Well, traditionally back then—"

"Yes, back then. I'm thinking about now, 1895. I would like my portrait done, but done as I am so I can be remembered as I am now and not like some decrepit old lady riddled with arthritis and wrinkles, her face full of bitterness," I said. "Don't deny it. You've made similar comments about those portraits from time to time."

He stared at me, and then he smiled. "That's a rather good idea. Years and years from now, I'll be able to point to it and say, 'You can see why I wanted very much to marry her.'"

All about himself, I thought, always.

"Yes, exactly. You can boast for as long as you live."

"Okay. You probably don't have an artist in mind, but I can—"

"It so happens I do. He is an up-and-coming artist, and he's done a number of ladies in Charlottesville. The last was Amanda McKnight. He's booking his new client very soon, and I'd like to contract with him before he gets on to someone else. These things take time, and it could be most of the year away from being done if I don't."

"William McKnight hired him to do his wife's portrait?"

"You know him, I assume?"

"He has a steamship-building company. He and I have had some financial doings. Happens to be a good businessman. Certainly not one to waste money on some amateur. What's the artist's name?"

"Beau Dawson."

"Never heard of him. Did Mrs. McKnight indicate the cost?"

"Of course not," I said. "How common it would have been for her to have done so or for me to have asked. People would think you were concerned about money."

He nodded. There was nothing easier than stroking Garland Foxworth's ego.

"Yes. Well, I do like to know what I'm spending before I spend it, but . . . if this is what you want, I'll send a message to him from my office tomorrow, and as long as it's not something ridiculous, I'll hire him to do your portrait. I don't suppose you know where he resides."

"I heard him say he was with his cousin in Charlottesville for the time being, Beverly Morris."

"Beverly Morris . . . Ethan Morris's widow? My father used to play cards with Ethan Morris.

Said he was stupid at it because he talked rather than paid attention and usually lost money."

He paused, obviously in deep thought about his father for a moment, and then his eyes seemed to snap on like just-lit candles.

"All right. I'll take care of it. I'll make sure he chooses to do you before anyone else. When it's finished, if I like it, I'll decide where we have it hung. Perhaps in here," he said, looking about and nodding. "I assume that would please you."

"Oh, yes. I'd like to think of it as a gift for you more than one for myself."

He liked that. "Well, then, I'll get Lucas to deliver a message for me right after he drops me off at the office tomorrow morning."

"Thank you, Garland," I said. I started out and then turned at the door. "I'm sorry you missed our trip to Virginia Beach. You would have enjoyed watching Malcolm behave more like a little boy."

"Well, why shouldn't he? What do you think he is if not a little boy?"

"A little Foxworth," I said.

His eyebrows went up, and then, completely missing my sarcasm, he laughed heartily. I could hear him still laughing when I started up the stairs. But he didn't hear mine. I was laughing harder on the inside.

Two days later, Garland sent me a note from his office. He had negotiated what he considered a good price for my portrait. The artist, this Mr.

Dawson, would contact me about the date he would begin next week. He was happy about it because he was leaving on another business trip in three days, and he thought having my portrait done would fill the empty hours until he returned. It so excited me that I reread his note three times.

So much of my younger self seeped into the Swan Room. Sitting on the bed, I imagined my younger self, Corrine Dixon, coming into the room giggling. She had just received a note from a lovesick boy who claimed his feelings for her dominated his every waking moment. He couldn't eat; he couldn't sleep. He pledged that no other boy would ever be as devoted. All he asked for was a chance to persuade her in person.

I remember how much I had enjoyed dangling my permissions to walk with me, send me letters, and, the highest prize, which I rarely bestowed, visit me, with my mother nearby chaperoning, of course. Then I would, usually abruptly, become inaccessible, stop responding to any correspondence. In my dreams I saw raining broken hearts, but I justified that by asking myself, what did they expect? Someone like me didn't commit to any one boy so early in her life.

My imaginary self turned to me with her head shaking, her eyes full of pity. *But didn't you?*

Like a popping bubble, she was gone. But I would not give in to the depressive shadows rushing in to fill her place, shadows that wanted to embrace me tightly like a too-small corset and squeeze all hope from my heart. I shook them off the way you might shake off a chill and opened my closet to search for the right dress to wear when I was sitting for my portrait, sifting and sifting through the garments like a prospector panning a promising stream for gold. Nothing satisfied me.

Frustrated, I screamed for Dora. She was across the way giving Malcolm his lesson. I went to the door and opened it to shout for her again, but she was already coming. Malcolm stood behind her in his doorway, his arms folded, his face his father's, incensed that I had interrupted his lessons and extended his study time. He had asked for both Dora and me to go down to the lake with him today so he could play with his new sailboat as soon as his lessons were done.

"Ma'am?" she asked.

"Go fetch Lucas, and have him prepare the carriage to take me to Miller and Rhoads on High Street immediately."

"Yes, ma'am."

She hurried to the stairs.

Malcolm stepped closer. "You said you would watch me sail my new boat. You said we'd even have a picnic lunch on the dock. Why are you going shopping?"

"If I'm not there, Dora will be."

His expression didn't change. It embarrassed me to be so affected by the glare of a child. I was actually intimidated, but lately I couldn't think of him as anything but a miniature version of his father. The older he became, the more of Foxworth emerged.

"Just go back to your room and wait. Dora will be right there to finish your lessons. If you do well, maybe your father will agree to your attending a boarding school someday."

"I don't want to go to a boarding school." He stamped his foot. "I'll never go to a boarding school."

"Don't you want to be with other boys and girls?"

"They can come here."

I laughed. "No, Malcolm. Dora can't be your teacher forever. Now, go wait in your room. I have important things to do."

Defiantly, he stood there. I returned to my room and prepared for my shopping trip. An hour later I entered the department store and began to study the displays of new fashions. I was immediately drawn to a robin-red blouse and a skirt so dark blue that it looked more like black from a distance. The blouse had a collar of ruffled silk fastened in front. Beside the two was a waistcoat that matched the skirt but on closer look was a shade or two lighter. I thought the colors were exciting.

"I was going to buy that, but my husband thought the colors were too bright. 'Blinding' was the way he put it," I heard, and turned to see Melinda Sue standing behind me. "Oh, hi." She giggled.

"Hello. They are bright, but I like it."

"For your portrait?" she asked with a sly grin.

"My portrait?"

She nodded, holding that idiotic smile.

"Does everyone in Charlottesville know already? Gossip is faster than the telegraph here."

She laughed. "Beau Dawson's cousin likes to brag about him, and you missed our Charlottesville Women's Club meeting. It was the most popular topic, of course. I wanted him to do my portrait, too, but my husband thinks I'm too young. He says a woman has to establish gravitas before she should have her portrait done to hang on family home walls or anywhere, for that matter."

"Gravitas? Might I say, from what you've told me and my meeting him at the Halloween party, that your husband is something of an idiot."

She laughed again but nervously checked to be sure no one was close enough to overhear us. "Well, he's right that most women we know wait until they're a bit older to have their portraits done," she said, trying to justify her husband's stinginess, especially when it came to her.

"There's nothing but money to stop any woman

from doing it again when she's older, if she wants to. I don't want to be remembered as an elderly woman, and those new photographs we have taken of us fade so quickly we look more like ghosts. I've never seen one that does me justice anyway, and there's no color. Besides, an artist, a good artist, doesn't only paint what he sees on the outside."

"What does that mean?"

"Haven't you ever heard of the artist's eye?"

"No, but it sounds so right." Like the child she was, she burst into a new idea, first giggling around it. "Maybe after you've had it done, my husband will change his mind. Or you can ask your husband to tell him to do so. He respects Garland very much. Most businessmen in Charlottesville do."

"How nice. I'll be sure to let him know he should do that. Right now, I have to attract a saleslady. I want to see how this looks on me."

"I can stand by if you want another opinion."

I didn't want to say her opinion wouldn't matter in the slightest, but I smiled. "Thank you."

Just as I turned to fetch someone, she put her hand on my forearm. "Look," she said, nodding to her right. "Over at the shoes. That is your famous Catherine Francis."

I turned to look.

"That woman has a bottomless expense account," she said.

"What? Why do you say so?"

"She brought home new fashions from London recently, and now she's here looking for more."

So much for her losing money and being in a desperate situation, I thought. And she bought them in London? Melinda Sue wasn't simply dropping that in. Jealousy had the key to every woman's house here in Charlottesville as well as anywhere. Little green-eyed monsters would seize on anything that would cause another, more attractive woman to suffer mere embarrassment, if not disgrace. It made them feel superior to me even though they were so far below me that they couldn't see up past my knees.

I stared at Catherine Francis, the rage swirling under my breast. First, she was far younger than I had imagined and, to my disappointment, quite stunning. She had rich, thick coal-black hair and a beautiful peachy complexion that made her even more exquisite. She looked a little taller than I was and carried herself with confidence.

"How do you know all this about her?" I asked Melinda Sue while I continued to watch Catherine Francis talk to a saleslady and then sit to try on a pair of shoes.

"Louise Mason is one of her best friends. You met Louise at the Halloween party."

"Did I?" I turned to her. "What other little bits and pieces about Mrs. Francis did she share? Did she talk about her trip to London in any detail, for example?"

"That's all I know," she said, quickly looking away. It was as good as confirming what I had always suspected.

"When did her husband die?" I asked, not that it would have mattered to Garland if he hadn't.

"A few years ago. She lives in a nice house and has servants, but I can't imagine her not being lonely. Most of the time," she added. "Maybe that's why she travels so much."

"Maybe there is more than one reason, although loneliness can make you do things you'll regret."

Her eyes widened. Perhaps she could see the fury in mine. "Oh, look at the time," she said, gazing at the watch she wore in a necklace. "I didn't realize I'd been here so long. I must apologize. I'd better go. I'm sure you'll choose the right clothes for your portrait."

"Sorry you have to rush out."

"I just remembered that my husband wanted me home with him. He thinks it's time we discussed having a child," she added in a whisper.

"Does he? How nice. I hope he or she looks like you, especially if it's a little boy. When they look like your husband, you feel like you have a little spy in your house."

She laughed, but I had already turned away and signaled to a saleslady.

After I had chosen my clothes, I had Lucas

take me directly home. I had come inches from confronting Catherine Francis. She either didn't know who I was, didn't care, or didn't see me. In my mind I envisioned my first words if she had said hello. They would be *How was my husband in London? Did he behave himself?* My words would be like knives.

But it didn't happen. I rode home with them burning under my breast, cutting into me instead.

I was sure Lucas had told Garland that he had brought me to the department store. I had deliberately told Lucas why I was shopping, but when Garland arrived home, he didn't ask to see what I would be wearing for my portrait. I decided I wouldn't mention it or show him until he asked. The result was that he didn't see the dress until my portrait was completed, but that was a journey that would change everything anyway.

Days later, as was his plan, Garland left to go to New York and then, because of a last-minute problem, he claimed, said he would have to go on to Maine. That morning he said he was leaving from his office in Charlottesville in the evening because it would be the fastest route to New York. When I looked at the train schedule, I saw none leaving for New York in the latter part of the evening. I believed he would spend the night at the Caroline and leave in the morning. Did he really think I was that stupid? Maybe by now he didn't care. The more occupied I was with my amusements, like having my portrait done, the more he could violate our vows.

If it weren't for Beau Dawson's impending arrival, I would have been depressed about it, depressed at what a fool he was making of me. I knew if I kept thinking about it, I wouldn't sleep well, and I would not look my best for my first portrait sitting. The following morning, I informed Mrs. Steiner of Beau's impending arrival. She looked surprised but happily so. Mrs. Wilson promised to have a hearty lunch prepared, because "artists are usually starving folk."

"Not this one," I told her. "But he'll enjoy whatever you prepare."

When Dora explained it all to Malcolm, prefacing and finishing with warnings to be extra polite to our special guest, he looked angry at first and then asked if he could watch.

"Absolutely not," I told him. "An artist cannot be distracted."

"What's that mean?"

"He has to focus on his subject so hard that he doesn't see or hear anything else, not unlike the way you are when you play with your train and other things and don't listen to either Dora or me."

His eyes narrowed with that characteristic Foxworth skepticism, and he walked away with his hands in his pockets and his shoulders hoisted just the way his father hoisted his after he had a conversation that didn't satisfy him. But I was too occupied with my own thoughts about my portrait sitting now to worry about him. The biggest question was where in the house I wanted it done.

I decided that the ballroom was too big and open, with servants marching back and forth in the hallway. No one could resist looking in at us, and there was something about using the library that soured me on the idea quickly. The area was too close to Garland's personal office. Would some unused bedroom in the less-traveled portion of the mansion make sense? Most would be too stuffy and dark. I'd have to get Mrs. Steiner and Dora there to spruce it up. Anywhere outside was too dependent on the weather. Of course, I could ask Beau Dawson for his opinion and find out where other women had their portraits painted in their homes, most likely in front of grand fireplaces, but even before I had the idea to do this, I wanted to be different from them. I didn't want to model anything I did after what these women did.

The one place I thought would be most comfortable and effective carried so many other negatives: my bedroom, the Swan Room. But there was one unspoken fact that made it very attractive to me. Garland avoided going into the

Swan Room. Most likely, when he was home and Beau was working on my portrait, he would not interrupt. He would not even peek in.

From the very first moment I contemplated doing this, there was a titillation around my heart. Even though it was something so many women in society were doing or having done, it felt "forbidden" to me. Certainly the idea of having a man stare at me in my bedroom, even for hours on end, didn't frighten me or make me nervous. I was used to men staring at me. Of course, no one would have done so this long, not even Garland in the early days, but I knew, expected, that Beau Dawson's stare would be more . . . analytical. He had a job to do and a challenge to meet. Others would see the results, and his career, his livelihood, could benefit or suffer. He would see what an artist has to see when he looked at me. That's all it would be, I told myself.

Why, I asked myself instantly after, was it always so easy to lie to myself?

I went up to the Swan Room and considered what I might rearrange. Beau would surely want the best lighting. Would he have me standing in one spot the whole time? Would he decide that painting me on the chaise might be interesting? Should I be near the vanity table? I couldn't rearrange anything yet, I realized. *I have to wait for him. He's the artist.* Now I was nervous. What if he didn't want to be in the Swan Room at all? Shouldn't I give him permission to search the mansion for the correct setting? Would that anger Garland? This was all making me quite fidgety. I couldn't give anyone instructions until Beau Dawson arrived and decided.

I hurried up to my room after eating practically nothing for breakfast because I was so nervous. I changed into the clothes I had bought for the portrait and then sat in front of the vanity-table mirror suddenly feeling quite helpless. Should I have my hair this way or that? Did I need some tint? Would Beau Dawson be upset by that? What about jewelry? I shook my head at my lack of self-confidence and my indecision. I should greet him totally nude and have him decide how I should look, I thought. The idea both excited and amused me.

I was able to make a firm decision about something. *I'm not going to wait for him below,* I thought. *I want him to see me descend those stairs, drifting down to him like some goddess. Maybe he'll never stop looking up at me.* I looked at the clock. He would be here very soon. My heartbeat matched the tick-tock.

And then, listening hard, I heard Mrs. Steiner greeting him. That was followed by Dora's approaching footsteps.

"The artist is here, ma'am," she said, after I had told her to come in. I remained sitting at the vanity table and looking at myself in the mirror.

"I will be right down," I said. "Go so inform him."

"Yes, ma'am."

*Let some time pass,* I told my anxious heart. Since my early days with Garland, it was simply not in my nature to reveal how anxious I was to meet or see any man. There were few men so handsome or intriguing these past years anyway. Finally, I took a deep breath and rose. It was so unlike me to be this insecure. *He's not going to like the clothes I chose,* I thought as I started to descend.

Lucas had brought all Beau's supplies in and was talking to him as I appeared. They both stopped talking and looked up at me. Lucas, as if caught doing something untoward, turned and rushed out of the house. Mrs. Steiner, standing in the library doorway, didn't move. Dora came out of the dining room with Malcolm. As I descended, I was afraid I'd miss a step and look absolutely grotesque.

"Good morning," Beau said when I drew closer.

"Mr. Dawson," I replied. When I reached the final steps, I turned toward Dora and Malcolm. "This is my personal assistant, Dora Clifford, and my son, Malcolm. Malcolm, say hello to Mr. Dawson."

Malcolm looked at me with that initial defiance.

He was born hating orders or commands. Dora pulled him forward, and Malcolm, true to his training, extended his hand.

"Pleased to meet you," he said. "I'm Malcolm Foxworth."

Beau smiled at me and then extended his hand. "Mr. Foxworth, my pleasure," he said.

"You're going to take my mother's picture?"

"No, not take it, paint it," Beau said.

Malcolm smirked. "Takes too long," he said. Dora tugged him.

"Only as long as it takes," Beau replied.

Malcolm didn't understand. I dare say Dora didn't, either, but Beau smiled at me.

"Shall we discuss the setting first, Mr. Dawson?" I said. "Perhaps we can talk in the library." I nodded at Dora, who whispered something to Malcolm and took him back toward the ball-room.

"Some tea?" Mrs. Steiner asked.

"Mr. Dawson?"

"Would love it," Beau said. "Thank you."

I gestured at the library door, and he walked in with me. He contemplated the room.

"It's a nice setting," he said, "but I don't see you. Not that I know if you read or not," he quickly added with a smile. "It's too . . ."

"Erudite?" I ventured. He lifted his eyebrows. "I confess I looked it up recently."

He laughed, and I sat on the settee and gestured

for him to sit directly opposite in the matching one.

"I imagine there are many possibilities in a house this large."

"Yes, but so much of it is hardly in use. There's dreariness in some sections."

"Well, living rooms or grand rooms are often used."

"I venture to guess that you need little or no distraction."

"I'm famous for my concentration once I begin."

"No doubt. I'll show you some of the house, but there is only one room that is . . . what's the word . . ."

"Sacrosanct?"

I thumbed through my vocabulary.

"Sort of sacred, sanctified?" he said.

"I don't know if I'd go that far. Only my personal maid spends any time in it. To clean, of course."

"Surely your husband . . ."

"He's not fond of it. He rarely goes into it."

"You have me intrigued," he said, just as Mrs. Steiner brought in a tray of tea and crumpets. She placed it on the table between us. "Thank you," he told her.

She nodded, glanced at me with an expression that spoke volumes of warnings, and left us. He poured us both a cup.

"I do warn you, although settings provide some feelings, I will probably see nothing but you no matter where we are."

"Is this what you tell all your clients?"

"Yes, but not as assuredly."

He sipped his tea and stared at me. I saw only his eyes and his lips forming that slight soft smile. I hadn't trembled inside this way for years. It was as if all the time in between had evaporated.

And I was truly Corrine Dixon again.

# 13

Feeling more like someone giving a tour in a museum, I showed Beau Dawson all the possible settings for my portrait in Foxworth Hall. He nodded when I described the possible disadvantages of each and, looking thoughtful, said nothing favorable about any. I was afraid he had settled on one of the fireplaces. Before he could suggest it, and even knowing how it was going to shock everyone, including him, I led him up the stairway and brought him to the Swan Room.

He stood in the doorway and stared at the image of the swan in the headboard, studying it so long that I thought showing him the room was truly a mistake. He gazed around but said nothing. I began to feel uncomfortable. After all, the only men in here since I had married Garland were he and Lucas for a very quick few moments.

"If you don't think this is appropriate, there are many other rooms we can consider."

"No, no. There's a certain sad but graceful beauty to it," he said, nodding at my headboard and walking farther into the room. "It's fascinating." He looked at the small swan bed. "This was your son's?"

"Intended to be. It didn't work out, but once I had it made, I didn't want to put it into forgotten storage. There's enough of that here, especially in the attic."

He continued to look around the room. Then he went to the windows and opened the drapes as far as they would go.

"Enough lighting. You wouldn't mind all my paraphernalia in here?"

"As long as I won't trip over anything," I said.

"Once I begin, I wouldn't fancy changing in midstream. As I said, although I don't use the setting in a portrait dramatically, I do pick up a feeling that carries into the work."

"Yes, I understand." I didn't completely, but I was ready to accept anything he told me.

"And a portrait is not something done in one day or two. You understand that as well, right?"

"Yes."

"I'll cover it every day when we stop, and I don't want it looked at until it's completed. It takes time, development, before it truly emerges as it is meant to be."

"I'll swear on a stack of Bibles," I said.

He laughed. "One will be quite sufficient, but your word is as good as that."

"Such trust on so little evidence. I'm flattered."

"A true artist cannot paint something that is

301

untrue. I'll ask you every day if you cheated and looked. If you should lie to me about it, my fingers would stumble with the brush."

"Lie? Why, sir, what do you take me for?" I asked with an exaggerated posture of offense.

He laughed again. "Do me a favor, and stand beside the chaise."

I did. He stared for a moment.

"Now, put your left hand on it, not leaning on it, just touching it. Yes. It's not that I would include it. It's just the attitude; your posture beside it seems right. As I've said, we don't want anything to distract from you in the portrait. Now, look at the swan," he said. "Tell me what you see, not with words, with your face."

"With my face?" I smiled and did what he asked. "Am I saying anything?"

"You see yourself under that wing, don't you? Protected in a way?"

"Yes," I said in barely above a whisper. How could he read that in me so quickly? Perhaps there really was what I had described to Melinda Sue, an artistic eye.

His eyes brightened with conviction. "We'll do it here."

"What about my clothes? I bought these for the portrait recently, thinking . . ."

"We'll see. I will do sketches first, from different angles. I'll get the answers from that. Good. Perfect." He slapped his hands together.

"I'll go down to get my supplies, and we'll begin immediately."

"I'll help," I said. He started to shake his head. "It is a journey carrying your things up and down those two sets of stairs. Why do it twice?"

"All right. You can take my case of pencils and pens, brushes. I'll bring the rest," he said. He started out and then stopped. "You're sure this is not going to upset anyone?"

"It's what I'd like if you like it, and that's all that matters. This is my portrait, and how and where it is done is for me alone to decide," I concluded firmly.

He raised his hands. "I won't get in your way, Mrs. Foxworth."

"I think by now you can call me Corrine. The way you say 'Mrs. Foxworth' makes me feel older, much older. And I brought you here to help me feel younger . . . forever."

He laughed. "Corrine it is, then," he said, and walked to the stairway with me slightly behind him, hiding my smile.

When he heard us bringing up Beau's things, Malcolm ran out of the ballroom, where Dora was giving him lessons.

"I wanna help!" he screamed.

"Go back to your lessons, Malcolm. There's nothing for you to do."

He stood there pouting until Dora tugged on him to return to his lessons. He continued to loudly voice what he wanted until he was out of sight.

"My son is quite spoiled," I told Beau. "Be firm with him if I'm not around and he approaches you. He'll take advantage if he sees an opportunity."

"It is often difficult to distinguish between high-spirited and too aggressive when it comes to young boys," Beau said. "I won't deny I was quite high-spirited."

"You won't have difficulty deciding when it comes to Malcolm Foxworth."

We brought everything into the Swan Room.

As he set up his easel, he said, "You do that often, do you?"

"What?"

"Call your son by his full name? Sounds so formal."

"You're in Foxworth Hall, Mr. Dawson. Someday he will be the master of it. Sometimes, even as young as he is, he thinks that time has come. It won't be long before he will refuse to answer to anything but 'Mr. Foxworth.'"

"Even when his mother addresses him?"

I didn't answer, because I had no doubt that as soon as he could command that, he would, even of me.

"Speaking of names, I do hope you will start calling me Beau rather than Mr. Dawson. An artist and his subject develop a rather intimate creative relationship. I suspect you already understand all that. Whether my subjects want to or not, they reveal much of themselves when they pose. We can never again be strangers."

"Sounds unfair. Too one-sided."

"I'm an open book. I assure you. Just turn the page."

"Maybe I will. All I really know about you is that you're from New York. What did your parents think of your pursuing a career as an artist?"

"Oh, boy," he said. "You go right for the jugular, don't you?"

"Pardon?"

"Let's just say my father didn't draw up papers, but for all practical purposes, he disowned me. He thought I was a philanderer just using the pursuit of art as an excuse. He was a real estate developer, building and renting buildings for businesses, office buildings, warehouses in Richmond. He wanted me to step into his shadow, but I was always off doodling, as he put it, and missed important deadlines, information, and so on. When I did my first painting and sold it to a wealthy family, he was quite annoyed. He told my mother that now I would think I could earn a living with my foolishness. He wanted me to give the money back to them."

"And your mother?"

"She was a gentle, very pretty woman who

supported me, but I was the only son in the family, so it was assumed at my birth that I'd be in my father's business, or shadow, I should say. I have two younger sisters. My father took my disinterest in his business as disrespect for who and what he was. My mother contracted typhoid fever and died when I was eighteen. She was only thirty-eight. Shortly after, I left home with practically nothing but my paintbrushes under my arm. I had met Jean-Paul, who was already a somewhat successful artist, my mentor, as I told you, and followed him to Europe to study. He became more than a teacher, more of a second father, maybe a truer father. When he returned to America, I did, too."

"Did you see your family?"

"I saw my sisters. My father had died by then. They're okay. The cash still flows, but I'm afraid they might be confirmed spinsters, Effie and Pauline. Only two years' difference, Effie the older in her mid-twenties."

"I'm sure they're not unpleasant-looking."

"No." He thought a moment and then shrugged. "I don't see them much at all now."

"Why not?"

"I think . . ."

"What?"

"They want me to be a father to them. After my mother's death, he made them quite . . . dependent. His shadow was there, waiting for me.

306

I practically fled," he said. "But this biography is taking me out of the place I want to be. When I paint, I don't want to be anywhere else or have another image in my mind."

"Before you even said we won't be strangers anymore, I thought it might make it better for us both if we knew more about each other."

"In a short while, I'll know more about you than you might want anyone to know."

"Sounds . . . dangerous," I said.

He laughed. "Okay," he said, after he had his large pad on the easel. "If you're ready, we'll begin. When you're tired, just speak up. I don't want to see fatigue in your face."

I took my position, and he took off his jacket and rolled up his sleeves.

"I must admit," I said. "Now that you've told me how much of me you will see and know, I'm a little afraid."

"Not as much as I am," he said.

He paused, pencil in hand, and began his intense artist's look at me. I saw the way his whole face changed, his eyes seemingly seeing past any facade I might cast over myself. They grew smaller as his face tightened. I tried not to move, but it felt as if my whole body was blushing, as though with those penetrating eyes he was touching me beneath my clothes, rushing up along my hips and tracing the curves in my body, gently lifting my breasts and with the tips of his visual fingers outlining my suddenly erect nipples.

I shifted my feet and wet my lips with the tip of my tongue. His expression didn't change. His hand was moving rapidly over his canvas. He paused, looked harder at me, and then began drawing again. I saw him switch to a thicker chalklike utensil.

"What is that?"

"Charcoal," he said. "For background, so I can envision how I will bring out the colors I want. You'd make no sense of this if you looked at it. I was once told that a sculptor sees the sculpture he wants to do in a block of stone and simply chips away to bring it out. I think the same way. I see you standing there, but I want to bring you out. Understand?"

"Honestly? I'm not sure."

He smiled. "Maybe you will be when I'm done."

He tore off the paper on which he had worked and tossed it to the floor, then started another. I didn't look at the clock, but it felt like over an hour had passed. He showed no sign of wanting to pause, and despite feeling a bit uncomfortable holding my pose, I didn't ask him to take a break.

"I'm getting up a rough shape of your face for now. At this point I don't have to be that accurate. I'm determining where I'll have the lighter areas, where the edges will be soft. I call this the fetus."

"What?"

"An artist, any creative person, essentially goes through a sort of birthing. Just like a child develops inside a woman, the work gradually finds its shape and its . . . soul inside the artist."

"Well, I do hope it doesn't take nine months," I said, and he stopped to laugh harder than ever.

"You are very clever, Mrs. . . . Corrine. Somehow I have to capture that. Just a little longer, and then we'll take a rest. Promise."

"I'm fine," I lied.

When he stopped, I felt all my muscles relax. They actually ached a little. I hadn't realized how much of the time I had gone in and out of holding my breath. As he wiped his hands, my bedroom door was thrown open, and Malcolm rushed in. As soon as he saw the papers on the floor, he seized some.

"Ugh," he said. "This doesn't look like you. It's stupid. I could draw better."

Beau laughed.

"I told you so many times, Malcolm Foxworth, that you knock before you come into my room."

Dora stepped up behind him, obviously out of breath. "He just got up and ran out of the ballroom before I could grab him, ma'am, and then he ran up the stairs. He wasn't doing his work. He wouldn't stop asking questions about the portrait."

"He doesn't go out to play today. He goes right

to his room and stays there until dinner," I said.

Malcolm looked at me, his face in a rage. And then he started to tear the papers apart, dropping the pieces to the floor, until Dora grabbed his arm and turned him toward the door.

"Now he has his dinner in his room as well, Dora," I called after her.

She closed the door, and for a moment it felt as if a blizzard had gone through.

"Well," Beau said, looking a bit overwhelmed himself. "You do have a handful there."

"I'm so sorry."

He picked up the pieces of his drawings. "My first critical review," he said, smiling. "It wouldn't have been much longer before I did the same."

"That door has a lock. I think I'll begin to use it."

His expression of surprise was tinged with a little fear. "Wouldn't that be . . . indiscreet?"

"This, Beau, is the only space I have in Foxworth Hall that is, as you suggested, sacrosanct. When I told you my husband was not fond of this room, I understated the situation. He won't come into it, spend any time in it, if he can at all help it."

"Oh." He glanced at the bed.

Before he could ask why, there was a knock on the door.

"Yes?"

Dora stepped in.

"I'm so sorry about all that, ma'am."

"I assure you that I know you do your best, Dora. Thank you. Let's just enforce the discipline this time. It's all he understands, I'm afraid."

"Yes, ma'am." She glanced at Beau and then backed out and closed the door.

I sat on the chaise. "I fear I'll be forever apologizing for what Malcolm does to people."

"Relax," he said. "I'll dabble while you sit there."

"How long did it take you to do Amanda McKnight?"

He leaned forward to whisper. "I could have done it in four days but stretched it to ten; otherwise she would have thought it too simple."

"Should I use that time line as a guide?"

"I'll work until it's done if you let me," he said.

"I'm in no rush. Unfortunately," I added.

He paused, debating whether he should ask his question or not.

"My husband is on a business trip. It could last longer than he described before he left. It usually does. For lots of reasons."

"I see."

He worked quietly. After a while, I asked him if he wanted me to stand again.

"It's fine for now. Did you want to do something?"

"You mean go to the loo?"

He laughed. "Brilliant idea." He put his pencil down.

"I'll show you the closest convenience," I said, starting to rise. He rushed to give me his hand. When I stood, we were inches from each other. For a moment, neither of us spoke or moved. Perhaps he was seeing if I would, or perhaps I was testing him.

"When I was a little boy, my father would put a chocolate on a plate in front of me after dinner and have me sit there looking at it until he decided if I deserved it or not. He was a bit of a tormentor. Lots of times, he decided I didn't deserve it, so I had to get up dreaming of it. After a while, I got so I could taste it even if I didn't eat it."

"And then?"

"I would ask to be excused as if I didn't care. He was more frustrated than I was."

"And you're telling me this because . . . ?"

"Are you going to make me say it?"

I smiled. "Yes."

"I think of your lips as that chocolate."

"You had to taste a chocolate once to imagine what it tasted like afterward, didn't you?"

"I'm afraid of one thing," he said.

"What?"

I expected him to say Garland's name, but he didn't.

"Anyone who looks at your portrait after I've done it will know."

"I hope so," I said, and he kissed me.

I think from the moment I had seen him at Amanda McKnight's house, I had envisioned this moment. It was in my daytime fantasies ever since and even in my dreams.

"Better than chocolate?" I asked when he pulled back.

He pretended to be giving it serious thought. Then he smiled. "I know you won't believe me," he said, "but I've never done this."

"Kissed a girl?"

"Kissed someone I was painting."

"Why me, then?"

He glanced back at the swan. "She told me it was all right," he said.

I wondered what else she would permit. I wondered what he really thought of me, being so permissive so quickly. Had he pieced together all the hints I had dropped? Did he sense my unhappiness that quickly, perhaps the first time we had met? Or was he just like Garland when we first met, seeking a new conquest? What did he think would come of it? Did he care? Did I?

Neither of us spoke of it for the remainder of the day. It remained like a fine jewel we both could turn over and over in our minds. We broke for lunch. Mrs. Steiner had set it up in the nook where I had my lunch with Melinda Sue. While we ate, he talked more about his travels in Europe. I told him he was sounding a lot like my husband in the earlier days of our marriage.

"Perhaps he was trying to get you to want to go with him on those trips."

"No. I did ask to go often, and he always had some reason why I wouldn't enjoy it, but that was also always followed with the promise of our visiting some of these places as honeymoons. I must warn you, not because of his failure to fulfill these pledges, but because I've never liked the idea of it."

"Of what? Traveling?"

"No, no. Promises. I don't believe anyone who makes one. To me, they're setting up excuses not to do something. At least, that was my experience most of my childhood."

"Interesting. I find myself agreeing. A healthy skepticism helps us avoid disappointment."

Whenever either of us paused in our conversation, we fell back into each other's eyes, gazing at each other in a way that would tell the dullest observer that we were filling our cups of desire rapidly and willingly. Every time Mrs. Steiner or Mrs. Wilson walked in or even just passed the doorway, we both blushed as if we thought they had seen our kiss in the Swan Room and could see another coming any moment.

*Stop this while you still can,* a little voice of conscience told me. It sounded quite like my mother's voice. I wanted to smother it but obediently turned away from him instead. After lunch, we returned to the Swan Room, where he continued to explore with his drawings. Strangely, we both fell into a deeper silence, as if we knew that words led to touch and touch led to a storm of feelings that would easily sweep over us both.

"I like where this final drawing is going," he finally said. "I'm going to take it with me and study it tonight. If I'm right, I'll begin the portrait tomorrow."

He began to put away his things. I slipped onto the chaise and watched him. I could see how hard he was trying not to look at me.

"You don't want to show me that?" I asked.

He looked up from fastening his case of pencils and brushes. "It won't mean anything to you," he said. He put his right forefinger on his temple. "I'm going to begin filling it in with what is being shaped in here."

"Such a mysterious process," I said. "You make it sound more like magic."

"It is to me."

"You wouldn't want to stay for dinner?"

"Oh, no, thank you. I have homework," he said, smiling. He rolled down his sleeves and put on his jacket. I rose when he started for the door. "Your coachman was kind enough to feed and water my horse," he said as we started out and toward the stairs. "I have a little buggy. It's really my cousin's."

"I have one, too, but I rarely use it. My father had one as well as his coach, and he'd let me be the driver when I was barely nine," I said.

We descended. The house was very quiet. When we reached the entry hall, he paused to look back and up.

"I don't know if I could be comfortable in a mansion this size," he said. "It makes you feel . . ."

"Small? Forever a stranger?"

He smiled without saying anything, and we walked to the door. As if he had been waiting all this time, Lucas was out front with Beau's buggy.

"Did he hear us coming down the stairs?" Beau asked.

"Maybe. He lives to please—my husband, mostly."

"It's getting chilly, Corrine. We can say good night here," Beau said.

"As long as it's not good-bye," I said.

He smiled and shrugged. "That day will come."

"Will it?"

I stepped back, wanting to have the surprised look on his face be the last one of his for the day that I held in my thoughts.

As I started for the stairway, Mrs. Steiner appeared, just like one of those Foxworth ghosts

I often imagined. I was thinking that she had been watching us from some doorway. Did she, too, make reports often to Garland? Had she done so all these years? Why should she be any more loyal to me, after all?

"Oh, Mrs. Steiner," I said. "I'm a bit tired tonight. Standing for hours was a great deal more tiring than I had imagined it would be. Would you be so kind as to have Dora bring my dinner to my room tonight? Be sure there is that wine I favor, too."

"Very good, Mrs. Foxworth."

I went up the stairs slowly. My heart and my head were filled with conflicting emotions and thoughts. Everyone seemed to be arm wrestling the other for dominance. I did feel exhausted, but unlike the impression I had given Mrs. Steiner, it was a good feeling of exhaustion. When I stepped back into the Swan Room and saw the things he had left, I easily envisioned him still there. It had been a long time since I had felt this young, felt like a girl with a crush on some handsome boy, which was usually a short-lived flirtation.

I changed into my nightdress, brushed out my hair, and washed my face before returning to the Swan Room and lying in bed. I closed my eyes and drifted through my memories of the day, highlighted by that forbidden kiss. Just then, there was a knock on the door. Dora was bringing me my tray. She helped fix my pillows and reported that Malcolm was refusing to eat.

"Don't force him or argue with him, Dora. In fact, take the food out, and tell him you won't be bringing him anything more tonight."

"But later . . ."

"Later he'll feel some pebbles of regret. If we don't teach him that his misbehavior can also be painful for him, he won't change, Dora. I fear he won't change no matter what, but at least we'll make an effort."

"Yes, ma'am."

"Take his food," I emphasized.

She nodded and left. Imagining Malcolm wishing he had not been so insolent and regretting his defiance now helped my own appetite. I ate well, drank all the wine, and then opened a book to read myself to sleep. The words drifted, constantly interrupted by the vision of Beau standing there, concentrating so hard on me. Garland's escapades and absence were painful, but for now, at least, Beau Dawson helped me put all that aside.

It was as if I had never married.

Was that a feeling or a wish?

Whatever it was, it helped me sleep, because the faster the evening went by and the faster the morning came, the faster Beau Dawson would return.

I curled up and embraced my big, soft pillow.

Somewhere in Charlottesville, he was sitting by a lamp and gazing at his drawing of me.

Perhaps he would go to sleep with the same impatience for morning and the same dreams.

# 14

Every one of the next four days was special and different in some way, even though we did the same things. Malcolm always asked to join us whenever we took breaks, but I told him he had to show me he was going to behave before I would include him in anything. He did try to be meek and obedient, but I held him back. I knew he would take up all of Beau's attention with incessant questions. "Perhaps in a few more days, if I see you're not misbehaving," I told him. He glared at me with his father's suspicious eyes, but for now, I held him at bay.

If the weather permitted, Beau and I left the house to get air and a walk, usually ending at the dock and looking out at the lake. The first time we did that, I found I could think only of Garland during that day my parents and I first had arrived at Foxworth Hall to talk about the wedding. Garland had already started to build a stage and a dance floor. My mother had seen a great deal of the house, with Mrs. Steiner guiding and explaining, and had gone in to take a rest. My father had continued to walk about the grounds with Garland and talk about the reception, deciding where kiosks would be set up for food and drink, what to do first after the ceremony, who would speak to the guests, and more about who was invited. They left me out of the discussion. After all, who was I? Just the bride. But this was a man's world, and there was no greater example of that than the planning of my wedding at Foxworth Hall.

I had left them talking to Olsen about construction of the stage and walked close to this very spot by the lake. It was June and warm, so I had sprawled out on the plush grass to look up at the clouds sliding across the deep blue sky. Now that I was there with all this happening around me, I had never felt as swept away. All my childhood friends and experiences had drifted back. It truly had been like being reborn, a new name, a new life, and with people I knew less than a day.

I had been so young, so frightened, and so lost. Garland had come to me, and for a while at least, he was quite romantic and loving, putting my unease to rest. Obviously, I had been filled with a natural fear of all things new, but especially new here, with so much to know and learn about the Foxworths and the property. Now, when I recalled his assurances, full of promises, I realized they were as light and out of reach as the geese we could see flying south. They disappeared in a cloud. It was the way I felt now, so much of my early life here disappearing into a cloud.

"The grounds of Foxworth are a gold mine for a landscape artist," Beau said as he gazed out over the lake. "Even now, with all the leaves and color disappearing, there are so many inspiring scenes. I can envision you everywhere, with this beautiful background around you." He laughed. "I'd paint you standing on the just-frozen water or standing on this dock with the wind blowing through your hair. A landscape of any of this without you in it is nothing more than pretty wallpaper." He turned to me.

I smiled softly to myself and said nothing. I could feel his eyes on me. His breath, like mine, was visible in the much cooler air. I imagined the wisps of it joining before disappearing.

"You seem to grow younger as soon as you step out of the mansion," he said.

"Like it's my first day here? That young?"

"Yes. I can picture that big-eyed, overwhelmed girl. How lonely and frightened you must have been."

I held my smile and walked along to my right, because I knew the grounds dipped there and unless you were in the attic, looking in this direction, you would not see anyone. I was sure our servants were talking about Beau and me taking these walks. We didn't hold hands or walk particularly close to each other, but Garland Foxworth's wife alone with a man, even in broad daylight, was something of great interest for them.

"You go rowing here often?" Beau asked, starting after me.

"No. I don't do anything particularly often," I said. I turned to him. "Don't you know what the women in Amanda McKnight's women's club call me? Didn't she mention that?"

He smiled, his eyes telling me that she had. "The Lady of Shalott?"

"Maybe they're right," I said. "Most of the time I find myself somewhere in the mansion looking out."

"I find people are right about you only when you let them be," he said, drawing closer. He was only inches away.

I looked toward the house. Again I thought, no one could or would see us. My courage, but more so my desire, rose to the surface.

"Was that taste of chocolate enough for you to imagine it whenever you wished and therefore not need to taste it again?" I asked.

"No, but I'm afraid of how much I want it again and where that could go."

"I'm not," I said.

He looked at me so hard and was so quiet that I thought, or rather feared, it was all he would do. In a moment he was going to turn and say, "We should start back to the house." But he didn't. He stepped closer and put his hands on my shoulders as he brought his lips to mine, so gently at first that it felt more like he was brushing his lips across mine, and then he pressed harder, firmer, as his hands moved down and around me, pulling me tenderly against him. I felt myself going limp, sinking into the strength of his arms, as his kiss parted my lips and his tongue touched mine, sending a streak of lightning down through my neck to my breasts. We pulled our mouths away from each other only to catch our breath so we could kiss again.

Then he stepped back just a little and lowered his head while he slipped his hands down my arms and took my hands in his.

"What are we really thinking about each other?" he asked, as if there was some mind reader standing beside us.

"You could be thinking I am a frustrated wife trapped in a mansion with a spoiled child doomed to become his arrogant father, and I could be thinking you are a self-confident young artist who falls in love with his prettier portrait women easily and enjoys knowing they will keep what he has done secret because they have no choice."

"Very possibly true," he said, "except for one detail you left out."

"Which is?"

"I have never had a prettier, more beautiful woman to paint than you."

"But there were others? You didn't tell the truth about that when I asked?"

"Not really others. I had women who posed for

me while I was developing my talent, and one or two were . . . attractive, but I wouldn't say I fell in love or do so easily. I fall in love with what I've painted more than the woman I've painted, if you can understand that."

"Is that what's going to happen here?"

"I don't know. Perhaps there'll be no difference between the painting and the woman this time."

He looked back toward the house.

"Maybe we should go back. I can get a lot more done today, and—"

I pulled him back toward me.

"Corrine—"

I put my finger on his lips to stop him from saying anything more.

And then he kissed me with such tenderness that I longed to be naked beside him, my body touching his. This feeling was never as strong with Garland as it was now with Beau. I was a child then; now I was a woman, I thought, and it was a world of difference.

"Corrine . . . we're gone too long. Let's go back. I do want to get to the painting."

"Let's," I said, and started away abruptly, digging my heels into the hard earth.

"I hope you're not upset with me," he said, catching up.

"No. More intrigued, if anything."

We both were silent all the way back to the house, me walking with my head down, my arms embracing myself, and the taste of his lips remaining on mine even after we entered the mansion.

I could feel something had changed, or perhaps the better word would be *deepened,* between us after that walk to the lake. Beau worked with more intensity, stepping back and looking at the canvas, constantly shaking his head and then returning. We hardly spoke when he arrived in the morning and seemingly rushed through lunch to get back to the work. There was definitely a new intensity to everything he did. I had the oddest dream in which I saw myself being drawn out of my body slowly and then being painted onto the canvas. Soon I would be simply an empty shell standing there. I woke with a start. What I feared in the dream was that I would be a prisoner of my portrait, hanging on a wall in Foxworth Hall forever and ever, silently.

Indeed, sometimes during the next two days, I felt that my part in this was over, that he could continue the painting solely from what he had captured in his imagination. Often I was afraid to speak, fearing that I would make his artistic eye blink and he'd lose me. At times, when I watched him contemplating his work, I half-expected he would lunge at the easel, tear the canvas off, and declare we had to start over from day one.

Finally, when he took a breath right before we were going to break for lunch this time, I asked him if he was always this highly critical of his work.

"Why do you ask such a thing?"

"I see only a face of dissatisfaction most of the time these past few days," I said.

He smiled. "I'm afraid no painting, no artist, can do you justice. All I hope to do is approach the height of your beauty, touch it enough so that anyone looking at this work would think, *She had to be one of most beautiful women in all of Virginia.*"

"Your compliments will do me in. My mother used to say I couldn't pass a mirror, even a pane of glass, without looking at myself. How will I ever come back to earth, live with mere mortals, if your painting is that good?"

"Don't return to earth. Let them come up to you. From what I hear, many would like to be you. They look up at Foxworth Hall and dream of it."

"Do they?" I grimaced, thinking of their green eyes of jealousy as they whispered behind my back.

"Does that displease you?"

I shrugged. Why give them the satisfaction of my caring? "I don't think about it. Can we have lunch? This angel is starving. Posing is more work than you artists know."

He laughed, put down his brush, and gently covered the canvas, and we went down.

Mrs. Steiner had the table set. She served us silently. I had no doubt she sensed what was in the air between Beau and me.

"How much longer do you think you'll need? Not that I'm bored with you or anything," I quickly added.

"Maybe I'm really like Penelope."

"What? Who is that?"

"The wife of Odysseus, who remained faithful to him by promising to choose a new husband when she was finished weaving a burial shroud for Odysseus's father. Each night she unraveled the day's work."

I laughed. "You're not unraveling anything, but . . . I do suspect you are being a little more critical of what you've done in order to keep it going longer."

"Suspect or hope?"

I looked toward the door. "You know it's hope," I said in a whisper.

He had started to reach under the table for my hand when Lucas knocked on the open door.

"Yes, Lucas?"

He looked first at Beau.

"Mr. Foxworth will be home today," he said. "After four. He sent word that I should let you know."

"Thank you, Lucas."

"I guess I should get back to the weaving," Beau said after Lucas left us. "I think the work will be ready for him to view."

"It's for me no matter what he thinks," I said firmly.

Beau smiled. "No. It's for me," he corrected.

I could see that there was truly a sense of finality to the work in the afternoon. He was doing so little now with his brushes, and when he stepped back to contemplate it all, he began to look more satisfied.

"You're not rushing it just because Garland is returning, are you?" I asked.

"No. Now I am wondering where you intend to have it hanging."

"Garland said something about putting it in the library, close to his office."

"I would do the same," he said. "I cannot imagine that he doesn't love you very much, Corrine."

"And I thought an artist was supposed to have deeper vision and insight. My husband's ability to love someone other than himself is quite limited."

He smiled. "I really haven't met your husband, so I can't say."

"He doesn't have to be here for you to see him," I said, or more like muttered. "I haven't been able to change a shadow once cast by the Foxworths. Sometimes I imagine that the mansion literally has their blood pulsating through the walls."

Beau was silent. Perhaps he felt helpless and saw no point in encouraging anything. Instead, he studied and studied the portrait, and then he put down his brush.

"You've been quite honest about not sneaking a look, haven't you?"

"Yes. For some reason, I have trouble even imagining lying to you."

He laughed. "Am I the first man who can claim that?"

"I believe you are," I said, nodding. "Yes, I think you are."

"I will be holding my breath," he said, and stepped to the right.

"Really? It's time?"

"Really, it is."

I was actually a little afraid of walking across the room. I glanced at the swan before I took a step. Beau saw where my gaze was going.

"She's been watching with that one eye of hers," he said. "The whole time. To make sure I do you justice."

"Yes, I think so."

I stepped around and looked at my portrait. It took my breath away. I think I gasped. I did feel a glow as he stood there watching my reaction to my portrait. It was joy but also the embarrassment that comes with being totally exposed, naked, because I thought anyone would look at it and see my affection for the artist.

"I didn't believe I would say it," I said in a whisper. "None of the artists who did any of the Foxworth ancestors succeeded in doing this."

"Doing what?"

"You've made me more beautiful than I am."

"That's who you are . . . to me," he said. "There's nothing exaggerated there."

I studied my face, the way he had my eyes turning in his direction as he painted. There was no far-off, postured look. Those were my eyes every moment he worked, and what I was looking at was very clear, at least to me.

"Do I see what you saw?"

"What's that?"

"The way I'm looking at you." I turned to him. "My desire? In my eyes."

"It's what I saw, yes, but for a long while, I wondered if I was painting what I hoped rather than what I was seeing."

"Now you know."

"Yes," he said. He stepped closer. "Now I know. But we are trapped, you and I, in that painting. I fear it's as close as we'll ever be."

I nodded, feeling the tears beginning in my eyes. "Maybe I won't give it to my husband," I whispered. "Maybe I'll have it hanging in here."

"That might be a mistake," he said. "As I recall, you told me you convinced him to have it done by telling him it was for him."

"Everything's for him," I muttered.

"I'll send a framer around with a few of my suggestions. I'm not a political man, but you might want to let your husband make that choice."

*"No,"* I said firmly. "This is mine. I make that choice. It's not finished until it's framed."

"Okay," he said.

I smiled as an idea took hold.

"What?" he asked.

"Perhaps we'll have a party to celebrate it and you. Lots of potential new customers for you. If I can keep you busy, I can keep you in Charlottesville."

"Weave and unweave?"

"Yes."

"I'd paint the portrait of a hyena if I knew it would keep me close to you."

I stepped toward him, and he brought his lips to mine. Our kiss was sweet and long, until we heard the door swing open. Before I could take a breath, I realized I had forgotten to lock it this time.

Malcolm stood there looking at us. We had pulled apart quickly, but did he see?

He was holding a sheet of paper with a drawing on it. He stepped forward and looked at the finished portrait. His eyes widened, and then he pressed his lips together, ballooning his cheeks.

"Doesn't look like you," he said.

"I've told you many, many times that you knock before you come into my room, Malcolm. You know better."

"I wanted to show you this," he said, and tossed the paper at us. "It's better than that."

He stepped out, closing the door behind him. Neither Beau nor I moved for a moment. Then he picked up the sheet and smiled.

"He did a picture of you," he said, and showed me the crude drawing with some basic resemblance. "Pin it on the wall or something to make him feel better."

I nodded but put it on my vanity table and then watched him gather his things.

"For now, leave the portrait on my easel. The framer will be here in late morning with samples, and you can have it brought down."

He snapped his case together.

"Will you be back to help decide?"

"No. As you said, it's your decision, and whether you like it or not, your husband will have some say, I'm sure."

"But . . ."

"Let time pass. You know where I'll be," he said. He put on his coat.

I took out the key to my door lock.

"I don't trust Malcolm," I said, looking at the portrait on the easel.

"Really?"

"He's capable of sneaking in here and

destroying it. He did something like that with my wedding album."

I locked the door behind us, and we started for the stairway. I saw our groundskeeper, Olsen, speaking with Mrs. Steiner. They both looked up as we descended.

"Lucas has gone for Mr. Foxworth, ma'am," Mrs. Steiner said. "Olsen will bring up Mr. Dawson's buggy."

"Thank you, Olsen," I said, and he hurried out.

"And how is the work going, if I might ask?" Mrs. Steiner said, her face full of suspicion. She wasn't really asking about the painting.

"I believe it's finished," Beau told her. "I want to thank you for your kindness and ask you to pass my gratitude to Mrs. Wilson for her wonderful lunches."

"I will," Mrs. Steiner said, surprised. Maybe she thought he'd be here for months. "I do look forward to seeing the portrait."

"We have a framer coming tomorrow," I said.

"How nice to have it ready for Mr. Foxworth to see on his return," she said, and walked off toward the dining room.

"How long has she been working here?" Beau asked.

"Centuries."

He laughed, and we headed toward the front entrance. Once there, he looked back to be sure there was no one within hearing.

"Whether your husband wants a party or not, I will see you again," he said.

"You thief of beauty. You stole my words."

He smiled and opened the door. Olsen had his buggy at the front.

"Mrs. Foxworth," Beau said, with a small bow. We both felt Olsen's eyes on us. "It's been delightful. Please give my regards to Mr. Foxworth."

"He'll be happy to receive them," I said.

Beau nodded and hurried down to his buggy. Olsen told him something about his horse, and he thanked him. I watched him get in, put his things in safely, and then pause to look at me as if for the last time before he started away.

My heart fluttered as an ache of disappointment traveled through my body. I did feel like a shell of myself, with a heavy emptiness turning my heart into stone. I stood there, embracing myself. Olsen gazed at me and then hurried away as if he had seen something in my face that he shouldn't. I didn't reenter the mansion until Beau and his buggy dipped below the drive and were gone.

*He has left himself upstairs,* I told myself, to stop the tears that were building. I hurried in and started up the stairway. Dora, holding Malcolm's hand, was standing at the top, waiting for me.

"Master Malcolm has something to say," she told me.

I looked at him. "What is it, Malcolm?"

"I'm sorry I didn't knock," he said.

I softened my face and lowered my shoulders. "Well, just so you remember for the next time. There are other women in this house as well, and you're old enough now to respect their privacy."

"Mrs. Steiner has told us Master Malcolm's father is returning this afternoon," Dora said.

"Ah. I hope you're not apologizing because you're afraid of what your father will think and do, Malcolm."

He didn't reply; he just stared at me.

"There's no reason to tell your father anything now. Maybe he'll have something nice for you. He always does when he returns from a long trip."

"Not always," Malcolm said sharply.

I smiled inside. He probably remembered exactly which times Garland hadn't. Even at nearly five, he had grave doubts about his father.

"Well, let's wait to see. We'll have to get ourselves ready for dinner soon. I'm sure your father will be hungry. We want to look special tonight, Dora."

"Yes, ma'am," she said, and hurried him off to wash and dress.

I opened the door to the Swan Room and went to the portrait.

"Who are you, really?" I asked the woman staring back at me, looking in what was Beau's direction.

Then I went to choose something for dinner, wondering what the remainder of this day would bring.

Less than an hour later, as I was fixing my hair after preparing myself, I heard Garland's voice as he was coming up the stairway. He'd have to come into the Swan Room whether he liked it or not, I thought. I looked at my portrait. What would my husband, who was probably off womanizing, dare to think? Would he realize my beauty and how lucky he was to have me? Would the painting make him feel guiltier for betraying our marriage vows? Would he be down on his knees apologizing?

I was sure he knew it all, knew just how long Beau had been here and where we had decided, or I had decided, to have the work done. This was, after all, a den of spies. Even Dora was more frightened of him than she was of me, and she probably said more than I would like. But I had no fear, not in the Swan Room. In fact, never since I had been brought here had I ever felt less interested in what Garland Foxworth thought or wanted. It was as if the painting gave me more courage. I'd be hanging on these Foxworth hallowed and revered walls. Now everyone who entered had to look up to me as well.

Even Garland.

He surprised me by knocking hard on my door.

"I heard your portrait is done," he said, before

337

saying hello or greeting me with a hug and kiss after so long a business trip.

Normally, I would have put that aside. It wasn't out of character, and it had happened this way often.

"You sent me nothing to tell me your trip would go on and on," I said.

Lucas passed behind him, carrying his things to his room.

Garland waited and then smiled. "While I was in Boston, a company I had been watching went bankrupt, and I scooped it up for pennies on the dollar. There was much to do, and the details would surely have bored you."

"I'm not a total empty head, Garland."

"Forget all that." He looked past me at the easel. "Turn it around so I can see it."

"Just come in," I said, stepping back.

He hesitated, and then he entered and looked at the portrait.

"I heard this artist was here all the time I was gone," he said, instead of commenting on the painting.

"Portraits are not photographs," I said.

"He left earlier today?"

"Yes."

"Maybe he was afraid of my opinion."

"What is your opinion?"

"It's a good job. Maybe a little too colorful, but that's fine. We'll keep it in the library."

"A framer is coming tomorrow," I said. "Beau is taking care of that."

"Beau?"

"Mr. Dawson, the artist you hired. The one you think might be afraid of your opinion."

"Oh, right. Well, then, we can say it's money well spent. Let's talk more about it over dinner. I'm famished from all my traveling to get here this early."

"You weren't back yesterday and staying at the Caroline House?"

"Enough of that," he said sharply. "I'm still repairing the damage you did with your suspicions."

"Really? I happened to be in the department store recently when Mrs. Francis was buying herself new things. Word was she brought back a lot from London, especially for someone who just lost all that money in one of your enterprises."

"I never said she was desperate."

"You said she had to tighten up on her expenses."

"I don't watch everyone else's bank account, Corrine. That was what I would have done. Since when do you take notes on my exact words?"

"Only when I think it involves me, too," I replied. I did not cower before his burst of anger. I did have more courage.

He saw it in my face and blew out a breath to get control of his anger. "Okay, okay. Enough of that. Mrs. Wilson is preparing a roast. Let's enjoy our dinner to celebrate my return."

"And the completion of my portrait."

He grunted and started out, then paused, glanced again at the portrait, and kissed me on the cheek.

"It's certainly good enough to make my friends jealous," he said, smiling.

"I was hoping it was good enough to make you happy."

"It is. Damn it, woman. Since when did you become a nag? I'll make more of it when I'm not as tired and hungry. Okay?"

"Garland," I said when he stepped to the doorway.

"Yes?"

"Perhaps we should have a little celebration, invite some of those friends and their wives, and highlight the portrait."

"To celebrate you or celebrate the artist?"

"Why not both?"

He thought a moment and then shrugged. "Why not?"

When he left, I closed the door. I felt as if I had been holding my breath the entire time.

Had I convinced him of the innocence of all this, or was it that he simply didn't care?

Somehow, thinking of the Foxworth ego, I was skeptical. Like all men in this country, maybe on this whole planet, he believed forgiveness was his right. It followed quickly on the heels of any sin he might commit, especially adultery.

But for a woman . . . there wasn't any forgiveness.

I gazed again at the woman in my portrait. She looked like she didn't care if she was forgiven or not, as long as she was loved.

And now she knew where that love awaited.

# 15

Anyone sitting at our dinner table would surely conclude that nothing new had happened in my life while Garland was gone, certainly nothing interesting enough to justify any attention on me. From the moment we sat to the moment we rose, Garland talked about his achievements, his travel, and his prospects for becoming one of the richest men in the state. Dora and Mrs. Steiner stood off to the side, listening and nodding whenever he turned to them.

"People have asked me to seriously consider running for governor," he boasted.

"Oh, you should, Mr. Foxworth," Mrs. Steiner said. "Anyone who can run all the businesses you do can certainly run a state."

He looked to me to second her, but I sat dumbly. Malcolm doodled on his napkin. Suddenly, for him, being an artist was more important than being a train engineer.

"Yes, well, we'll see," Garland said. He looked at Malcolm. "Stop that. You're at dinner."

Malcolm put his pencil down quickly.

"So," Garland began, sitting back, "it seems we might be planning a celebration of sorts, Mrs.

Steiner, an event in the ballroom to introduce a new portrait to Charlottesville society."

"Really? When would that be, Mr. Foxworth?"

I looked up. Was he teasing, or did he mean it?

"Let's give it a month to plan," Garland said thoughtfully. "There are some people I might want to come from afar, some investors. Wine and dine, Mrs. Steiner, wine and dine. More big deals have been made over too much wine than anything else."

Mrs. Steiner nodded as if she approved completely.

He turned back to me. "I imagine you'll want all those women in the women's club, eh, Corrine?"

"I don't know. I haven't given it that much thought."

"Oh? Well, when you do, give me your list to approve. There are a few husbands out there I'd rather not see."

He laughed and looked at Malcolm, who was staring at him with a strangely dissatisfied expression. He could look so hateful and mean sometimes. Whatever adorableness he projected with his good looks would evaporate before your eyes.

"Tomorrow I want to hear all about what you've done since I've been gone, Malcolm. I want to see how well you do with your letters and numbers, too. Dora, you'll take care of this?" Garland ordered.

"We'll have him ready, Mr. Foxworth."

"Good," he said, wiped his lips, and stood.

"You didn't bring anything for me," Malcolm blurted. "Nothing from your trip."

Garland looked speechless for a moment. To be reprimanded by his almost-five-year-old son uncovered a jar of angry bees.

"How dare you speak to your father like that? Is this the discipline you're being taught around here?" he asked, looking at me and then at Dora.

She wilted quickly.

He leaned down so his face was inches from Malcolm's. "I brought myself home safe and sound, didn't I? You should be happy you have so successful a father. Someday you'll have to run all this, so you'll have to be well educated. Your mother and I have been discussing a good boarding school for you," he added. "Maybe the time has come."

Malcolm looked at me as if I had done something behind his back.

"I told you about that, Malcolm," I said.

The truth was that Garland and I hadn't really discussed it, but on a number of occasions, I expressed my opinion to him that it would be a good idea to have our son exposed to other children, even though most would be from families almost as wealthy and surely as arrogant.

"Don't want to go to a boarding school," Malcolm said, looking down and away from both of us.

Garland stood straighter but hovered over him, poised at any moment to slap him on the back of his head. "Yeah, well, what you want to do and don't doesn't count for years, Malcolm. My father made all my decisions until I was nearly eighteen. It will be the same for you."

Malcolm bit down so hard on his lower lip he looked like he would draw blood.

Garland turned to Mrs. Steiner. "I'd like a cup of tea in the library, Mrs. Steiner."

"Yes, Mr. Foxworth."

He looked at me. "Let's get that portrait and the easel down to the library in the morning. Doesn't do any good hidden away in that room," he said, and walked out.

Malcolm leered at me, capturing his father's face in his. "You'd better not send me to a boarding school," he said, his eyes washed in threat.

Now I was the speechless one. Forget respect for your parents, our son had no fear and no worries about being liked or cherished. What had we created?

"It's up to your father," I said, and rose. "You'd better read yourself to sleep tonight. If he thinks you're not learning at home the way you should, he'll send you to a boarding school tomorrow, and I might just agree."

I left before he could respond, practically charging up the stairs. Were our family dinners doomed to always be like this? I looked forward to sleeping with my portrait beside the bed and dreaming of Beau.

I had just gotten myself ready for sleep when I heard a knock on my door. Dora was standing there with her fisted right hand pressed against her lips. She was trembling as if she was freezing. For a moment the sight of her took my breath away.

"What's wrong, Dora?"

"I couldn't stop him, ma'am. He just got up and shot out of the room, shouting that he wasn't going to go to a boarding school. He ran to the stairway. By the time I got there, he was halfway down. I thought he would trip and spill himself over those steps."

"Where did he go?"

"He ran into the library. I followed him, but by the time I arrived, he had already told Mr. Foxworth, shouted it at him."

"Shouted what?"

She shook her head. "Mr. Foxworth asked me if I had seen such a thing happening, and I told him no. He ordered me to take Master Malcolm up to his room, put him to bed, and come back.

He didn't believe me, ma'am. I think he wants to question me further, harder."

"What did Malcolm tell Garland? What did he say?"

"He told me he was going to tell because you were going to send him to boarding school, and then he ran out shouting what I said."

"Tell what, Dora?"

"That you and Mr. Dawson were kissing," she said. "On the lips." She looked like she was choking on the words, choking with fear.

"Don't go down, Dora. I'll go see him. You go to bed," I told her. "Make sure Malcolm is asleep."

"He'll be angry at me if I don't go, ma'am."

"I said I would go down to him."

She nodded. "Yes, ma'am." She turned and walked away.

I put on my robe and slippers and stepped out, wondering how a boy almost five could be so conniving. He kept what he had seen to himself until he thought he could use it to his own advantage. How much of that did he inherit from Garland, and how much did he inherit from me? Perhaps he was doomed to be who he was. I hated to think, however, that someone who would become so deceitful, so full of himself, had come from me. Was this something my own mother had thought when I was younger and I was scheming and manipulating, especially when it came to getting my father to do what I had wanted? I locked the door behind me, put the key between my breasts, in my cleavage, and descended the stairs.

Garland was sitting on the settee in the library, an opened bottle of his limoncello on the table with two glasses. He poured them both full and smiled.

"Ah, Corrine. Perfect. Join me." He lifted one of the glasses.

"You know how I have come to despise that drink, Garland. It does not bring good memories."

"Well, maybe it will be different now. You have so many new memories."

He held out the glass. I didn't move.

"Surely you wouldn't mind toasting your successful portrait," he said, his smile sharpening. His eyes seemed to come from another face, a face that wasn't smiling, a face that was full of rage. How much, I wondered, had he already drunk?

"I thought you had asked Mrs. Steiner for a cup of tea."

"Oh, I had that." He jerked the glass toward me. "I do apologize for not making more of your portrait. Such a work of art. Our artist captured so much of the inner you. Anyone seeing it will blush thinking you're looking at him. There's something quite sexy about the way he drew and painted your neck. Think of all the women who will be jealous. I'm sure you are pleased."

Again, he jerked the glass toward me. Reluctantly, I stepped forward and took it. Instantly, he stood and reached out to tap our glasses.

"To the wonderful portrait," he said.

He held his to his lips and waited for me to bring my glass to mine. We drank. I tried to only sip, but he put his left hand out and under my glass. "It deserves more of a toast than that, Corrine. I did spend a lot of money on it."

I drank some more, and he reached for the bottle. I started to shake my head, but he poured it into my glass.

"There's more to toast," he said. "You wouldn't deny me that."

"Why are you doing this?"

"Joy," he said. "Celebration. What a husband and wife should do on these occasions." He tapped my glass again with his.

"Can't we do it with something else, some wine?"

"Oh, no, no. Besides, it doesn't carry only bad memories, does it? Out of the limoncello your son was born," he said, smiling. "You do love your son, don't you? To Malcolm," he said, and watched me sip. "He deserves a little more than that."

"I'm going to get sick if I drink too much of this, Garland."

"Nonsense. This was made with the finest

ingredients. It can only make you feel good. It doesn't look good that you won't drink to your own son, Corrine," he added, the rage swirling beneath his mask of a smile and rising up through his lips and cheeks to add fire to his eyes.

I drank more. He reached for the bottle.

"No more, Garland. My stomach is churning."

"Oh, no. This is our final toast," he said. "We must." He poured my glass full. "Let us toast your artist. We will celebrate him and reward him for his ingenious view of a woman who is really not much more than a stranger to him. What he's accomplished in so short a time is nothing less than amazing. I'll put that portrait right up there," he said, nodding at the wall anyone would first see on entering. "Guests will inquire constantly."

He tapped my glass.

"Don't you think he deserves a toast? Is there any reason not to?"

He stared hard. *He's already quite drunk,* I thought. *Humor him.* I took a long sip. My head felt full of steam. I quickly put the glass down with what remained. He stood smiling and staring at me oddly.

"How much of a disservice I've done not taking immediate pleasure in your beautiful picture. Forgive me. I'm stirred by your beauty. You want that to be true, don't you? You welcome such a reaction in me, don't you?"

What I wanted was to sit and start to contradict what Malcolm had told him.

"Dora is upstairs terrified," I began.

I started for the cushion chair, but he reached out and seized my arm, squeezing it so hard that I cried and tried to get myself free of his grasp, but he tightened it even more.

"Wait."

"You're hurting me."

"Oh," he said. "Sorry."

He released my arm, and I went to rub it, but he stepped closer, so aggressively that I lost my breath. The limoncello was rushing through my veins.

"I feel sick," I said.

"We don't want that. You were speaking of Dora? You said she was terrified?"

"You frightened her with your questions."

"Poor Dora. She's so easily frightened, isn't she? Fragile, but she's been that way all her life and I suppose will never change."

"What she said Malcolm told you . . ."

"Yes?" He held his cold smile.

"Malcolm is just angry that we might send him to a boarding school. He's . . ."

"Lying? I . . . don't know, Corrine. Foxworths can be devious, I won't deny that, but when it comes to us, to ourselves, we are naturally protective. My father taught me that, as did his father. It's in our blood. We can't help but support ourselves."

I shook my head. "No, listen . . ."

Now there wasn't even a suggestion of a smile on his face. His rage was so hot that he was nearly unrecognizable.

"No, *you* listen. So I'm to be a cuckold, made a laughingstock in Charlottesville? I know I have my share of enemies, jealous failures, and people I've bettered in business. They'll welcome this, won't they? Why, this artist himself must be bragging by now."

"No. Garland, you must not—"

I wasn't sure what I was going to say, but before I could say it, he slapped me so hard I spun and fell. The shock of it kept me from crying or screaming. The whole left side of my face was stinging.

"You accuse me of adultery, and then you perform it yourself? And in front of our son?"

"No."

I struggled to stand.

"There is only one way for a wife to prove it's untrue. She must make love like she has never before. In a way, it will be a little celebration, too. Shall we, my sweet, innocent wife? Shall we show each other how deeply we love each other?"

He reached down and pulled me to my feet. Then he brought his glass of limoncello to my lips.

"Drink now to us, to your love for me. Drink,"

he ordered, pressing the glass so hard to my lips I could only open my mouth as he poured what remained in his glass into it. I choked and tried to spit it out, but he put his hand over my mouth and kept me from opening it. "Drink to us," he said.

I swallowed and started to cry. He turned me hard toward the door.

"Shall we go up and bond our marriage even more securely?" he said, pushing me toward the door.

I stumbled forward, and when I looked back, he stepped toward me. I hurried through the door and to the stairs. *Get to the Swan Room,* I told myself, *and lock the door. He'll give up and go to sleep. Everything will be different in the morning. I'll convince him that Malcolm was only trying to get out of attending boarding school, and this will pass.* I had reached for the banister and pulled myself up the first few steps just before everything swirled around me and I fell. He was walking slowly, determinedly, behind me, smiling and gesturing for me to keep going up.

I turned, looking for some help. I thought I saw Mrs. Steiner in the dining-room doorway watching us, but before I could cry out, she was gone. Pressing forward, I tried to rush up the second set of steps ahead of him. He was quite close but paused to catch his breath. Maybe he was too drunk to continue. I took the last few steps quickly and then, keeping myself from falling, leaned on the wall for a moment before I charged toward the Swan Room.

When I got to the door, I reached into my cleavage to pull out the key, but before I could get it, he had his arm around my waist and swept me up. Laughing, he carried me like a sack of potatoes toward his bedroom.

"No swan will help you tonight," he said, and shoved me into his room, slamming the door behind us, before he came forward and lifted me to toss me onto his bed. Finally, I found a scream, but his laughter was louder.

"Stop!" I cried, as he began to tear away my robe and then my nightdress.

"Stop!" he mimicked. "Don't worry," he said. "I'll be artistic."

He laughed and came at me, pulling apart my legs so roughly that my hips ached. He was in me before I could offer much resistance. I felt myself being pushed and shaken. It was far worse than the last time because I was so helpless. The limoncello was as strong as it had been that first night. It swirled inside me. I felt myself black out and regain consciousness and then black out again when it seemed he was finished.

Sometime during the night, however, I woke because he was at me again. I was crying loudly and trying to push him away, but he was still in a rage. Before morning, he woke and again pressed himself into me. He brought his lips close to my ear and whispered, "I will not be a cuckold."

When I awoke again, he was gone, but my body was screaming with pain. He had been so rough. I sat up and saw blood on the sheet. I panicked and got out of his bed. For a few moments, I just stood there looking at the dried streams of blood on the insides of my legs. My heart was pounding. I gathered up my robe and my torn nightdress and luckily saw the key to the Swan Room on the floor. After I put on the robe, I opened the door softly and looked out. It was still very early morning. I heard no one stirring.

Almost frozen with fear, I went to the Swan Room and for the first few moments just stood inside. I was too tired and frightened to cry. I went to the basin and cleaned the insides of my legs, but I didn't feel right at all. It was as if some bees had landed between my legs and stung me repeatedly. As quickly as I could, feeling pain all over my body, I put on clothes and then looked at myself.

There was a large black-and-blue mark where Garland had slapped me. It started at the crest of my cheek and reached to just under my eye. Sobbing softly, I found my warmest coat and left the room. As quietly as I could, I descended the stairs. When I reached the bottom, I started for the front entrance. Gazing into the library, I saw Garland sprawled and asleep in the large cushion chair. He was still in his nightdress. His mouth was open wide, and his arms hung off the sides.

As softly as I could, I slipped out of the house, and, as painful as it was to walk, I made my way to Lucas's quarters on the side of the stables. He was already up and working. The sight of me at his door was quite shocking, I'm sure, but he hurried over.

"Ma'am? What do you need? What happened? Did you fall?"

"Hook up the buggy, and take me to Charlottesville. Do it quickly, Lucas. I'll tell you where to go."

"The buggy?"

"You can get it ready faster. Just do it," I ordered.

"Yes, ma'am."

I lowered myself to a bale of hay and waited. When the buggy was ready, I rose, and he helped me board. He had a blanket for me and put it around me. After we had started and were traveling a good ten minutes, I told him where to take me. He nodded, as if he had been anticipating those directions.

"When my husband demands that you tell him where you took me, Lucas, please tell him you took me to the railroad station. He'll think I went home to my parents. Do you understand?"

"Yes, ma'am."

"I know you might not do it, Lucas. You are my husband's closest confidant, but it's a small white lie that might save me much pain."

He nodded. "Whatever helps you, ma'am, is more important."

I sat back.

I believed him. I believed him because of the way he always looked at me when he could do so unnoticed. I was sure I was often in his dreams.

And that was stronger than any loyalty he had to Garland Foxworth.

When we arrived at Beverly Morris's house, Lucas leaped out of the buggy and ran ahead of me to the door. He knocked hard. Beau appeared with a cup of coffee in his hand. He was in a shirt and pants. Whatever Lucas told him shocked him. He put down his cup and rushed out to the buggy.

"Oh, Corrine," he said, reaching for me.

"I'm hurt, Beau. It's not only my face. I was bleeding."

He stopped trying to get me off the buggy and turned to Lucas to rattle off an address. Then he stepped up and into the buggy to embrace me. Lucas got back on board and turned the buggy.

"Where are we going?"

"There's a new doctor in Charlottesville, a young man from New York, Daniel Isaacs. We've become friends. What did Garland do to you?"

I laid my head against Beau's shoulder and

closed my eyes. Just remembering, much less talking about it, brought back more pain.

"He was in a rage. More than once," I said.

He understood. No one spoke until we arrived at Dr. Isaacs's home and office. His wife was his receptionist and greeted us. She didn't have to do more than take one look at me to bring me immediately back to the examination room. After she had me sit on the examination table and then lie back until she brought in her husband, I passed out.

Afterward, if anyone knew I was at Beverly Morris's recuperating, they did not tell Garland. I had no doubt that Lucas had told him I had boarded a train for Alexandria. Ashamed of what he had done to me, perhaps, he did not contact my parents. He was confident I would return.

No one but Beau, Dr. Isaacs, and his wife in Charlottesville knew I had run away from Foxworth Hall. I didn't leave the house. Beverly, a sweet lady in her late sixties, had curly white hair but with shades of strawberry red still in it here and there. Her round, jolly face was still peppered with fading freckles on the crests of her cheeks, and she had the most orange-red lips I had ever seen.

Beverly obviously adored Beau and loved having another female in the house. I needed no other entertainment. She would sit with me for hours on end, describing Charlottesville when she was a child. She talked about Beau's parents and teased him with stories about when he was a little boy, calling him their own Tom Sawyer. He sat with me in the evening, holding my hand, and never once demanded that I describe in detail what Garland had done.

Dr. Isaacs had advised my staying off my feet, and although he didn't come right out and say it, it was clear he didn't want me to have any sexual relations for weeks, strongly suggesting a month. Maybe in his mind I eventually was going to return to Garland and Foxworth Hall. What real choice did any woman have in 1895? There were many marriages that to me looked more like indentured servitude.

On the morning of the fourth day, Beau came into the guest room I was using. He brought breakfast on a tray and pulled a chair up while I ate. I could see he was in deep thought. Perhaps he was thinking I shouldn't stay much longer, that it wasn't good for his cousin.

"I might do what I told Lucas to claim I had done, Beau, and return to my parents for a while, maybe a long while, whether they like it or not."

"No," he said, shaking his head. "That would be horrible for you, from what you have told me. And the way other people would treat you . . ." He shook his head. "Not a good idea."

"I'm not ready to go back. To be honest, I'm afraid to go back."

"You'll never go back," he said. He pulled a letter from his pocket. "Jean-Paul has written to me. It's what I would call serendipity."

"Why?"

"He has gotten me an art teacher's position in that small French village I have talked about from time to time, Villefranche-sur-Mer. He's always wanted me to end my career as a portrait painter. He advised me on how to become one successfully, but only in order for me to support myself. Now he claims it's time I do what I should be doing, more landscape art, which I've told you is closer to my heart. He's seen my work and he thinks that now I will do very well."

"Oh."

"Don't look despondent. What I propose is you come with me."

"What?"

"We'll leave right away. You can rest there as well as here. I have all the arrangements planned. I've accumulated enough money to give us a good start, and Jean-Paul has already acquired a small house at the seaside for me. I've written to him before about you," he added, confessing. "He's anticipated this."

"I don't know. If Garland finds out we're leaving together . . ."

"He won't, and by the time he knows anything, we'll be long gone."

"But . . . France?"

"You'll learn the language. We'll have a home, and we'll have our own garden. It will be infinitesimal compared to Foxworth Hall, but in time, after I become a famous artist and I'm earning thousands . . ."

"That was never what was important to me," I said.

"Now, don't go hating being rich because of Garland Foxworth," he chided with a smile. "What do you think?"

"I have nothing, and if I went back to get some of my things . . ."

"We'll have what you need to leave."

I thought about all the reasons to say no. Of course, I thought about Malcolm, but I didn't worry that he would suffer unduly. Perhaps I should have, but I kept thinking he was more Garland's son than mine. Maybe it was my fault, but it was what he was. Besides, Garland would never let him leave with me, and there was no way judges here would rule in my favor. Maybe when he was old enough to understand, I would write him and explain, just so he wouldn't hate me. Of course, by then, Garland would have poisoned him against me.

"I'm thinking about the painting," I said suddenly. "Do you think he's destroyed it by now?"

"No. I think something would make him hesitate. Not the investment so much as the proof that he could have the most beautiful women whenever he wanted. 'See my first wife,' he'll say."

"Maybe. I do know where he might keep it if he remains angry about it. It won't be in his library."

"Wherever," Beau said. "You're not imprisoned in it anymore. Neither of us is."

I smiled and reached for his hand. "You're such an optimist."

"If an artist isn't, his work will be dark and depressing, and he'll die in poverty in some gutter, proving the world is miserable.

"Besides," he said, "I'm chafing, imagining you standing on some hill with the Mediterranean behind you. You'll never feel as free, as out of the darkness. Will you go with me?"

"Yes," I said.

He leaned over to kiss me.

I closed my eyes and lay back with a smile on my face. I felt so much older, so much wiser. Corrine Foxworth was disappearing, but so was Corrine Dixon.

*Tomorrow, tomorrow, I will discover who I am.*

# EPILOGUE

Happiness torments us with its promises.

Beau had his cousin buy what I needed for the trip we were to take. I was wearing a hood when we boarded the train in Charlottesville. No one was looking for me in particular, but I wanted to be as unrecognizable as possible. As I had hoped, Garland had told people that I was visiting my parents in Alexandria. Despite that, practically every waking moment, I anticipated someone stopping us.

From New York we took a steamship to Marseilles and then traveled by coach to Villefranche-sur-Mer, where Jean-Paul awaited us. The little house we had was probably not much larger than the Swan Room, but right outside the front door was a patio facing the sea, just as Beau had promised. For weeks, we were both occupied with setting up our home and with me learning more and more French.

There was a girl living with her family nearby named Yasmine, who at twelve spoke English so well that she could tutor me in French. She was pretty, with dark-brown hair and the deepest brown eyes speckled with rust. In time she was more of a companion to me than any woman my age had been in Virginia. During those early days, her laugh drove away any sad thoughts before they could take hold. We walked the beach almost every morning. She was filled with questions about America, and I admired her hunger for knowledge. We traded well, my American facts for her French.

A letter from Beau's cousin arrived months later. She described how Garland Foxworth first had made my disappearance a national crisis. Everyone in Charlottesville was talking about me, but suspicions energized by gossip, especially emanating from the Charlottesville Women's Club, centered on my running off with the young artist Beau Dawson. The suspicions were strong enough for Garland to have our marriage annulled. He did control the judges. However, nothing I heard pleased me more. It was as if I had been given a reprieve, a pardon, and set free.

My father cleverly tracked us through Beau's cousin and had a letter forwarded to me in which he condemned me for my actions, wailing about how much I had damaged his and my mother's reputations. He didn't come right out and disown me, but his words were the closest to it that words could be. I cried about it. Beau comforted me, assuring me that in time they would soften. Not my parents, I thought, but I would learn to live with it.

Beau and I had gone gently with our affection for each other, even after I was quite past the period of time Dr. Isaacs had prescribed. Ironically, it wasn't until the first time we made love that I realized what was happening. I rose from our bed that night and, wearing only a robe, walked out before Beau knew what I was doing. Barefoot, I was halfway to the beach when he caught up.

"What is it? What's wrong? Were you in pain?"

"No," I said.

The sea was gentle, the moonlight drawing a silver path to the horizon. It was so bright that we couldn't see many stars.

"Corrine?"

I took a breath. "I'm pregnant," I said. The words seemed to fall like rocks to his feet.

"What?" He started to shake his head.

"No, I know it. I'm carrying Garland's child."

I laughed insanely.

"Ironic, isn't it? He could create a child in me only when he abused me."

Neither of us spoke for almost a minute as we took a few more steps together on the beach. It was over, my escape. I felt like continuing into the sea to stop the existence of another Foxworth.

"No," Beau said, suddenly stopping and turning me to him. "Not true."

"Beau, I'm quite aware of the symptoms, my own body, and . . ."

"It's not Garland's child."

"But we never made love until now, and I never made love with anyone else since I was married. It's . . ."

"It's my child; it's our child," he insisted.

"It's a Foxworth."

"Not here," he said. "I don't even want to think of it as a secret. It's a fact. We'll never say this again to each other or anyone, Corrine. Our child will be born here. *Our* child," he emphasized.

The breeze lifted my hair and then brushed the strands over my cheeks and forehead. He pushed them aside and kissed me.

Seven months later, our son was born. Whether it was wishful thinking or not, I believed he looked more like me than Garland. This time there would be no wet nurse. He was on my stomach the moment the umbilical cord was cut. Afterward there was food and music with all our new friends. I held my baby, whom we had decided would be named Yvon, which both of us thought without saying it that it was a name no Foxworth would want.

It was also more of a reason for me to be more attentive, more sensitive, to anything, everything, about my baby. This boy would not be another Malcolm, I thought. He was being raised in such a different world with truly loving parents, for Beau never hesitated in showing his love for Yvon. As he grew, he leaned more and more toward my more gentle features, with my blue eyes. Unlike Malcolm, he was full of smiles and laughter. I never saw the same, almost eerie look in those eyes when he paused and studied the world around him. The moment he could walk, he was holding Beau's hand and moving down the beach. Beau even put a paintbrush in his hand when he was capable of manipulating it and mimicking his father. Watching them together filled my heart with hope.

Yvon took such delight in learning both French and English, and Beau took a father's delight in his every achievement. I was convinced he had escaped Foxworth. When Yvon turned three, we had a special birthday gift for him and for ourselves. I was pregnant again.

The day our Marlena was born, Beau knelt at my bedside, took my hand, and swore.

"There'll never be any difference between them in my eyes. I promise," he said.

We kissed to seal the promise.

But I knew in my heart what I always believed about promises.

People who make them make them about things they already know can't be true.

## Center Point Large Print

600 Brooks Road / PO Box 1
Thorndike, ME 04986-0001 USA

**(207) 568-3717**

**US & Canada:**
**1 800 929-9108**
www.centerpointlargeprint.com